AMÁNE
OF
TERAVINEA

THE
CHOSEN ONE

D. María Trimble

ISBN: ISBN-10: 0985575301
ISBN-13: 978-0-9855753-0-4

To my dad, who met with his ancestors before I could finish the series. I'll meet you on the other side when it's my time and let you know how it ends.

CONTENTS

To Orchila

Kep

KINGDOM
OF
SERISLAN

Serislan Castle

Castle Beag

Trivingar
Arevale
Outpost
Arevale

Tramoren

Nunn

City
of
Teravinea

Castle Outpost
Castle Teravinea

KINGDOM
OF
TERAVINEA

Anbon

Nicobar
Nicobar
Outpost

Keose
Outpost

Glinfoil

Dorsal

Dorsal
Outpost

Behold the mighty Dragon hatch,
It has chosen one, has found a match.
By gazing into eyes that spin,
The Chosen One will be drawn in.
Like lightning strike the venomous fangs,
The Chosen's life in balance hangs.
Burning venom spreads like fire,
The hope to die is the One's desire.
If both shall live, then they will soar,
Together linked ... forevermore.

~ Dragon Hatching Song

CHAPTER ONE

I raised my sword to block and deflect yet another blow. The dark armored lord set upon me throwing strike after strike. My breath became short and raspy as I struggled for air. With no time to thrust or lunge, I could only parry his attacks. I couldn't hold him much longer. His bulk towered over me as he pushed me back. Back toward the precipice that would finish the battle. *Why hadn't help arrived?*

Sweat stung my eyes, my head throbbed where the flat side of his sword had made contact. My muscles no longer burned, but had reached the stage where they would no longer obey. The end was close. The void from the edge of the cliff echoed behind me as I lost ground.

With a gleam of death in his eye, my enemy lunged for his final blow. I stepped back but my boot couldn't find footing. The ground broke away and I tumbled backwards. I felt the swish of his sword as it just missed taking off my head. Helpless, I grabbed at nothing — both arms beat the air. My stomach leaped to my throat as I plummeted into the chasm.

From out of nowhere a large fiery dragon swooped in. Its talons wrapped around my waist as it snatched me from the air. At that same instant, I jolted upright in my bed. My nightclothes stuck to the sweat that drenched my body. My breathing matched that of my dream. The throbbing in my head was real.

Lately, my dreams always ended the same — rescued by a dragon. But there haven't been any dragons in our skies for a long time. In truth, I'd never seen one in my nearly fifteen years. That fact did not lessen my hope of the future for which I longed — one filled with weaponry, swordplay and a distinct journey all my own — which included dragons. Ever since I can remember, I'd aspired to be brave and strong; to have a mission in life; to be worthy of a quest. But one problem plagued me — I was born a girl.

CHAPTER TWO

"Amáne," my mother called. "It's a market day. Get up. I need you to help me load up the cart and hook up Ezel." Ezel was our donkey.

My mother, Catriona, made fine ceramic utensils, bowls and plates that she sold in the marketplace. Her wares were not unknown throughout the kingdom. Her family's guild had made the tableware for the House of Drekinn, the royal family that had ruled Teravinea for the last several hundred years — before Galtero seized the throne by treachery.

We rode into town together and she dropped me off at the Dragon's Fang Tavern. It was a classroom by day and a pub by night. People were frugal in our township of Dorsal. They saw no purpose in a building where the sole use was for academics. A pub was a perfect location — students occupied the place from early morning until early afternoon, at which time the pub patrons would start trickling in. They caroused until the wee hours of the morning — vacating just in time for the students the next day. It worked.

Like other girls of Teravinea, I was educated. In addition to reading and writing, we were expected to learn our history songs and ballads, although most of them had been altered and had lost their beauty and power. They had deviated from the beautiful works our ancestors had written. My mother took it upon herself to teach me the original songs. I was thankful for her efforts because it is in ignorance that we lose our direction.

Entering the tavern, I took my place on a bench at one of the long tables. The stench was enough to aggravate my progressing headache. The straw on the floor had probably been there when the last dragon lived — which was a few years before I was born — and had only been added to instead of changed. The spilled ale, wine, urine and whatever scraps had fallen on the ground, along with the heat and the rare humidity, made the odor nearly unbearable. It certainly didn't improve my mood.

A new teacher arrived in town only a few weeks before. My mother contended he had been sent to Dorsal from the City of Teravinea to try to bend or break us. Evidently our previous teacher lacked in forceful persuasion. We were unwilling to move too quickly into accepting the usurping King Galtero, never mind he had been on the throne for over seventeen years. If this teacher could indoctrinate the younger generation, in a matter of a short time we would forget our ancestors and our history, and yield completely to Galtero's corrupt rule.

My headache refused to relinquish its hold — I struggled with it for most of the day through writing and calculating figures. I just wanted to close my eyes and make it go away, but found myself, instead, staring at the confusion of carvings in the table. Decades and decades of "art," some quite rude, scarred the long tables of the Dragon's Fang Tavern. Lost in thought, I contemplated the unsung stories of the people who had sat here.

The sudden silence in the room brought me out of my musing. To my horror, I realized the teacher had called upon me.

His angry glare confirmed he had tried more than once to get my attention.

"I beg your pardon, Teacher," I said, standing up too quickly, which caused my head to feel like it would explode. "I didn't hear you."

"I asked you to sing the ballad of *The Battle of Sregor's Field,*" he said, "which I hope you have been studying, as I gave you two weeks in which to learn it."

I felt the heat rise in my face. Being called to sing in front of the class always made my stomach churn. I became paralyzed whenever attention was drawn to me. But I had to comply with Teacher's request. To my consolation, the *The Battle of Sregor's Field* was one of my favorites — I knew all of the verses.

"Yes, Master Teacher." My hand clutched the table to steady myself. I closed my eyes so I could imagine I was alone, and began to sing in a shaky voice.

The ballad described a battle that took place in a field owned by Hon Sregor, near the City of Teravinea. It told of how Nara, the last dragon rider, and her famous dragon, Torin, had swooped into the battle at the last moment when things looked bad for King Emeric. Flaming the forward line of the enemy army, Torin and Nara gave King Emeric's soldiers the inspiration they needed to rally in one last heroic effort. With Nara and Torin's help, they turned the tide of the battle and allowed victory for King Emeric.

I had not gotten far into the ballad when Teacher shouted, "Stop singing! Those are not the proper words."

"Excuse me. With all due respect, sir, these are the proper words, written by a minstrel who was present at that battle. My mother told me."

"Don't be insolent, girl. Now sing the proper words."

I felt the eyes of my fellow students — their interest sparked in our exchange — alert and eager to hear my response.

Under his breath I heard Teacher say, "This is the result of a child being raised solely by her mother. There should be a law against that."

Only with extraordinary effort did I manage to hold my tongue. How dare he insult my mother. I started again, and sang it the way my mother had taught me.

"Silence!" He pounded his fist on the table. "Those are the antiquated words and you will not sing it as such. King Galtero has forbidden it."

Fully aware of how he expected me to sing it, I refused to offend my ancestors. The ballad had been revised and completely left Nara and Torin out in an effort to brainwash the youth with the lie that dragons never existed. Instead, it boasted the battle was won only by the intervention of King Emeric's step-uncle — Galtero. I would pierce my foot with my dagger before I would sing anything in honor of that man.

"Now, Amáne, will you sing it correctly?" He was losing his patience. I had already lost mine.

"Yes, Master Teacher, I will sing it correctly." My eyes blazed as I locked eyes with him. My head pounded and I began again. I sung it — the way it was originally written.

The girl beside me gasped.

The teacher charged at me with the stick he was in the habit of carrying and struck my arm, leaving a welt. He roared, "Out, you contemptuous girl! You may not set foot in my class again until your mother comes and speaks with me. I want a written apology from both you and your mother."

THE CHOSEN ONE

I was more than happy to leave. I didn't care if I ever stepped foot in his class again. Gathering my satchel, I stormed out without giving him the satisfaction of my tears, or the acknowledgment of the painful sting he had inflicted on my arm.

CHAPTER THREE

Being born here in Dorsal is truly the only way anyone could love and understand this place. The furthest township from the throne, we have our traditions passed on from generation to generation. We're loathe to part with them any time soon, regardless of the efforts of our current king — or any teacher intent on changing our ways. Our allegiance, in reality, should be to King Galtero, but our allegiance in our hearts remains with King Emeric of the House of Drekinn, who has rested with his ancestors since before I was born.

Perched at the edge of the desert, Dorsal is a modest seaside township on the southernmost tip of the Kingdom of Teravinea. It overlooks a large bay of sapphire blue, dotted with a scattering of islands — an incomparable view.

Not to be misled by its beauty, our seemingly alluring corner of the kingdom truthfully presents a harsh environment with draconian shifts in the weather. One minute the bay shines as smooth as glass, the air dead calm with unbearable heat. Then, without warning, white caps appear — breaking the tranquility of the sea. Suddenly, the furious wind lashes out with a vengeance — like a scorned female who has lost control of her temper. Anything not secured is tossed about, only to be found battered and broken at quite a distance from its point of origin. Then, satisfied with the punishment inflicted, her anger abates with no apology. We call this wind a Valaira. She commands our respect and is never to be underestimated.

On more than one occasion I heard my mother lament the fact she named me Amáne and not Valaira.

Despite the weather, and our small size, our township boasts quite a bustling location. Merchant ships still find it worthwhile to gamble on the temperament of a Valaira and enter our harbor, depositing their goods in trade for our fine crafts as well as salt and other delicacies of the sea.

It was just the two of us, my mother, Catriona, and myself, living in a small cottage outside the walls of Dorsal, at the southwest end of the township. My father, Duer, left on a mission for the king shortly after I was conceived. He never returned. Personally, the fact he was involved in this king's business left me feeling fortunate I never knew him — King Galtero will be the ruin of our once-great kingdom. Duer's affiliation with him, and his abandonment of my mother and me, would be his life's greatest regret if he were still alive — and I were to meet him face to face. I vowed he would have no mercy from me. My mother, knowing my feelings, didn't speak often about Duer, but when she did, it was without animosity. She never fully got over him. I think she always had hope he would return. I, however, shall never forgive him for deserting us.

Once girls reached fifteen, most parents began to look for suitors for their daughters. Thankfully, my mother didn't believe in that archaic practice. Instead, she supported my inclinations and did what she could to make me feel like I wasn't a complete oddity for my gender. We never made public my attraction for learning the arts of weaponry and defense.

I didn't have many female acquaintances as my interests varied too greatly from those of the other girls. There was a group I would join occasionally. We wandered the marketplace and flirted with the handsome young men who tended the colorful stalls. We were thrilled if we caught the eye of a rich young foreign merchant. Then I would enjoy their fantasies as they dreamed of being whisked away to live forever in a palace in some exotic kingdom.

One of the girls, Fiona, whose disposition matched the sweetness of her looks, was the closest of my acquaintances. Although we didn't spend much time together, we were comfortable in each other's company. I could more or less be myself. But, there remained one thing of which I was extremely envious of Fiona — her younger twin sisters, Rio and Mila. Twins were rare in our community because of the high mortality rate, unless they were delivered by the Healer. It just so happened my mother assisted the Healer in their birth. Rio and Mila were about five years younger than I. Being an only child, I longed for siblings. They were my ideal of the perfect sisters — little ones who would look up to their older sister with such love and admiration in their eyes. It pained me to know I would never be the recipient of that kind of devotion.

Unusually perceptive, not much got past Fiona's discerning eye, even when there were quite a few of us together. It was just the day before our group had stopped at every stall selling silk, ribbons and lace, for which I had very little enthusiasm. My inattention was not lost on her. However, when we passed a stall with an inventory of swords, partisans, polearms and daggers, I would hang back and feast my eyes on these masterpieces of the cutler. Then my own fantasies formed in my head. Instead of being whisked away by a handsome foreign merchant, I would travel throughout the kingdom, join in raging battles to save lives and put all things to right.

"Amáne," Fiona brought me out of my reverie. "You would do better paying attention to the ribbons and lace — you'll never find a suitor looking for a wife who wields a blade."

"Unless it's a six-inch blade to cut the meat and vegetables for his meal," piped in one of the other girls. We all laughed, but I kept it to myself I was not the least bit interested in finding a husband.

I had one male acquaintance, Kail, the grinder's youngest son, who was a year or so less than I. I referred to most of my peers only as acquaintances, because "friend" was a much more powerful relationship than I held with anyone in Dorsal. Only my mother deserved that title. Kail was a rebellious young man, and it seemed he lived to fight authority. This worked out to my advantage as he was only too happy to take issue against the king's edict of no swordplay for females. This gave opportunity for him to dissent. He happily taught me the art of sword fighting. We practiced most afternoons behind my mother's workshop. She made sure to keep a close eye on us. She held some concern at how much larger and stronger Kail was than I — and at his lack of restraint when we fought. We never used metal swords for our practice. Instead we'd spar with the wooden ones called wasters. Our practice often ended in large bruises for me, but I could smugly say he never left our sessions unscathed. In my efforts to avoid bruises, I learned very quickly. I knew I could learn more from fighters who were more skilled than myself — and Kail was quite capable in the defensive arts. Again, it was to my benefit, as my lessons in self defense were more enhanced. What hurts, teaches.

My mother also offered verbal lessons and critiques to help me improve. I loved that she also had an interest in defense. Her knowledge of weaponry was impressive.

Although I preferred the masculine education and conventions, I was completely satisfied with the gender into which I was born. Never would I be that helpless maiden in search of a husband to take care of me. If and when I finally decide to find someone, contrary to what Fiona might think, he would be someone who accepts a wife who wields a blade. But such a topic was so far in my future, it was almost non-existent. I never wasted much time or effort dwelling upon it.

CHAPTER FOUR

I didn't think it possible my day could get any worse. Storming out of the Dragon's Fang Tavern, I made a concerted effort to hold my tears until later, when I could confide in my mother. Heading to her stall in the marketplace, I hoped she would want to leave the market early. When I arrived, I found her booth empty and sealed up for the day.

The man who sold teas and spices in the neighboring stall noticed me as I stood before her deserted booth. "Amáne, your mother went home early. She said she wasn't feeling well."

Alarmed, I rushed away.

Disregarding my headache, I ran most of the way home. I burst in the door of our cottage and found her in bed, wincing in pain. Something was seriously wrong and the sight of her pale face terrified me. She was my rock and my strength, and was not supposed to get sick ... she was my mother.

"Mother," my voice trembled, "what's wrong? I'm going back into town for the Healer."

"No, Amáne, that's not necessary, yet. Please, just stay with me and let me rest. If I'm no better tomorrow, then you can go first thing in the morning. I'll be okay tonight." She calmed my uneasiness. It couldn't be as serious as I had feared. Needless to say, I didn't burden her with the events of my horrible day. I tucked the incident away in a safe place to bring out later when she felt better.

At the break of day, after a feverish night for my mother, she sent me on my way for the Healer. I'm small for my age, but I'm fast and I love to run. I decided I would get there more quickly on foot than if I had ridden Ezel, our donkey. Running in a gown, however, posed problems for me, so whenever I took a path where I would meet with few passers by, I would tie a sash around my waist and pull the back of my skirt forward through my legs, bringing it up and tucking it into the sash. It made it much easier to run. So, I tucked up my skirts and headed for the Healer's apothecary shop. I went as fast as I could, running most of the way.

The Healer — the only name I've ever known her by — lived at the most northeastern corner of Dorsal, inside the town walls. I had known her all my life and her age was debatable — at times she seemed ancient and at other times she gave the impression she was as young as my mother. A highly respected member of our township, I suspected she was well known throughout the kingdom. Her past was shrouded in mystery. The Healer took care of the ills and injuries of the inhabitants of Dorsal, but yet there was more to her — a certain vigilance or protectiveness about her. I couldn't quite decide what made her so unique.

I turned in at the east gate, and zigzagged through an alley, and then one more lane, finally arriving at her apothecary shop, which took up the front room of her large residence. She had a substantial expanse of land that started at the lane on which her shop opened. Then it stretched back and butted up against the cliffs to the north.

I charged in the door, breathless, and found her assistant, Gallen, at the front counter grinding herbs with a mortar and pestle. I had known and loved this man all my life — he was the closest to a father figure I'd ever had. Many hours were spent in this front room of the apothecary shop as I watched him prepare herbs and seeds. It was he who had acquainted me with the dragons who had been the heart of Teravinea. He told of how dragons hatched and linked to their riders. Along with those of my mother, his accounts had kept the lore of dragons alive for me. The fact he lamented their absence was not lost on me, but he never shared his theories regarding their disappearance.

"Good morning, Gallen. I need to see the Healer, please." I didn't waste time with the formalities and manners of greeting him. I knew he would understand my abruptness. Before I finished my sentence, the Healer came in through a door at the far end of the room.

"Greetings, Healer. Please, my mother has sent me. She said to tell you that she is now at the stage you discussed with her, and she will need to see you." I didn't really know what my message meant, but delivered it as instructed.

The Healer was a very good friend of my mother's — and had been such long before I was born. I caught a deep sadness in her eyes at my message. She exhaled quickly and her shoulders dropped. I got the feeling she was expecting me.

Because of the urgency of the situation, the Healer announced, "Meet me in the courtyard. We'll take Thunder and you'll ride with me." She quickly exited the way she had come.

Confused by her haste, I looked with shock at Gallen and was met with sympathetic eyes. He remained silent and with a hand of comfort on my shoulder, he led me back through the kitchen to the courtyard. Their behavior had only solidified my terror that my mother's illness was life-threatening — they didn't convey much hope. I refused to believe it.

Thunder was the Healer's beautiful grey stallion that ran like the wind. I used to imagine he could outrun a Valaira. No one that I knew of had ever ridden on Thunder, besides the Healer. On any other day I would have been elated with the expectation of being the only one to ever fly with them — which was the appearance they gave as they glided over the land. But this day did not allow any excitement, I was too busy building a corner of my mind to hide in — denial was my only hope.

The Healer and Thunder rapidly approached from the barn. Upon reaching the courtyard, the Healer put her arm down. Hardly slowing she locked wrists with me, and with ease swung me up behind her. "Hold on!" she shouted as she gave Thunder the reins.

I wrapped my arms around her waist and off we shot. Her horse was well-named. His powerful legs pumping and his hooves striking the ground echoed like peals of thunder. My stomach lurched and I bit my lip to keep the scream in my throat that was fighting for release. The experience was exhilarating, but again, in a dulled version, as I couldn't allow myself to enjoy it. We arrived at our cottage before I even realized where we were.

I waited alone outside while the Healer spent time with my mother. Finally, the old woman came out, looking most ancient. She turned to me with eyes full of sorrow and pity.

"Your mother has some things she needs to tell you."

She gave me a lingering hug, walked slowly to Thunder and was gone before I could ask anything.

In terror, I rushed to my mother's bedside. She smiled weakly and beckoned me closer, taking my hand in hers. I couldn't hold my tears back, I couldn't face what, in fact, I knew was inevitable. I let out a moan of despair, and tried to will away the fact I knew my mother was preparing to rest with our ancestors — how could this be happening? Panic and anger fought for command of my emotions.

If I closed my eyes it would go away. It was my standard solution to situations of which I wanted no part. She waited patiently while I struggled for composure — to get a hold of my anger, which continued to be my own worst enemy. If I lived for a hundred years I'm not sure I would ever be able to fully master it.

I had every right, I thought, *to be angry.* It was not fair that my best friend, my mother, was being taken from me. In truth, I had no choice but to resolve myself to that conclusion — she will be joining our ancestors. Finally, with great effort, I was prepared to listen to what she had to say.

"Amáne, my only child — sometimes as unruly as water — most of the time obedient — always my strength. I've known for a while now I would soon be leaving this life. I'm sorry I kept it from you, but I didn't want you to have to suffer any sooner than necessary."

My heart threatened to break. I earnestly hoped this was one of my bad dreams, and I would wake up soon to the smell of her bread baking in the oven.

"Your fifteenth birthday is quickly approaching. Don't worry, I haven't made marriage arrangements for you." A corner of her mouth turned up as she tried to make this as light as possible. I breathed a sigh of relief — my mother knew me too well. "But I've discussed your care with the Healer and she insists you stay with her. She has been a close friend and soon you'll understand our friendship. I know you will continue to make me proud."

She took a shallow breath, "I want to give you my blessing. I see a monumental change coming in your life, a fire burning in your soul, a time of decision and perhaps danger." My mother was somewhat prophetic and not often wrong. "Be sincere of heart, Amáne. Accept whatever befalls you, in great misfortune be patient; for in fire gold is refined.

"Now you're nearly of age. I'm sincerely sorry I will not be able to watch you turn into the beautiful young lady you're already becoming. You'll need to use your intuition and your intelligence in deciding which paths you choose — remember to follow your heart. In your resolutions, please do not neglect your own happiness. Your life is in your hands. Direct it well."

Her weak smile faded and her expression turned serious, "I want you to know, my sweet Amáne," she paused to make sure I was truly listening to her. "You need not worry about me. I'm at peace with this and I will see you on the other side with our ancestors when it is your time. Do not forget that, my precious daughter."

She is at peace with this? What about me? I selfishly thought. *I'm the one being left alone!*

And then she finished off with one devastating request. "But the one thing I ask of you, please, I do not want you present when I take my last breath."

"No!" I cried out. This request was more than I could take. "I am not leaving your side. I'll be here until the end. You can't tell me not to be here, Mother, please!"

No more was said on that subject.

So, the days went by, slowly creeping one day after the next. I struggled to exist as my world got darker, but I couldn't let my mother see my sorrow. She was at peace with her fate. I wasn't, but couldn't let it show. Each day she held on, became another day

I couldn't bear. I put on a brave face in her presence and took care of her as she slowly drifted closer to our ancestors. I read to her and talked to her to pass the long hours, but still she remained here in this life.

Every few days the Healer would arrive on Thunder to check in on us. Hoping knowledge of what my mother was going through would help me in my suffering, she explained, "The body will shut down slowly, as each organ finally gives in. Crossing to our ancestors is different with each person. Some go quickly and for some reason, others do not. It is a mystery."

She advised me to keep talking to my mother, because even if she couldn't respond, she could hear me from whatever path her departing spirit traveled. I told my mother that I loved her and accepted that she was leaving, then assured her I would be fine. She taught me well, to persevere until I achieved my goal — whatever I set my mind to. We were fighters, she and I.

I silently cried myself to sleep every night, but it was a fitful sleep — it did not restore or revitalize. Instead, I tossed and turned, listened to my mother's labored breathing and wondered which breath would be her last. But she would not let go. My agony increased.

One day, no different than the rest that had dawned grey and dreary, the Healer came to visit. She held me in her arms for a few minutes and then looked at me closely. She could see I was not doing well.

"Amáne, I would like to ask a favor of you. First, you need to clean yourself up. You look a fright, child. Go wash your face and change your clothes. What would your mother say if she could see how you looked now?" She held up a small leather pouch and said, "Please take this to Dorjan, the blacksmith's home. Their baby is sick and these are some herbs to help him. I will sit with Catriona and watch. It shouldn't take you long. Now go."

"What?" I asked with less civility than I should have. Was I to believe that while I was numb with grief, this woman dares to ask me to leave my dying mother's side to take some herbs to a sick baby?

"I can't do this! They live all the way on the other side of Dorsal, outside the west wall. I can't leave my mother when any moment could be her last. I won't chance it," I said, trying in vain to control my anger. I realized with increased remorse, the disrespect I directed toward the Healer.

I was mortified by my bad behavior, yet not enough to hold my tongue. Surprisingly, she didn't reprimand me as I deserved, but simply tilted her head, looked with pity into my eyes, and said gently yet incontestably, "Amáne, go clean yourself up."

I sidled off in shame and went to make myself presentable to deliver the herbs. Taken aback, I stared in shock when I saw my reflection in the glass. My eyes had dark circles under them and my unbrushed hair hung in a tangled brown mass, as twisted as the sage brush that grew outside. I hadn't realized how bad I looked. I scrubbed myself, brushed my hair and changed my clothes.

Back at my mother's bedside, I took her cold hand and put it to my cheek where a fresh flow of tears was unleashed. Explaining to her what I was about to do and that the Healer would stay with her, I kissed the palm of her hand and then her forehead. I told her I would be back soon. Feeling an ever-so-small twitch from her hand, I knew she understood. I took the herbs from the Healer, charged out the door, tucked up my skirts, and ran toward the blacksmith's home.

As I ran, I almost let myself enjoy the feel of the wind on my face. My hair blew in long waves behind me. The Healer was a wise woman. I don't know how long I had been in that house, suffering. I actually felt better than I had for days — it may have even been weeks since I came home to find my mother in her bed.

I delivered the herbs to the thankful mother, and felt good about it. I knew it was something my mother would have encouraged me to do. She would never hesitate to help a needy family, no matter the sacrifice to her.

As I stepped back on the path to head home, I heard a dog's mournful howl in the distance. My heart skipped a beat and my stomach twisted in a knot. I ran faster than I had ever run before. The tears started again, stinging against my cheeks as the wind hit the salty wetness that flowed from my eyes.

I bounded up the path and rushed into our cottage. The old Healer's eyes told me all. It was over. My mother was now at rest. A pressure that started at the bottom of my lungs released itself in a wail drawn from the very depths of my heart. At that moment, even a Valaira could not have muffled the sound that came from me.

I ran to her bedside and threw my arms around her now cold body. "Mother. Mother. No. Don't leave me." Although I thought I was ready to accept this moment, no amount of preparation could lessen the devastation of this ultimate separation. My body shook with uncontrollable weeping. I cried until I was spent. My sobs continued, even though there were no more tears left in me. My mother was gone. I had never experienced anything so shattering.

The Healer lit her herbs and candles around the room, softly sang her dying songs and waited patiently until I was silent. Mother was her good friend — this death was obviously difficult for the Healer as well. She took me by my shoulders, gently guided me away, and lovingly pulled the burial cloth over my mother's now peaceful face. My grief renewed, she held me as my shoulders heaved while I sobbed dry tears. Staying with me for quite a while, she watched and waited until I at last calmed down.

She had come prepared with her donkey and cart to take my mother away. It is our custom for the Healer to take the deceased, to prepare the body for crossing, and then to cremate it. Once a year, when the desert flowers bloom, we have a gathering in the fields outside the south wall to celebrate the lives of those who had passed that year. The deceased's family is then given the urn that contains their loved one. It's a beautiful celebration, but much easier if it was not your own mother's ashes being handed to you. I was not looking forward to the next Life Celebration Gathering.

Another solemn practice we have in Teravinea is called a memorial journey. It's a pilgrimage in honor and thanksgiving for our loved ones. The family must decide on a location significant to the deceased, and travel there to sing our memorial songs. It could be far or close, of short duration, or long. As it was only Catriona and myself and no other family, I would make my memorial journey alone. I wasn't in the least opposed to going by myself.

I assisted as the Healer dressed my mother in her favorite gown. The one I will always remember her in — the blue one. She was fond of saying it was her favorite, because it matched my eyes. We gently lifted her into a box that waited on the cart. The colorful cloth lining will forever echo in my memory. The Healer slowly let the lid down, as I caught my last glimpse of my best friend, my mother.

Trudging back inside, the Healer followed me. She put a hand on my shoulder and turned me to face her, "Won't you ride with me back to my home and begin your stay with me? It would be better that you don't stay alone tonight. Also, if you need me, I would be honored to accompany you in your memorial journey, when you decide to go. I've always considered you and your mother as family."

"No thank you, Healer, I'll be fine by myself here ... and when I make my journey. I'll come and stay with you afterwards." I wanted nothing more than to be alone with my misery.

She hesitated and appeared to struggle with my decision, but then relented. I felt she left something unsaid, but with a look of intense sorrow, she left my home and climbed onto her cart. She clicked to her donkey and rode off slowly. I stood at my doorway and watched until the cart was no longer visible as my mother — my life, was taken away.

At that moment I forced myself to face the fact I was truly alone. I turned, closed the door, and looked around our humble little home as I tried in vain to fight off the approaching depression. *Maybe I should have gone with the Healer.*

My breath then caught in my throat. I could barely breathe. The stark realization hit me as suddenly as a Valaira — Mother hung on for so long because of me! It was my fault she wouldn't let her spirit go. Her words echoed in my head, "... please, I do not want you present when I take my last breath."

A wave of guilt and desolation spiraled around me as darkness wrapped me in its embrace. I had not honored her dying wish. I never left her side after she said that. Not until the wise old Healer gave me the bag of herbs to take to the sick baby. The Healer, for whom I had shown such disrespect, knew my mother didn't want me to witness her last breath. She sent me away, so Catriona could finally rest. This truth was more than I could bear. I crumpled to the floor, wrapped my arms around my legs and curled into a ball in the corner of the room, succumbing to despair. I lost track of time — I didn't care if it was day or night. It was all the same to me as I headed down a tunnel of shadows and nightmares. My mother wandered in and out of my dreams as if attempting to lighten my heavy load. She drew near to me with a loving look but there was something else in her gaze — something unsaid. A look similar to that of the Healer. She softly called my name, told me she was at peace, and then faded away to be replaced by fire and wind, lizards and snakes writhing in my disturbed sleep.

CHAPTER FIVE

Awaking before light the next morning, still curled up on the floor with a pain in the pit of my stomach, I recalled that my mother was gone. But something in me had shifted, a decision made. I would leave today for my memorial journey. This day — my 15th birthday, that had for quite some time been the anticipated pivotal point in my life — I would start my journey in thanksgiving for my mother. Not sure if I was coming back or not, I had made my choice.

I rose from the floor stiff and hungry. It took an immense amount of effort for me to grasp at some substance of hope to blot out my feelings of utter desolation. My thoughts turned to my mother for strength. She would have expected more from me. She deserved better than a cowering, sniveling daughter.

Straightening up, I took a deep jagged breath and said out loud, "I am Amáne, daughter of Catriona, and I will push myself to go forward and make my plans for my journey."

My mother's words echoed in my ears, "Accept whatever befalls you, in great misfortune be patient; for in fire gold is refined."

Whenever she and I felt a need to break from our daily activities, we would pack up some provisions and make the long hike to our special cove on the bay. Nature and beauty and our little family all came together in that one location. This cove would be where I would make my memorial journey. My mother had taught me survival and that was how I would honor her memory and give thanks for her guidance and love she had shown all my life. I owed her that much.

Comforted by the fact I now had a direction to follow, I lifted my chin and took another deep breath. I moved forward slowly, step by step and repeated, "I am Amáne, daughter of Catriona. I am Amáne, daughter of Catriona." Finally, I was sure of myself and the course I'd chosen.

Changing my clothes, I put on a simple gown — the less skirts, the better. I washed up and brushed my hair until it returned to its original state — long and straight. Then I braided it and secured it in a queue down my back. Once satisfied with my appearance, I turned my attention to my home and put it back in order. Not without effort — it held so much sorrow.

I gathered a bed roll and our small wedge tent, and put some clothing and other necessities into my pack. It was easy to recall the excitement we used to feel when collecting our supplies for a journey. I took the water skins off of their hooks and filled them, then wrapped up some stale bread, some dried fish and squid, and the last of the apples in the larder. Slowly, I lifted from my darkness and willed myself to keep moving. When I hesitated, my depression threatened to take hold again. I fought it as I poured my entire self into the preparations for my trip.

Before the sun began its ascent into the cloudless sky, and before the heat of the day made itself felt, I slung my pack over my shoulder. My dagger was secure in its sheath on my belt, and my fishing gear hung from my pack. I was ready to leave. After a last look at my home, I backed out of the door, secured the latch, turned, and walked away.

The narrow path led straight from our cottage toward the water. I turned left and trekked the long distance along the rocky shore, making my way to our sandy spot at a curve in the bay far ahead. I walked until the sun shone high in the sky. Sweat ran down under my pack as the heat increased with the progressing day.

After more than two hours of hiking, I finally arrived at our cove. I found the trip was not as enjoyable traveling by myself. *Should I have given more thought to my brash decision to make this trip on my own?* Pushing aside my fears, I set myself to my chores.

Further up from the beach, between three old and twisted scrub trees, I set up my small tent. It was now low tide, so the shoreline was a ways off. If I were to pitch my camp closer to the water at this time of day I would be in for a rude surprise in a matter of a few hours when the tide would rise. This spot, my mother and I calculated, was the perfect distance from the water at high tide. A freshwater spring that poured out of a fissure in the cliffs behind my camp completed the ideal location. The scrub trees hovered over my shelter with branches that spread like gnarled arms, prepared to fend off any harm that would dare to come my way. The familiarity of the location and the fond memories offered me comfort.

Wandering the beach, I gathered some large stones to repair the fire ring that still stood from our last trip. Not often, but occasionally, others would pass through and rearrange the rocks or use them for other purposes. I searched close to the cliff to find large enough ones to use. A fire would be necessary, not only to stay dry if the dew came in, but also to cook my dinner. In addition, it was a deterrent for wild animals. At last, I took inventory of my setup and came to the conclusion my camp was complete — Mother would have approved.

Perhaps tomorrow I would look for shells to decorate my surroundings — a comforting ritual we had always enjoyed. A smile came to my lips as I recalled how we would create an elaborate system of shell-lined paths leading from our camp to the stream, to the beach and other destinations, bound only by our imaginations. I could still see some remnants of paths we had created the last time we visited.

Tired from my exertions, I lowered myself silently next to my cold fire ring and allowed a few tears to escape. I wondered if I would ever really be able to enjoy sunshine and happiness again. Nothing could convince me it could be possible. A scar was left upon my heart. I went through all the thanksgiving and memorial songs that I knew, and also sung a few grieving songs until my sobs would no longer allow me to sing.

Staring at my fire ring, I sighed and decided to start gathering wood. I needed the distraction. I also had to think about preparing my tackle to catch a fish for my dinner. Angling would give me an activity to keep myself busy, but it was not imperative, as I did have some dried food if the fish decided not to bite. It was, however, the way my mother and I would always start our trips — with a contest of who could catch the first fish or the largest. We were both very competitive and I was up for a challenge. This day, it was only me competing with myself. But it was another ritual that would comfort me.

I had a nice blaze going before I gave my attention to catching my meal. Living in a fishing town had its advantages. We had several shops that specialized in tackle. Rather than having to make our own, my mother had saved some money to buy each of us a rod, some horsehair line and a few metal hooks. We cherished these items, not only because they were costly, but because they were very much a part of our escape to our cove.

Wading into the water, I netted some small fish that swam close to the shore. Impaling one on a hook, and silently thanking it for its life, I cast the hook and bait as far as I could and waited. Angling is an art and is not to be rushed. It was one of the most enjoyable activities we had shared. We were able to use the time to discuss issues important to us or just merely talk about the oddities of the local people. My mother would often tell me of her childhood and early adulthood in the City of Teravinea. She wasn't originally from Dorsal, but was a city girl, the daughter of prominent ceramic artisans that ran the pottery guild. The family had a permanent booth at the Teravinea Marketplace where they sold their wares. They also filled orders for the Royal House of Drekinn. It was there she met my father, Duer, with whom she fell in love and moved to Dorsal. I was allowed no more details of that part of her history.

As my mind wandered, thinking about some of our adventures in this cove, I felt a small tug on my line. I was fully attentive now to see if the fish would take my bait. Another stronger tug prompted me to yank back on my rod, which set the hook. The fight began. Its pull told me it was a large one. Time flew by as I pitted myself against the fish. It looked like it would win the battle as it headed out to deeper water — not what I was hoping it would do. Unexpectedly, the fish changed direction and headed toward me. Its scales shown colorful in the sun. I ran backwards to keep the line taut. Fighting for its life, it tried several more tactics to loose itself from my hook. In the end, I was able to get it close enough to pull my pole quickly and beach the fish.

I ran to where it flopped on the sand, gasping for life, as it tried to get back into the water. Pulling my dagger from my belt, I quickly ended its struggle. I whispered a short song of thanks for its life and began filleting it on a nearby flat rock. It was a big one and I would have to cook what I could eat today and then try to prepare the rest with salt and smoke to preserve it. I had never done that by myself, it was always my mother who would process it. I was going to have to learn.

Later, after eating a portion of my catch, I lounged by my fire. Humming another grieving song, I resumed my doubts. Perhaps my decision to come here was a little premature. My memorial journey may not have been such a great idea after all. *What was I thinking coming here alone?* I was a long way from anywhere or anyone, and I told no one where I would be.

A fear seized me. I began to consider maybe I was not as brave as I thought. It had gotten too late to head back to the cottage. But I was also too stubborn to end my journey just yet, even if there had been time to go back home.

As I struggled with the whirlpool of emotions that threatened to pull me under, I felt maybe I should just succumb to my spiral of despair and let it take me down again. It would be so easy to sink back safely into my depression. Then I wouldn't care what happened to me.

I missed my mother. She used to tell me when I got frightened to start singing, so she could hear me. It always worked. It made me feel safe. I fought off the depression once more and followed her suggestion from the past. I softly started a favorite ballad about an ancient battle.

I closed my eyes and began to sing louder as my fear intensified. In spite of my increased volume, I could hear a soft humming sound that began to accompany me. *Had someone arrived while I was distracted?* My nerves reached their breaking point. I turned quickly to see who had entered my camp. There was no one. Turning back to my fire I decided the sound originated from the vicinity of my flames. At first, I thought it may have been the wet firewood, but usually that sound came out as more of a hiss. This was definitely humming. It was, truthfully, a very soothing sound. I found that my body started to relax, comforted by the beautiful tune — almost hypnotic — like a sedative herb the Healer had once given me when I was very ill.

Slowly, I was drawn to the rock that sat directly in front of me — part of my fire ring. I found myself pulled strongly toward the stone. It was one of the larger ones I'd carried from the cliffs behind me. I remembered it wasn't as heavy as I had expected from its size.

As if called to do so, I reached out to touch it. I felt it vibrating, drawing me in still closer as it continued to hum its mesmerizing strain. The volume and the vibrations intensified. Still I held my hands on its warm resonating surface. Subconsciously, a song began to surface. It tickled the edge of my memory but I couldn't get it to reveal itself. If I could remember, I felt it would tell me what was happening. Something about a Chosen One, but the details would not come to mind.

Then, without warning, cracks appeared in the rock as it vibrated more violently. The humming was at a feverish pitch, although it didn't hurt my ears. Something inside of it was pushing out. A fissure appeared in the top of the rock — which was not a rock at all. A small horn or tooth knocked the opening larger. A glow of yellows and reds radiated through the cracks, as if there was a fire inside. My eyes went wide as a creature thrust its head out of the opening.

A small dragon appeared. It tumbled out in front of me, fatigued from its struggle to release itself. A beautiful being that I wanted to scoop up in my arms. No fear was left in me as I gazed in wonder. It had tiny horns on top of its head, and large golden eyes. Lifting its short body on its four legs, it unfolded its wings, still wet from the moisture in its egg. It looked like a living flame. Iridescent scales of red, orange, yellow and hints of blue played through its body. I was held spellbound.

My mother taught me many dragon songs, and I had seen her detailed drawings from when she was a young girl. Song or painting could do no justice in comparison to this creature. Its beauty hypnotized me. I had never seen anything of its equal. Raising its head to look at me, its eyes locked onto mine. I became entranced in its whirling golden orbs. I couldn't release myself from their intense gaze — nor had I any desire to do so. Its eyes reflected a blazing, golden fire — comforting, like a hearth or a camp fire. They spun me ever inward into their depths — holding me there for an undetermined amount of time.

Then the creature blinked. The spell that engaged me was broken. I struggled to get my focus back — to grasp what had just happened. A part of me felt missing now that its eyes no longer held mine. I wanted to dive back into their comforting warmth. I watched in a stupor as its head pulled back slowly. Like lightning, it lunged and struck me on the right shoulder, burying its venomous fangs in my flesh.

Horrified a beloved dragon could do such a thing, a thought drove into me that maybe it wasn't a dragon. A flash of agony exploded through me, as if someone had taken a red hot brand and held it to my arm. The excruciating heat traveled across my chest. Breathing became close to impossible. The burn continued slowly to my opposite arm, spread up to my head and steadily down my body, paralyzing as it went. Acid-like venom flowed in an almost traceable path — like hot lava surging through my veins. The intensity increased every inch it progressed as my veins filled with the deadly venom. Over the throbbing sound in my ears I heard screaming. Then I realized the screams were coming from me.

Through my tears of pain, I could make out the creature's golden eyes as it stared at me. It must have been the effects of the venom — I thought I could read pity or concern. However, that naive observation dissipated quickly as fear overcame me.

"Why are you waiting to kill me?" I shouted. "Do you keep your prey alive and plan to eat me bit by bit?" My voice shook in terror before I lost my ability for speech. I began mentally begging it to finish me off.

As shock coursed through me, my body convulsed. My mouth foamed as my throat began to close. I prepared myself to meet my ancestors. As my consciousness slipped, a line of a dragon song nudged a corner of my mind. "The Chosen's life in balance hangs." Then, my eyes rolled back in my head and I fell into blackness.

CHAPTER SIX

I stood on a beach. It wasn't daylight nor was it nighttime. An eerie luminosity filled my vision, but I couldn't see clearly. The pebbles beneath my feet glowed phosphorescent in the half-light. I started running — looking for something. But what? The edge of panic closed in. I felt as though I had gone mad.

So, this is what it's like to join my ancestors? But I felt no peace. My mother told me it would be peaceful. Then I remembered I was looking for my mother, but I didn't know why I needed to find her. She told me she would meet me on the other side and now I wondered if this was where I might be. But she wasn't here, and I was in a state of fear instead of calm.

I found myself flying, but I didn't know if I flew like long ago in my childhood dreams, or if I was riding on something. Nothing seemed clear. I caught sight of a white figure below me on the beach. Upon landing, I saw it was my mother.

"Mother, where am I? Am I with our ancestors?"

"No, Amáne, you are in the shadows." Her soft voice filled me with an ache to remain with her.

"Am I dying, then?"

"That is not for me to say. The answer rests upon you and the healing powers of your dragon."

"My dragon?" She stood before me, but she sounded like she spoke from the other end of a long tunnel, echoing off the walls. I thought she said something about my dragon.

"Recall the song, Amáne," she encouraged.

" *'Burning venom spreads like fire*
The hope to die is the One's desire
If both shall live, then they will soar
Together linked ... forevermore.' "

The dragon hatching song touched the edge of my consciousness. My mother loosened the memory, but nothing stayed with me — I couldn't concentrate.

"I don't know what to do, Mother. I want to stay with you."

"Only you can decide, my daughter. But, it's important that you know, should you choose to stay, it would very likely mean the death of your dragon. The future of Teravinea would be at stake."

"What does the future of Teravinea have to do with me?"

Before she could respond, I heard a mournful wail from far away. A keening that started out low and raised its pitch until it would have been unbearable to human ears. I was torn. The dragon keened again. Instantaneously, my decision was made — *I must go to my dragon. She calls for me.* One last longing gaze at my mother, and I snapped in a flash back to intense pain.

My tongue was thick, my throat parched, but I couldn't find water. I came upon a stream and drank from it, but my thirst was not quenched. It was only a dream — my mouth felt full of sand that I couldn't spit out. I found nothing to bring relief.

The fact I was not dead was my only consolation. Although as I lay writhing in agony, I did wish for death. Thus I spent my hours passing in and out of consciousness. My head ached like it was split open. I could see the light through my closed eyes, but couldn't open them as even the light behind my lids was too intense. On the occasions when I forced them open, I saw the dragon's eyes hovering over me, watching. *Was this still part of my nightmarish dreams?* It looked larger than it did before — nearly as tall as I and even more beautiful than when I had first seen it as a hatchling. Had it grown that rapidly?

At last, my fever broke, and I awoke in my tent. As I moved toward consciousness, I became aware that my mind was incredibly clear. My hearing was sharpened, my body, unmindful of the torture it had just been through, felt stronger than it had ever felt before. I lay there wondering how long I had suffered as I sensed new strength coursing through me. Grabbing my water skin, I moistened my parched lips, letting only a small amount trickle down my throat, lest I choke. Still unsure of my condition, I sat up and found myself staring into the golden eyes of the dragon whose head was now in my tent, where she had dragged me.

"You're the one that's always been in my dreams." I said.

"Perhaps. I am Eshshah — which means fire. You are my Chosen One — my rider, as I am your dragon. My venom running in your veins commits us to each other. We are inseparably linked." I felt her relief at the fact I had lived through my dragon fever. The fever was a necessary part to linking. I noted her tone of regret as she repented the force she had used when she struck me.

I tried to ease her of her guilt as I sat entranced, drinking in her beauty, her spicy, exotic scent and the compassion in her warm eyes. I found no fault in her for whatever she felt she'd done.

At the same time my heightened senses noticed everything around me. The sound of the water lapping at the shoreline; the smell of the fresh morning air; the surrounding colors as I gazed outside of my tent at the azure bay. Even the islands scattered in the distance were more clear. I could see there were many more than I had previously thought.

"Hello, Eshshah. I'm Amáne, daughter of Catriona. My name means water," I said in a hoarse voice. I felt the strength of our bond — she was now a part of me.

"I'm so sorry for your suffering," she said, agitated and ashamed at the same time. "I wasn't able to restrain the amount of venom I injected into you. Our ancient memories recall grown men as riders. They require more venom to link. I couldn't believe I'd finally drawn you in. Before I realized it, I gave you the full measure and almost lost you. Can you find it in your heart to forgive me?"

"Eshshah, you've done nothing to warrant asking for my forgiveness."

I had to pinch myself to see if I was still not dreaming. I sat there holding a conversation with a dragon — the first dragon I had ever seen. In fact, as far as I knew, the only dragon alive in all of Teravinea. And, I was unequivocally linked to her. I was to be her rider. I swallowed hard. With some effort I managed to get my emotions under control. "What do you mean, you finally drew me in?"

"We dragons have an awareness before we hatch. We know there is a person out there who is destined to be our rider. There is no set incubation time, but we must wait until our chosen one is drawn to our egg. Some of us wait hundreds of years for our rider to be born, and when they are, we know. We entice them — lure them to us and hope for the proper conditions where we can draw them in and link with them."

"How long have you waited for me?"

"My egg was laid in this cove many years before you were born. I felt your presence when you and the other female came here many times. But I had to wait until you were old enough. I linked with you the day you came of age."

She backed her head out of the tent to let me out.

More alive than ever before, I left my shelter. Breathing in the salty morning air, I began to stretch, feeling every muscle in my body had been rejuvenated — improved upon. I raised my arms above my head, and winced. A burning pain seared through my right shoulder. If everything else felt so right, why should this shoulder throb? I lifted my sleeve and gasped as I took in the markings that had been left from Eshshah's fangs. It was not fang marks, but lines and symbols that resembled the body ink seen on merchants and foreigners who came to the marketplace. A tattoo. But more than just a tattoo, it was an intricate design incorporating a dragon, that was Eshshah, and fire intertwined in an elaborate device — an insignia. It was her linking mark upon me, claiming me as her rider. I gazed at it in awe.

Still distressed over the pain she caused me, she put her nose on my arm and breathed her healing breath. My discomfort disappeared.

"You must be hungry. You haven't eaten for days," she reminded me.

"Days? How long was I stricken?" It certainly didn't feel like days.

"Your arrival was three days ago. Your dragon fever should not have lasted that long. My memories tell me it should only have been a day, maybe two."

In an effort to console her, I explained, "But I'm fine now, Eshshah. Better than fine. Your attention and your healing powers pulled me through and now look at me, I'm so much more alive than I've ever been and I owe you thanks ... and, yes, I'm hungry. I'll get my angling rod and see if I can catch something."

"Please, let me do that for you. Let me catch your meal," she said, "I would like to do something for you in restitution for the pain I caused."

"All right, I'll start my fire while you're gone. But first I have to get a replacement stone for my fire ring. It seems somehow one of them has cracked to pieces," I teased.

"Imagine that," she responded with a low rumble in her chest that sounded a lot like laughter.

I laughed with her. It felt good to laugh, when not that long ago I doubted whether it would ever be possible — I missed my mother so much. Under these circumstances, I had been lifted up. I now knew I could be happy again. I didn't feel any shame in this revelation as I came to the conclusion I can miss my mother, yet still find joy. I understood she will always live in my heart and in my memories, making her never fully absent.

"May I start your fire for you? I'm still working on perfecting my fire skills. I may have all our ancient memories, but until I actually practice, I am functionally illiterate."

I had noticed little burn patches here and there throughout my camp, obviously her practice sessions. I tried to keep my amusement to myself.

Finding a replacement rock for my fire ring, I stacked the wood, and then, fascinated, stepped aside to watch while she concentrated on summoning her combustion skills. She inhaled deeply and then belched out a massive flame that exploded into the fire ring. The force of the inferno created such pressure the circle of boulders couldn't contain the heat and energy. Needing a direction of escape, the blast curled around the back of the ring and shattered many of the stones. It created a whirlpool effect, shooting a fire storm in my direction.

In alarm, I covered my face, turned my body and leapt away as the flames engulfed me. Not knowing my new strength, I flew several yards as my gown caught fire.

Eshshah leaped between the fire and me to take the brunt of the out-of-control blaze. Unharmed by her namesake, she shielded me from the worst of the blast.

Landing in the sand I rolled several times and managed to put most of the flames out before too much damage was done. I sat upright, singed hair smoking, eyes wide open, and tried to take in all that had just happened in only a matter of seconds.

I burst out laughing as I patted at the last of the smoldering embers on the disaster that was my skirt. I looked at Eshshah, "Well done, Eshshah! If we ever need to burn down a village with just one pass, I'll know who to call upon."

Poor Eshshah was stunned, but when she saw me laughing and that I was unharmed, that same rumble started deep in her chest. We spent the next few minutes trying to replay the last few seconds as we laughed at each other's reactions to the near catastrophe.

"Go! Catch us a fish, I'm starving." I entreated. "I'll start my own fire the old fashioned way."

I stood up, wiped the tears from my eyes and surveyed the irreparable damage to my gown. I never liked this one, anyway. I watched as Eshshah spread her wings and launched herself into the air. As she flew into the distance, I marveled at her beauty and her still undiscovered power. The only word I could think of was "magnificent."

As I rebuilt what was left of the smoldering fire ring and started gathering more wood, Eshshah said, "I'm sorry about your clothing, Amáne."

I stopped what I was doing, "How did you do that? I see you as a small spot on the horizon, but I heard you like you were standing right next to me."

"I communicate with you through thought transference. I don't have a voice like you humans. We can be a distance away and I can still be right there with you in thought. The distance at which we can still hear each other is yet to be discovered — it varies with each linked pair."

"Really? I didn't notice you weren't using a voice. I thought you were speaking to me like I speak to you."

"You really don't need to speak out loud either, Amáne. You can just think it and I'll hear you. I believe there are times that it's to your advantage to use thought transference, and not use your voice."

"So, you can actually hear me now, even though I'm not saying it out loud?" I tested.

"Yes, I can hear you."

"I think I prefer speaking out loud." I used my voice again. "It's more believable for me right now."

The rocks that had survived the inferno were still glowing and with no effort, my campfire was blazing. I got out my spices and my cooking utensils and waited for Eshshah to return.

I spotted her in the distance as she glided toward me carrying a large fish in her talons. It was nearly half her size — she was about as large as Ezel, our donkey, not including her long barbed tail. Swooping down, she dropped it on the beach, and landed softly beside it. I pulled my dagger and quickly dispatched the fish. Whispering a thank you song for its life, I cut a portion of it for myself.

"Thank you, Eshshah, the rest is all yours," I said as I placed my piece to sizzle in the pan.

"What are you doing?" she asked.

"I'm cooking it. I prefer my food cooked."

"That doesn't sound very appealing. In fact it seems a shame to destroy a perfect meal with cooking." She proceeded to rip into her portion with her sharp fangs, tearing large chunks of flesh and bones and tossing them down her throat.

"That doesn't look very appealing to me." I returned.

She rumbled her laughter.

We spent our first evening together by the fire feeling as if we had always been together. I looked forward to what tomorrow would bring.

CHAPTER SEVEN

The next day dawned bright. The heat pressed down on us quite early. Crawling out of my tent, I found Eshshah waiting nearby. I satisfied my doubts as to whether I had been dreaming of being linked to a dragon. It was not a dream. I threw my arms around her neck as I gazed at her and marveled at her beauty and her increase in size. She grew noticeably from the previous day, and had to lower her head down to my level for me to caress her jaws.

We used the morning hours to challenge our capabilities — before the heat became too unbearable. I had never run as fast as I now could. Exploring my new strength and speed, I started to run easily along the beach. I had an impulsive desire to test my limits in a sprint. Amazed at the unfamiliar power in my legs I picked up my pace on a long expanse of sand. Eshshah glided effortlessly beside me. I was quite exhilarated with my new skills, which made me a little careless of the terrain. Eshshah's smooth motion beside me attracted my attention. When I turned back to my path, I gasped. I'd come upon a rock that jutted up from the ground in front of me. Too late to stop, I had to dodge it. I veered toward Eshshah. The edge of her wing on its downstroke grazed my foot, and at the speed I was going, it took my legs out from under me. I tumbled for several feet and landed hard on my stomach. My breath forced out of my lungs. My chin smacked on a rock and opened a gash that flowed bright red.

Groaning, I grabbed my chin, and rolled to a sitting position. I found a clean, un-charred corner of my dress and pressed it to my chin. The sticky wetness soaked through several layers of cloth. "That's going to leave a scar," I said.

Eshshah skidded to a halt and hurried back to me. Her eyes whirled in concern. She lowered her face to mine and touched my chin. I felt the warmth from her healing powers enter the open wound. Immediately the blood flow stopped. My pain was gone and my injury was on its way to healing. Remarkable.

In the heat of midday, we took refuge under the shade cloth I had stretched between the scrub trees, and we dozed the afternoon away.

Eshshah hunted in early evening, this time going inland for some wild goats. While she was gone, I got my fishing tackle out and relaxed by the shore waiting for a bite. I didn't really care if a fish was interested or not.

As we lay by the campfire that evening, I poked at the wood absently and watched as the sparks danced in the flames. "Eshshah, in our ballads most dragons and riders had a mission or a quest after they had linked — or at least they had one deed of great note. Nara, my favorite of all of the riders, linked with her dragon, Torin, when she was twenty, according to the songs. There are countless ballads about their spectacular feats saving lives, winning battles and rescuing dragon eggs in daring quests.

Torin was the last dragon to live. I'm certain we're the only linked pair in all of Teravinea and we're in hiding. I'm worried. I've never heard of anyone as young as I am being linked to a dragon. And then add to that, the fact I'm a girl — with all of Galtero's new laws, I'm sure it would not be allowed."

"No matter, Amáne. It cannot be undone."

I turned to her. "I would never dream of it being any other way, but what I'm trying to say is I need to know our destiny. How are we supposed to know our duty as dragon and rider?"

"Our destiny is not for us to see at this time — dragons have memories of the past, and some of my kind had prophesying powers. Torin had such abilities, but I have no powers for seeing the future. Perhaps it would help if you knew my lineage is of royal origin in dragonkind. My line is linked to the human line of the Dragon Kings — the Royal House of Drekinn. Our threads have been interwoven for generation upon generation, and we have served that royal family for over seven hundred years. Many of that line of kings were riders themselves. You and I are ... brand new. Our direction has not yet been shown to us, but my — or rather our — ties to the royal family have been established. That may very well be our duty — to serve the king."

"I will not serve King Galtero!" I exploded, "I would rather exile ourselves to the farthest island and never see another person again before I would give myself in service to him. Besides, he is not of the House of Drekinn. He is King Emeric's step uncle. King Emeric and his family died, the last of the line of the Drekinns, so it may be we need to find new ties."

"I agree," Eshshah said, "but perhaps there is someone out there who has some Drekinn blood running in their veins. If there is, that is to whom we give our oath of fealty."

"Then, that will be our quest. To find a member of that family." I was satisfied. It was easier than I thought, to decide our destiny.

The following day I rushed out of my tent once again afraid to hope that my dragon was not just a dream. I half-expected to find only the sandy beach and the blue sea. But, there was Eshshah, watching me with her golden eyes.

"Eshshah, you are unbelievably more beautiful than you were yesterday." I rushed to her and threw my arms around her neck. She now towered above me.

"Thank you, Amáne."

"Why have so many of your scales fallen to the ground? Are you ill?"

"No, that's completely normal. We grow rapidly in the first few weeks. Each time we shed our scales they're replaced by new ones. You need to gather and keep them, for they are valuable. I'm not sure if it still holds true, but my memories tell me they were used to barter for services and wares."

"I know of no one that has ever used them in the marketplace. I doubt if it's safe nowadays to offer scales in exchange for goods. It would raise questions as to where they came from. No one would use any they might have. They would keep them safely hidden."

She gave out a saddened feeling, but continued on a different subject in her lesson. "We grow according to the size of our rider. You don't look very large. Will you be growing more?"

I laughed. It wasn't the first time anyone was curious about my small stature. "No, human females are about as big as they will get when they reach my age. Males grow for a few more years. I'm afraid this is all you get — I am small for my age."

"You are the perfect size."

Picking up one of her scales that lay on the sand, I examined it closely. They varied in size, but most would fit in the palm of my hand and were longer than they were wide. The one side that attached to her body ended in two spikes, the other end had a rounded point. It had a bit of flex to it, but was unbreakable. I proceeded to gather all that had fallen around our camp and placed them in my satchel.

"Another thing you need to know," she continued, "is that our scales exhibit the properties of the dragon from which they came. For example, you can start a fire with mine."

"Would this be a simple fire, or an inferno?" I couldn't resist.

"Whatever you need it to be," her chest rumbled her form of laughter,

"Go ahead, try it," she said. "You just need to whisper my name and imagine the size fire you want."

I removed one of the smaller scales from my satchel. "Do I hold it in my hand or put it on the ground?"

"That's up to you. You can keep it in your hand, if you like. It won't hurt you.

I held it in my open palm, and bit my lip, hesitating. I whispered, "Eshshah," and thought of a small flame. Already iridescent, it began to glow, like an ember in a hearth. Then, a small flame ignited, the size of that on a candle. It didn't burn my hand, but when I drew my other hand over it, I could feel the heat. It was real fire. Incredible. With more confidence, I imagined a larger flame, and was not disappointed. Fascinated, I continued my experiment until it appeared that my entire hand was on fire.

Always hungry, Eshshah excused herself to hunt. She informed me when she reached her full size, she would only need to eat about once a week. In a short time she returned with a large fish. I took a small piece and threw it in my pan while she looked on in disgust. I mirrored her disgust as I watched her tear her prey apart.

Our cove was our sanctuary where we could be assured that we would not be seen by anyone, but still I spent a better part of the day brooding about our situation. I could come up with no solution. No one had seen a dragon since before I was born. Anybody my age had never seen one. Their existence had become a tale of the past — especially when my generation was being convinced they never actually existed. There was no telling what kind of commotion it would cause if we just flew into town. That was not an option.

I went to sleep that night very uneasy about our being discovered, fearing the worst — that somehow she would be taken from me. I would rather join my ancestors than ever be separated from her. Now I understood the songs of riders who had gone mad at the death of their dragons.

On the third day after I had awakened from my dragon fever, the morning broke cooler and damp. The dew was dripping inside my tent. As I crawled out, I saw Eshshah was not in her usual place outside.

"Eshshah, are you hunting?"

"Yes, I have an idea of what we can do today, but I had to feed so I could have all my strength. I'm on my way back."

As I collected her scales, I saw her coming from a distance. The rising sun was at the perfect angle to reflect off of her. It gave the appearance she was glowing. She literally looked like a ball of flames as she glistened and shimmered fire red with hints of orange, yellow and blue. As she soared closer, I was conscious of a change in her. She not only looked so much larger than yesterday, but the stroke of her wings was more powerful. Eshshah was truly magnificent. I gazed at her in wonder almost forgetting to breathe.

My dragon landed lightly in front of me and I could see as well as feel her increased strength. She put her nose down to me as I hugged her large head and drank in her spicy fragrance.

"Amáne, would you like to fly with me?"

CHAPTER EIGHT

Eshshah's question echoed in my mind, and will always remain etched in my memory. This was the beginning of our true relationship as dragon and rider. It brought it to a new level — the objective of our existence. As the sunrise set fire to Eshshah's iridescence, I stood there, mute in voice as well as thought.

"Amáne? Do you not want to fly today?" I felt her confusion about my silence.

"There's nothing I want more ... I just can't believe this is not a dream. I know I keep saying that, but each day with you is more incredible than the one before. So, tell me what do I do? Do I just climb on? What do I hold onto? We don't have a saddle or any of the equipment I have seen in the paintings of dragons and riders. Can we do this without?" My excitement increased with each question.

"This is another case of my functional illiteracy. I don't really know. But we may as well face the challenge. We'll have to do without any equipment," she answered.

"I can't imagine I could walk up to the saddler and order a dragon saddle." I laughed.

"I don't think that would be wise."

Pulling my skirt through my legs, I tucked it into my sash and proceeded to figure out how to get up to the base of her neck, which was way above my head, at about the height of a large workhorse. She stooped down low and put her foreleg out for me to climb on. I clambered up and threw my leg over her shoulders, just in front of her wings. She had no ridges in this area, of which I was glad. But there also wasn't anything I could readily see to hold on to. I squeezed my knees and leaned forward, then placed my hands on either side of her thick neck. I hoped this would give me some kind of balance.

"Well," I gulped, nervous, excited, terrified. "I guess I'm ready."

Eshshah's emotions matched mine as she positioned herself for takeoff.

I braced myself as she spread her wings and gathered her legs under her. With a mighty thrust of her hind quarters, she leapt into the air, initiating a powerful downstroke of her wings. The sheer intensity of her actions caught me off guard. I thought I'd braced myself for her takeoff, but in my ignorance, I was not prepared at all. My head violently jerked backwards and then shot forward at the same time her neck lifted. They collided somewhere in the middle. The force of impact was like running into a stone wall. The crunch of cartilage and the explosion of pain in my face revealed every star I had ever seen in that cove. I cried out as blood spurted from my nose. My lips swelled immediately where my teeth broke the skin.

Instantly concerned, she landed abruptly. I barely recovered from the first blow, when the jolt as she touched ground threw me forward. My face crashed into her neck once again — doubling my pain. Another series of stars joined the first.

Tears streamed from my eyes as I slipped from her shoulders and crumpled to the ground. I landed on my hands and knees, and watched as my blood seeped into the sand.

Eshshah was beside herself as she turned to me. Her alarm echoed in my head.

"I'm okay. I'm okay. Don't worry Eshshah. It might not be broken. It just looks bad." Truthfully, it felt bad, but she was already upset, so I didn't share that with her.

"Look up, Amáne. Let me help you." I felt her distress.

I raised my face to her as she put her nose up against my nose and mouth. Directly, a warm soothing sensation radiated in my face. The relief was almost instantaneous. The pain and swelling subsided and the healing began.

"Ah," I sighed. "Thank you, Eshshah. You have a great gift. Now you have my blood all over your nose." I found the last clean spot on my skirt and wiped her clean.

"Wait, I have an idea," I said as I jumped up and wiped my bloody nose on my sleeve. "Hold on a minute and we'll try that again."

"You want to try again? Perhaps that jolt was a little harder than I thought. You're not thinking right."

"No, I know what I need, I'm okay, really."

I ran to our camp and retrieved some ropes from my supplies. Eshshah, waited on the beach, eyeing me like I had possibly gone mad. Making two loops, I pulled them up her front legs, and tied them on the top. Then another loop around her neck. I secured it with the first configuration, making a harness I could grip.

"I apologize, you deserve a silken harness, but have to settle for crude rope, instead. Such disrespect pains me."

"We take what small gifts we have been given, Amáne. Then we use them to the best of our abilities. It will make us stronger in the long run."

"Okay, are you ready?" I climbed up on her shoulders and took hold of the rope reins. This time I was able to sit up straighter so I could avoid a repeat of our collision.

Eshshah and I prepared for another take off. A little more gently, she launched into the air . She spread her wings for the first downstroke once she cleared enough height. It was still a powerful thrust that jarred me, but this time I had some knowledge of what to expect. I relaxed my body and tried to move with hers so I could, in effect, act as a spring and lessen the force of her lift.

"Much better!" I rejoiced as we climbed high above the beach.

My exhilaration was like nothing I had ever felt as we soared over the water. The sea wind rushed in my face — my hair flowed behind me. Flying was nothing less than glorious.

I recalled how I used to sit on the rocks at the beach and watch the pelicans ride the wind. Many times I would dream that I could be one of them. Now, even beyond the imaginings of my childhood, I was riding the wind — on the back of a dragon. Inhaling the cool salty air over the sapphire water, I came to the conclusion that this was the ultimate freedom.

She pumped her wings and flew higher and faster. I learned her rhythm and we moved as one. My skirts had to be readjusted several times to keep them a barrier between her moving scales and my bare legs.

My eyes teared up in the force of the wind as we sped over the sea, but there was not much to do about that. The elation I felt, however, was unmatched, even after riding on the Healer's horse, Thunder. I fervently hoped my whoops and screams of delight were not heard all the way in Dorsal.

"Now let's try the landing," I said.

Again, moving with her and trying to anticipate the landing jolt, the result was greatly improved. I let out a shout of joy. "Let's do it again!"

We practiced all morning, taking off and landing, each time an improvement over the last. I made adjustments on the harness and on my position on her shoulders. She made adjustments on her launches and landings until by late morning we were quite satisfied with our results. We made a few longer flights to nearby islands so I could get used to the speed and the wind.

The two of us were quite spent by the time we decided to take a break. We passed the heat of the afternoon sleeping in the shade after a cool dip in the water. I took a mental inventory of what was left of my supplies, including my clothing. Both of my gowns had been destroyed, the one being irreparably burned and the current one, so full of dirt and blood, it looked like I had been in a battle. No telling what the rest of me looked like. Toward evening I announced we should fly to my cottage in Dorsal after dark. It had been nearly a week since my memorial journey began. As unbelievably joyful as my life had been here in the cove with Eshshah, truthfully, I needed to feel clean again. I looked forward to being salt and sand-free for a little while.

Tomorrow I could mend and wash my things and also check in with the Healer so she wouldn't worry about me. I had no intention of telling her about our linking just yet. I had one more trip I wanted to share with Eshshah before we confided in her. We would rest tomorrow night, and then leave before daybreak the following day for a longer flight. Our goal was one of the further islands on the horizon.

When it cooled off that evening, Eshshah hunted while I broke camp. I managed to fit everything in the satchel I brought — my gear and Eshshah's scales as well the remains of her egg. Her hatching seemed like a lifetime ago.

After dark I threw my pack over my shoulders and put the harness back on Eshshah. I mounted, gave her the word and we took off. The new moon assured us we were in no danger of being sighted, and after a short but pleasant flight, we landed at the cottage. Even though not fully grown, Eshshah was too large to enter and had to stay outside. If ever we were finally revealed, I would have to make some changes so there would be room enough to accommodate her.

I hesitated at the door, and closed my eyes. Breathing deeply to control my grief, I stepped into the place that would bring back the memories of my mother's illness, and the darkness of her final days. What a contrast my life had become since I had latched that door.

My first activity would be a long hot soak. The one luxury my mother would allow was a bathing tub — both of us took great pleasure in the relaxing properties of hot water. We had a cistern on top of the cottage that collected water during the short rainy season. I had to merely open a valve to fill the wooden tub, then add boiling water for a perfect temperature. I soaked until my finger tips looked like dried fruit.

It was nice to sleep in my own bed that night and with Eshshah just outside my open window, it was the best sleep I'd had in a long time.

The following day, I repacked my satchel and got my provisions in order for departure the next morning.

Rummaging through the work shed, I found leather harnesses that belonged to Ezel, who now resided at the Healer's. Putting myself to the task, I fashioned a new harness out of the leather straps and buckles I had gathered. Still crude, but I felt better using leather than I did the coarse rope of my prototype. I had just finished adjusting it on Eshshah when she tilted her head to a sound she heard in the distance. As keen as my hearing now was, hers was even more acute. Shortly after, I heard it, too. Hoofbeats coming down the lane. It was Thunder and the Healer!

"Oh no!" I said. "I had planned on going to see her later, to keep her from coming this way. Eshshah, squeeze behind the work shed and the kiln, please ... and don't let your tail stick out."

Hurriedly, I scanned the area for any dropped scales or telltale signs. I ran inside to make sure there wasn't any incriminating evidence. Hearing the Healer's approach had given me a little lead time. With my newfound speed I removed anything questionable.

I put a pot of water on the hearth just as she knocked. Inhaling deeply and exhaling to slow my rapid breathing, I pulled the door open. I was surprised at how happy I was to see her. "Healer. Please come in."

I froze when her scrutinizing gaze swept over me — I thought I caught a hint of discovery flash in her eyes. It disappeared so quickly, it might have just been my guilty imagination. Her expression then changed to one of immense relief.

She gave me a hug and said, "I was worried about you, Amáne, out there by yourself. You didn't tell me where you were going. If I had not found you home today, we would have started a search. I told your mother I would watch out for you and I would be remiss if I lost you a week after I lost her."

"Don't worry, Healer, I'm fine. We ... er I ... actually just returned for the day and plan to go back again tomorrow — to the cove where we used to camp. I don't feel my journey is quite over. I think I need a few more days, but had to come home to replenish my supplies." I fervently hoped she didn't catch my slip. *Keep it together, Amáne*, I pleaded with myself. No need to be nervous, there is no way she would ever suspect I was now linked with a dragon.

She drew her face closer to mine and looked at my eyes, or rather at what was left of the bruising around them. "Are you feeling well? Were you ill or injured during your journey?"

Ugh, how do I answer? I can't lie. "Uh, yes, I was sick at the beginning of my journey." Which was the truth as I had almost passed on to my ancestors from dragon fever. "But I'm fine. Really, I feel fine, now."

She seemed satisfied with my answer, but I felt she knew I was holding something from her. *Why did she have to be so attentive?*

In an effort to change the subject, and as I remembered my manners, I offered, "Won't you stay for some tea? The water should be hot, now." I would have preferred that she leave. I couldn't be disrespectful, though, and I appreciated her concern.

I was torn — wishing I could have confided in her, but didn't want to take that chance. Not yet. If I'd broken some law and Eshshah was taken from me, I couldn't survive.

We sat at the table and she asked how I passed my time on my memorial journey, and if I sang all of the prescribed songs. I was preparing an answer in my head so I wouldn't give too much away when I noticed her attention drawn to the other end of the table. I followed her gaze and nearly gasped out loud at what lay there. In my mother's things I'd found a large leather bag with intricate beading of an exotic design. I don't know where she got it. Possibly she had traded it with a foreign merchant for her ceramic wares. Without hesitation, I realized it was a worthy satchel for keeping Eshshah's scales, and had placed them in it earlier. I overlooked it in my haste. Now, with eyebrows raised, it was that bag upon which the Healer's eyes settled. Not that she would ever guess what it contained, but my guilty conscience put me in fear of discovery.

My heart accelerated, but I recovered my composure. "Beautiful bag isn't it? It was my mother's. Oh, it sounds like the water's boiling over. Excuse me while I get our tea."

I stood up and in one swift movement scooped up the beaded satchel. I rushed to the hearth to take off the pot as I deftly tossed the bag into the other room. My hands shook. With my back turned to the Healer, I scrunched my face, gritted my teeth and closed my eyes, waiting for her to ask what that was all about. To my relief, she said nothing.

Eshshah then voiced her request. "Amáne, you should tell her. I feel she can help us. And besides, she intrigues me. I want to meet her."

"No Eshshah!" I said out loud.

"Excuse me?" asked the Healer.

"Oh, I don't know if I should pour your tea in this cup or the other one," I responded, turning to her. Now I understood why Eshshah had told me to practice speaking to her silently.

"Any cup will do," the Healer answered, perplexed — her eyebrows nearly touching.

I poured two cups and brought them to the table, trying in vain to calm my heart and my shaking hands. First my healing black eyes, next, the bag of Eshshah's scales and then Eshshah wants to meet the Healer. I didn't know if I could continue successfully with this deception.

The Healer took a sip of her tea in silence. *Was she waiting for me to say something?* It looked like she was wrestling with her thoughts. Then she said softly, "Amáne, are you all right? You've been through a lot in the last few weeks with your mother's passing — then going alone on your memorial journey. Do you have anything you'd like to tell me? Would you like me to accompany you on your continuing journey?"

"No!" *Ugh, that came out way too quickly.* "I mean, thank you very much for your concern and your offer, Healer, but I'll be fine. Truly I will." I wasn't ready to reveal my secret to anyone, yet — terrified that Eshshah and I would be separated, even though Eshshah assured me that could not happen.

"You know if you need me, I'm here for you. You can confide in me if there is ever anything you need to speak about. Just remember that, Amáne."

I nodded and thanked her.

Just then a shadow crossed the window and I saw Eshshah's large head fill the frame, trying to get a look at the Healer. She had an attraction to her for some reason and just couldn't control her curiosity. I swallowed the groan that was rising in my throat.

"Eshshah." I warned through thought transference.

I breathed a silent sigh of relief as I saw no indication the Healer had noticed. She slowly finished her tea, then stood up, "Well, thank you for your hospitality, Amáne. I must be going.

I'm relieved that I found you home and I'm pleased that your memorial journey has set you on the road to healing." She gave me a long hug and stated, "I'll await your return. We have a lot to talk about ... when you're ready."

All I could do was nod again. *Does she know? Would she have said anything if she had seen Eshshah?* My stomach twisted in knots as I walked with her out the door, struggling with my decision. *Was I doing the right thing keeping the truth from her?* I sincerely wished I could share my tremendous secret. Maybe Eshshah was right and she could help us. But what could the Healer do with a girl and a dragon? My stubborn resolve took over. I forced a smile and bid her goodbye, promising I would come to stay with her when I was done with my journey.

Standing on my front step, I watched the Healer and Thunder until the dust from their departure settled. The pressure of hiding my situation from someone I should trust, as well as my shame in my deception, then got the better of me and I fell apart. Slumping to a sitting position on the step, I put my face in my hands and sobbed. Eshshah rushed to my side and hummed a soothing tune.

CHAPTER NINE

Eshshah and I planned to stay at the cottage for the night, and then fly to our cove just before dawn. Once the rising sun began to light the sky, we would leave for the furthest island. We hoped to make it there in half an hour or less. If we felt like staying the night, we were prepared. I had packed extra provisions.

I went over the Healer's visit in my head. "Eshshah, you're probably right and we should confide in the Healer, but I truly want to do this ride. So, let's not stay long on the island, maybe just the day. I'll talk to her as soon as we get back. What do you think?"

"I guess another day won't hurt. But as soon as we return, we must reveal ourselves to her. I have a notion she may know more than we think — I sense she is a person we can trust. I like her."

That night I found it difficult to sleep. My unsettling dreams had me tossed about in a small boat while large waves crashed around me. I awoke with a start when I was thrown from the boat.

"We might as well get to the cove. I'm not getting any sleep, and it's close enough to dawn."

I gathered my pack and in the light of a small lamp, I secured the harness on Eshshah, quite pleased with my work. "At least this is an improvement over the rope. Again, I apologize for such crude gear."

"Amáne, I know your heart. Soon enough we will rise to our proper position, and we'll receive the honor we are due."

"You mean due you. I don't deserve any kind of honor."

"You'll need to stop thinking that way." Eshshah reprimanded, "Dragon and rider are equal. We are a linked pair."

"Sorry, I'll try to keep that in mind."

Everything was in order. I latched the cottage door and put out the lamp. Eshshah stooped down and put her foreleg out to give me a step up. I pulled myself up, swung my leg over her neck, grabbed the long leather straps and gave her the okay. With her muscular hind legs she kicked off and beat her wings in a powerful downward thrust. We were airborne and heading toward our cove. It was a swift exhilarating trip. My heart was ready to burst out of sheer delight.

We had about an hour before it would be light enough to leave for the island, and Eshshah was hungry again. I waited by the cliff while she hunted. She returned well-sated just as daylight broke.

I put on my pack and tucked my skirts up. A thrill coursed through me as I anticipated our upcoming adventure. Eshshah shared my excitement. It's always an elated rush whenever we'd take off — a wondrous feeling, unlike any other experience I've ever known. In no time we were gliding smoothly over the glassy sea. My screams of joy were not restrained. I was in utter ecstasy.

We relaxed as we took in the fresh ocean air and felt like we owned the world. Watching the calm azure water pass under us,

I could see to a great depth. A shark and several large schools of fish slipped by. Dolphins joined in a playful game as they danced in Eshshah's shadow, keeping pace with us. It was magnificent. The beauty and peace of our flight overwhelmed me as we soared. But there was a twinge of guilt that kept me from fully enjoying our freedom. Maybe I should have confided in the Healer.

A sudden blast of hot wind interrupted Eshshah's smooth course, and she lurched slightly. Pulled from my thoughts, I looked around and gasped — my stomach twisted. To my horror, whitecaps began to form on the waves that just moments ago were nonexistent. Out of nowhere, a strong wind whipped around us. A Valaira was surely brewing and we were in open ocean with no place nearby to land. The islands nearest us were small and offered no protection. It would have been more dangerous to be caught on one of them. Too late to turn around — our intended destination was closer than the beach we left behind. We had to continue on our current path, as we searched desperately to find a larger island — our only hope for safety.

The storm progressed and the waves grew in violence as they fell one on top of the other. The wind swept their mountainous tops and threw the salty spray in our faces — we were still flying too low.

As Eshshah lifted higher above the swells, a powerful gust rushed under her wings and threw her off balance. Unprepared for the sudden pitch, I lost my grip. I screamed as I slid off her shoulders toward her back. Panicking for something to hold on to, my hand closed over the leather strap just before it slipped out of my reach. My dragon fought to recover. She tried to hold level so I could pull myself back to the harness. The fury of the Valaira increased. Eshshah was tossed about like a ship on the raging sea

— with me banging around between her wings. I was terrified that as powerful as my dragon had grown, she may have been no match for a full-blown Valaira — which was what we were in for.

It took all my strength to hold on as I tried to avoid her wings. I fought my way back up to her shoulders. Hand over hand I painfully inched forward. My palms bled from the rough leather straps, making them slippery and harder to hold. Each time I thought I would succeed, the anger of the howling gale beat me back again. How foolish of us to think we were ready for such a flight. I shouted encouragements to Eshshah. We had to keep going — we had no choice.

Eshshah struggled to keep us above the furious waves. With sheer effort I managed to get myself back to the harness and into a sitting position. I wrapped the leather straps tightly around my left wrist and hand, then pressed against her neck and held on for my life.

My skirts came untucked, exposing my bare legs to her rough scales. I bit my lip to keep from crying out every time my flesh was pinched between them.

We were still flying too low and the rising waves exploded in our faces, drenching my clothes.

Eshshah rose higher again. "Amáne, our only chance is to get above the turbulence."

"Let's go then! Do what you need to do," I shouted.

She pumped her tired wings and slowly we rose high above the water. Higher than we had ever flown before. The height was terrifying, but the alternative was the Valaira. Our fear joined us closer, firmly linking us. We pushed ourselves beyond what we thought we were capable of. We were one as we fought — our minds melded together as I tried to offer her what little strength

I could. Higher and higher we climbed. We reached an elevation where the air became thin and bitter cold. Cold doesn't bother a dragon, but even as closely as we were linked, her venom running in my veins, I was still only human. The cold was numbing, especially with my wet clothing. I lost feeling in my hands that moments ago were screaming in pain. My legs burned with the effort of trying to hold on.

We finally rose above the Valaira, no longer buffeted, but riding smoothly in the frosty thin air. However, I wasn't sure how long I could endure the cold. My body became numb. Ice formed on my eyelashes and my wet clothes. Dizziness overcame me.

"Stay with me Amáne," Eshshah encouraged. "Hold on. I'm going to soar up here for a bit of a rest before we go back into the squall and find someplace to land."

"Okay, Eshshah. Don't worry about me, I'm all right," I stuttered. I shivered so badly, my teeth were in danger of breaking. My uncontrollable spasms violently jerked me. In a short time, the spasms subsided as the drop in my body temperature made me drowsy — all I wanted to do was sleep. Lethargy set in and nothing mattered anymore, I just needed to close my eyes.

Then in triumph, Eshshah cried, "Look, there's an island big enough for us to land. We're going to make it, Amáne. I see a cave in the cliffs where we can take shelter. I'll stay up here until the last minute, then I'll dive in and head for it."

"Eshshah, I don't care if I make it. Just save yourself," I slurred.

"Amáne you will stay with me. I need you. Fight! We're almost there. Hang on tightly, we're going in now."

With that, she folded her wings and dove into the savage storm. We plummeted faster than I thought possible. My stomach slammed to my throat as I was wrenched from my stupor. I screamed in terror. No longer listless, I clung desperately to the harness as the wind pressure pushed me back again toward her wings.

As if the Valaira were a living evil thing who knew we were about to win the battle for safety, she suddenly hurled a blast of hot dry wind at us. It flung me from Eshshah's shoulders. The leather straps, still wrapped around my left wrist, jolted me to a stop. They saved me from plunging into the water far below. But the force of my fall caused the leather to dig into my arm. It peeled my flesh to the bone as I swung from her neck by my wrist. My screams of pain competed with the howl of the Valaira. Eshshah fought to keep upright as she headed for the opening of the cave.

I strained to reach the harness with my free hand, needing to make it to her back before we landed. As my left wrist threatened to break with the force of our flight, I made one last lunge and caught the harness with my right hand. At that my strength failed. I couldn't urge my body to make the extra effort to climb back up.

"We're almost there. We're going to make it, Amáne."

Eshshah and I hurtled toward the entrance of the cave. She back-pumped with all that was left of her strength, but too late. She could not slow down enough as we approached the cliffs.

A strange calm came over me — I could see everything clearly. I resigned myself to the fact that the end of our lives was imminent. These last moments became like a vivid dream that moved slowly. There was a large cave halfway up the mountainside, like a mouth of a monster opened wide to swallow us. I noticed it was an unusual cave with colors that didn't seem natural. It intrigued me to see it come at us so slowly.

In my dream-like state I had plenty of time to gather the last of my energy to pull my legs up so they wouldn't get ripped off at the entrance ledge. We almost succeeded in entering the mouth without a mishap, but the tip of Eshshah's wing caught on the stone ledge and she tumbled head over tail. I felt my feet hit the stone floor, and was pleased my legs were still connected to my body. Propelled backwards full speed, my head struck the ground. I felt no more.

CHAPTER TEN

I found myself hovering over a beach where I knew I had been before, but couldn't remember when. The white pebbles below softly glowed in the weak light. A cave opened before me and I caught a glimpse inside. I saw a dragon, which for some reason didn't surprise me. She was very still. There was a smaller shape to her right, partially under her, and laying in a pool of blood. I looked more closely and found something familiar about those two figures, but I couldn't bring to mind what it might be.

Feeling a presence behind me, I turned around to find my mother. She smiled at me, and it warmed my heart to see her again. We both turned to observe the scene in the cave. The dragon stirred, and although quite tangled in her wings, she managed to turn her head and nudge the shape next to her. There was no response from the small figure. Then the dragon lifted her head and the most mournful sound came out of her — a sound I had heard once before.

Over her keening I could hear my mother's soothing voice, "Your dragon needs you Amáne. It's your decision, but I would counsel you to go. I long for you stay, but I don't believe it is your time, yet. Listen to her, Amáne. Go to her."

I faced my mother, yearning to remain with her, but my attention shifted to the dragon in the cave, and I realized I knew her. It was Eshshah, and she called for me. My decision made, I bid my mother farewell and then turned back toward the cave. Like a flash of lighting I found myself lying on my back in searing pain, next to Eshshah. There wasn't one part of my body that was not in agony as I shook from the cold, the shock and the pain.

"My head," I groaned, reaching my free hand to the mat of hair at the base of my neck. It was wet and sticky. My hand came away bloody.

"Eshshah?" I moaned.

Trying hard to focus, I could just make out Eshshah's golden eyes staring at me in anguish. She moved her muzzle toward me and breathed her healing warmth on my aching head to relieve my pain and begin my healing. Her warm breath was not enough to raise my body temperature — my tremors continued. I doubted I would ever be warm again.

"Eshshah, are you all right?" My voice quaked, barely a whisper.

Not answering my question, she said in alarm, "Amáne, I didn't hear your heart."

In truth, she was probably right, because there had only been one other time that I'd spoken with my mother after she joined her ancestors. It was on that same beach in the shadows. I must have been dead, or near dead, to have met with her on the other side. Eshshah had called me back — again. I feared had I not returned to Eshshah, it would probably have meant the end of her life as well. Shaking off that disturbing thought, I said to her, "I can't feel my legs."

"They're pinned under me," she said. "I can't move off of them without fear of crushing you. You're tangled too closely in the straps."

My body lay restrained in a twisted position. After tumbling into the cavern, I ended up on my back on Eshshah's right side, feet toward her tail. My left arm was painfully stretched across my face, held by the leather straps that made up my harness. Blood dripped down my arm and onto my chest from the laceration on my wrist. Moments ago these straps had saved me from being tossed into the sea. Now they held me bound to Eshshah.

My pack was trapped under me, adding to my pain — though fortune was with us it had not been lost to the Valaira. Groaning, I inched my free hand behind my back, slowly willing it toward the opening of my satchel until my fingertips felt the haft of my dagger. With stubborn persistence I succeeded in extracting my blade. I brought it around and sawed at the straps that held my left wrist. Concentrating on cutting the leather, I suffered through the added pain. The taut leather strap popped free. I squeezed my eyes shut, gritted my teeth and moaned, cradling my wrist to my chest.

"Ugh, that's going to leave a scar." I said, trying to make light of my agony.

Eshshah turned her healing warm breath on the carnage that was my wrist. It became instantly bearable — on its way to healing. Remarkably, it was not broken. Finally, I had loosened myself enough to shift my body so Eshshah could free my legs. I eased up slowly to a sitting position using her leg to support me. After a few moments waiting for my head to stop spinning. Clenching my jaw from the pain, I pulled myself to my feet — careful to not slip on my blood that pooled on the floor.

My first concern was Eshshah's wings, as I noted their unnatural angles. She rolled to her four legs and carefully opened them, testing for damage. I helped her search for rips as she stretched them out one at a time. She breathed her healing power to mend the few we found. Satisfied, she folded them properly. After such a violent crash, I was thankful she had escaped relatively unharmed. Still shivering, but aware we were at last out of danger, I threw my arms around her neck and hugged her tightly. My tears flowed as I gave in to my emotions.

The wind still howled inside the cave, creating spirals of dust and leaves that twisted around us. The deafening roar added to my aching head.

"Let's see what kind of place we've been cast into," Eshshah said. "I need to get you warmed up before you break all your teeth with your chattering. Maybe there's somewhere I can start a fire — your lips are blue."

"Where are we?" I stammered. "Eshshah, this isn't a natural cave. It looks like it was man-made — or at least humanly expanded upon. We've landed in some kind of entrance cavern. But entrance to what?"

Although dusty and uninhabited, I could see it had once been a magnificent entrance. The path we had cleared as we slid in the dust on our terrifying arrival revealed polished stone inlays of intricate designs. I knew of nothing like this in Dorsal.

Eshshah put her nose in the air and sniffed. "Dragon — but it's an old scent. There's been none of my kind here for a long time. This may have been a dragon and rider outpost to guard the outer reaches of Teravinea. My ancient memories recall such places."

One wall was occupied by a large fireplace, but the wind was too savage to even attempt a fire. Set into the back wall was a massive wooden door made from an unusual type of wood. I didn't recognize it as any I'd seen in Dorsal. It was ornately decorated with carvings — pastoral scenes of a castle I assumed was Castle Teravinea, and its surrounding hillsides and vineyards. There were dragons and riders flying above the castle. It was a beautiful work of art that I would have liked to enjoy more. It would have to wait for a later time. At that moment, I needed relief from the sound of the angry wind — and to find a place where Eshshah could start a fire. My tremors didn't let up.

With Eshshah's help, I dragged myself to the back of the cavern until we were in front of the door. Not sure about how to open it, I pushed experimentally in the middle. To our astonishment the door split in two and slid open silently in both directions, each half disappearing into the wall. It led into an immense corridor that extended left and right. The left passage dead-ended with a similarly carved door, several paces from where we stood. There were three other carved doors, one directly across the passageway from us, and the other two to the right. The corridor then led a little further and angled to an unknown end.

Moving into the main corridor, I turned and touched the edge of the door we had just entered. It shut silently behind us, at last bringing quiet relief from the fury of the Valaira. I turned to Eshshah and breathed a sigh.

The passageway was lit by natural light from an opening high up in the ceiling. Protected from the elements, the intricate stonework beneath our feet and the tapestries on the walls were beautifully preserved. More art that I couldn't wait to appreciate — later. Pain still wracked my body. I was too disoriented to even focus on my surroundings.

We felt no sense of danger in this place, but instead a calmness permeated. I was awestruck by the thought it had been a residence of dragons and riders. Dragon lore songs echoed in my mind and I wondered if I knew the names of any that had walked these same floors.

Eshshah and I decided to first try the door at the end of the corridor to our left. I applied light pressure, and like the previous one, it split and slid easily into the walls on either side. My mouth fell open at the sight of the room that spread before us. What we saw beyond this door was my idea of paradise at that moment. It was an impressively large cavern with tile mosaics covering the rock walls and a polished rock floor. But that was not what made me catch my breath. Directly in front of us were pools of steaming water. Underground hot springs fed into two bathing pools. There was a low waterfall pouring into the smaller one, which was raised with steps leading up to it. This smaller bath then overflowed into the larger bathing pool, which then emptied through an opening at the back of the chamber, then on into the sea.

I threw my pack down, then released Eshshah from the leather harness. Without further hesitation, I walked up the steps to the smaller pool, tested the water — which was perfectly hot — then stepped in, bloody clothes and all. There were no words to describe my bliss. I lowered my numbed body slowly into the steamy water, ignoring the sharp sting in my fingers and toes. Eshshah, pleased her rider would finally be warm, moved to the other pool. With an audible sigh, she sank down into the warmth of the hot springs.

"This has to be what it feels like to truly rest with my ancestors on the other side," I said.

"Don't say that, Amáne," Eshshah responded.

"Sorry."

I slipped out of my clothes while I soaked, and scrubbed them until they were as clean as I could get them. The blood stains would probably never wash out completely. Throwing them over the edge of the pool, I exhaled out all the terror we had experienced, and slid back down into the deliciously-hot water.

CHAPTER ELEVEN

After all my fears had soaked away, and Eshshah gave me another healing treatment, we emerged from the bathing cavern. Feeling refreshed, we began to explore our newfound palace, which was what it seemed like to me. I'd never been in any place so extravagant. Since we were the only dragon and rider in all of Teravinea, I felt like it belonged to us — there was no other way to enter, but by dragon.

The other three doors outside the bathing cavern opened to sleeping chambers. In the first chamber, there was a large four-poster bed with a canopy and heavy brocade curtains in a deep red color. They draped over a feather mattress, raised up on a dais. I sat on the bed experimentally and was more than pleased at how comfortable it felt. I should have had no problem laying back and letting sleep take me right then. But my excitement would never have allowed it. A short distance from the bed was a large hollowed-out indentation in the floor, perfect for Eshshah. Dragons are quite comfortable sleeping on a stone floor.

All the furnishings had dust covers, and upon removing them, we found a large ornately-carved chest, a matching wardrobe, and a small table with two chairs that occupied the corner. The furniture style and craftsmanship were completely new to me. Running my hand over the smooth surface of the table, I marveled at the beauty of the wood as well as the intricacies of the carvings. I wondered if they had been purchased and flown here by dragon from some exotic land, or if possibly the dragon riders who occupied this outpost had used their spare time in crafting these furnishing themselves. The work was certainly done by capable artisans.

Upon opening the wardrobe, I found it stocked with clothing — all men's, since all but two other dragon riders were males. I removed the smallest tunic and some leggings that I decided I would wash later and try on. As large as they still would be on me, they certainly made much better riding attire than my skirts and gowns. Once we got back to Dorsal, I could alter them to fit me better.

The other sleeping chambers were outfitted with similarly beautiful furniture. One was a bit larger and contained three smaller four-poster beds complete with the same ornate canopies and curtains as in the first chamber, except these were dyed a deep green. There were also three indentations for the dragons that would have occupied this cavern. The last sleeping chamber was done in a dark brown and had two large beds and hollows for two dragons. The outpost could accommodate at least six dragons and their riders — probably more if they made use of the entry cavern.

We made our way to the other end of the corridor finding a kitchen on the right that was fit for a manor. Long wooden tables for preparing meals were positioned around the room. A basin carved out of the rock gurgled with water redirected from a spring. Beside this, a larder for storing food. The brick stove took up the wall to our right. Three arches opened under it for the wood fire to blaze. A fireplace with a spit was on the far wall, as well as a stone oven, and quite a supply of pots, pans and cooking utensils. The kitchen itself was not that large, but had everything needed to cook for one dragon rider or ten.

Across the corridor from the kitchen was the dining cavern. It held a large long table with benches on either side. Along the walls were cupboards with bowls, dishes and tankards, spoons and knives. The walls were decorated with hanging tapestries depicting scenes from old Teravinea. So much beautiful artisan work that I couldn't wait to examine more closely.

At the end of the corridor we came to the last carved door. Pushing gently, it opened to reveal the endmost cavern. I gasped as we beheld a magnificent long room that was part library, with shelves of manuscripts and bound books; part art gallery with colorful paintings of dragons and riders as well as scenes of Teravinea; and part saddlery and weapons storage. The latter excited me as nothing else could. I had to remind myself to breathe.

"Oh Eshshah! Look at the swords, the spears, the glaives, the daggers."

Never had I seen such fine work. These blades could only have been created by master craftsmen. The smaller weapons were laid on a table as if being displayed. The spears and poleaxes, as well as shields, hung on the walls.

Attracted to one dagger in particular I gently lifted it in reverence, it was so beautiful. The hilt was made of what looked like bone and the pommel was a pewter dragon that started on the butt end. Its tail wrapped around the grip merging into an inlay down the haft. It felt so right in my hand. It was light, yet I could feel the strength and flex. The double-edged blade was wrought of a fine tempered steel with an engraved pattern on the shoulder — the end by the grip. It was so highly polished my reflection had practically no distortion. I couldn't take my eyes off of the dagger. Reluctantly, I laid it back on the table.

I would spend days in only this chamber if I could. Eshshah continued to the end of the room to inspect the saddles, and I turned back to the bookshelves. Taking a manuscript off of the shelf, I inhaled its leather scent as I carried it to a table to peruse. Caressing its ornate cover, I traced the tooled artwork depicting Teravinea with dragons and riders flying over the vineyards — which seemed to be the common theme in all of the artwork here at the outpost. The title was *Famous Dragons and Riders*. Opening the illustrated parchment pages, I sat back and lost myself in our history.

I spent quite a while studying one manuscript after another as I drifted in and out of sleep — my body made an effort to recuperate.

One thing, however, I noticed our temporary residence was lacking, was lanterns and candles. I couldn't find any method of lighting besides the sky lights, which would not be of much help once the sun went down. It was getting near that time. When we explored all of the chambers, I found the walls, as well as the corridor, hosted similar decorations that looked like shields made out of dragon scales. I recalled the conversation I had with Eshshah about her scales and how they take on the properties of their dragon and would react if you but spoke the dragon's name.

"Eshshah, I have an idea. Do your memories tell you any dragon's names that relate to light?"

"I wish I could tell you, but my memories do not hold names of any other than a few of my line."

I pulled out one of the manuscripts I had looked through earlier and started thumbing through it. Finding an index of dragon names, I tried translating to see if I could find one that would work. I was confident in my assumption. The only problem was whether I could find the right name before I completely lost my light to read. It wasn't critical, though, as I still had Eshshah's scales to light my way. But I truly wanted to get the light shields working. It was a challenge I welcomed — determined to figure it out.

Studying the book, I called out "Inara," which meant ray of light. Dragon of Keenu. Nothing happened. "Huelwen." Light from the sun, ridden by Koen. The shields remained dark. "Dinesh." The sun. Hajari was his rider. No success. I tried them as whispers, I tried them as shouts. Still no light.

"Eshshah, any ideas?"

She thought for a second, "How about starlight? Are there any names that translate? And what if the rider's name contains a meaning for light as well?"

"Sitara!" I invoked. Her rider was Leyna, which means bright light. To my gratification the shields in the room started to glow. They slowly increased their intensity until the room was lit as if it were mid-daylight. I jumped up from the table, and ignored the pain from my injuries as I danced around the room, quite pleased with our success.

"Sitara." I said again and the light diminished until the shields were no longer lit.

"Thank you, Eshshah, you figured it out."

"We worked together, Amáne."

As it neared sunset we went back to the entrance to see if the Valaira had abated. It had. It was dead calm and the west-facing entrance was glowing orange as the sun lowered in the sky. I had never seen a more beautiful version of my favorite time of day. We stood at the ledge marveling at our fortune in discovering this place. I sang a song of thanksgiving as Eshshah softly hummed beside me. We watched as the orange ball that was the sun slowly lowered itself until it was consumed by the dark sea.

I stepped closer to the ledge to look down and for the first time realized how high up the entrance actually was. The beach was a long way below us. I verified my earlier assumption that there was no other way to enter, except by dragon flight.

Without warning, my exhaustion overcame me. I'd been so excited at our discoveries, our harrowing events that started our long day had slipped my mind. I'd had no thoughts of our near-death experience, my head injury, nor my wrist, but it all came back to mind. And it weighed down fully on me at that moment.

My injuries had not completely healed, and the pain returned. Eshshah breathed her healing powers on me again. I sighed with immediate relief. She excused herself to hunt while I, barely awake, made my way to the first sleeping chamber. I pushed open the door, and whispered "Sitara" for the light shields to illuminate as I entered. In a stupor, I spread my bed roll over the feather bed, then fell into a deep sleep after one hastily murmured memorial song for my mother.

CHAPTER TWELVE

My comforting sleep soon filled with the horror of my nightmares. Raging wind and howling monsters were after me, ready to devour me. I ran for my life and found myself trying to climb a sand dune. The more I tried to scramble to the top, the more I failed. Someone was there to pull me to safety, but remained just beyond my grasp. The creatures closed in and poisonous tendrils reached out for my ankle as I clawed at the moving sand. I tried in vain to make the top of the dune.

I awoke with a scream and bolted upright in bed. Tears streamed from my eyes. Eshshah was there instantly and breathed her sweet and spicy breath in my face, as she hummed her soothing melody.

My bedclothes were soaked as I went from chills to sweating fever. My head throbbed, my injured wrist swelled. Eshshah worked to relieve my pain and fever. I began to relax, but was afraid to go back to sleep for fear of the monsters. They might catch me this time. Exhausted, I dozed off once more. No sooner had I reached sleep, my terror repeated and I ran for my life again.

One more time my screams woke me. One more time Eshshah calmed me.

"I'm sorry, Eshshah, you're getting no sleep with me in here. I'll go to one of the other sleeping chambers and give you some peace."

"No Amáne. It's fine, you're not bothering me. Stay."

Terrified of lying back down, I took my bed roll and dragged it to Eshshah's bed. I spread it out close to her head. Her nearness was all I needed. I fell into a peaceful sleep as she hummed beside me.

When I awoke it was nearly midday. My head still hurt but I felt much better. I made my way to the entry cavern to be with Eshshah. She lounged in the warmth, waiting for the sun's rays that would bathe the entry when it arced to the west.

A fear rose in my chest and I moved closer to Eshshah. My body trembled. "Eshshah, I don't know if I can fly again any time soon. I'm afraid. I thought I would be ready to go home today, but I just can't." Shame pressed down on me to think I was such a coward. The horror of what we went through yesterday, along with my nightmares was more than I could take.

"You need another day to heal, Amáne. We will not go back today. You have no need to fear another trial like we had yesterday. I believe I will now be able to sense a coming Valaira — what we experienced will never happen again."

She saw her consoling did nothing to relieve my fear. Turning her eyes toward mine, with an authoritative air she said, "Amáne, I need you to do something for me."

"Anything, Eshshah, what is it?"

She asked me to follow her into the library/weapons chamber. I was puzzled, but I did as she asked.

"I want you to put a saddle on me."

"What?!"

"Choose a saddle and put it on." She said it so firmly I couldn't argue with her, nor deny her request.

The rear area of this grand cavern had several types of saddles of varying sizes. I surveyed the choices. Having no knowledge of dragon saddlery, I decided on one that I thought would fit Eshshah the best. It was of beautifully tooled leather with ornate swirls and leaves, intertwined with a stylized dragon the length of the seat. Some saddles had leather straps at the foot rests to secure a rider by his boots, some had straps that fastened further up at the calf. This style had one strap in the middle of the seat directly in front of the rider and then divided into two. Each strap would be drawn across the upper thighs and buckle on either side of the hip — it looked to be the most secure. Referring to the illustrations in one of the manuscripts, I situated it correctly on Eshshah.

Satisfied, we made our way to the entry cavern. Only with a lot of coaxing and humming, was she able to get me to mount. She waited patiently while I struggled with the fasteners on the belt. My fingers refused to cooperate. Finally, I was securely buckled in.

Eshshah walked to the ledge as I shook in the saddle. Still humming for me to relax, she leapt off and easily took to the air. It didn't matter that she pushed off as smoothly as she could, I still let out a scream of terror. After just a minute in the air, my panic disappeared, replaced by the sheer pleasure of soaring with my dragon.

The difference the saddle made was like moon and sun. I felt completely safe, no fear of falling off. It was actually a very comfortable seat.

"Eshshah, you're a genius," I laughed. "You had the perfect cure for me."

We flew for a while around the island exploring our newfound second home.

Once we got back to the outpost, she suggested I soak again for a while in the hot springs. They had their own kind of healing powers, and when combined with Eshshah's, I was almost back to feeling like myself.

Confident in my improvement, Eshshah decided it would be safe to leave me while she hunted again. She seemed to always be hungry. I wondered when her rapid growth would slow down.

Eshshah craved fish and I accepted her offer to bring some back.

Since my injuries and disposition had improved, I needed an activity to keep me busy. I decided the entry cavern needed to be scrubbed to match the quality of the rest of the outpost. While Eshshah hunted, I got to it.

At close examination of the entry I noticed there was a large stone door hidden in the wall. Closing it would seal the outpost from any outside intrusion. I gave it a tug, but it didn't budge. The door looked like it should follow a track which I realized was lodged with dirt and debris. I removed the obstructions, then tried again. Once cleared, it just needed a gentle coaxing and it slid silently on its track. I repeated the closing and opening several times to make sure it worked properly, then left it open and decided I would test it later with Eshshah so we could figure out how to open it from the outside.

I found cleaning brushes and buckets in the storeroom by the kitchen and got to work on the entry cavern. The furniture in that room was made of polished stone to withstand the elements when the door remained open. There were couches and chairs and some tables all close to the walls, leaving the center of the cavern clear. Once I cleaned, scrubbed and mopped, the room looked just as impressive as the other chambers. I even managed to remove most of my bloodstains from the corner where we had landed the day before.

Finding some feather cushions in the store room, I figured they were intended for the entry furniture. I'd just finished placing them when Eshshah arrived with a large fish. She released it from her talons and laid it flopping on the newly-cleaned floor. I was surprised at myself that this didn't bother me. I quickly dispatched it and sang a song of thanks for its life. I cut a small portion for myself, and she carried the rest outside to devour on the beach.

Using one of her scales to make a fire in the kitchen, I soon had a tasty meal sizzling in my pan. Hungry and worn out from my exertions of the past couple hours, I was ready to eat and relax.

After our meal we went into the library where I pulled another book off the shelf. It was a pictorial with colorful hand-painted illustrations. Eshshah made herself comfortable toward the back of the chamber.

"Eshshah, in many of these illustrations people are making the same hand gesture. They have their thumb and forefinger of their right hand together forming an "O" with the other three fingers straight up, and then they bend their elbow and place it over their heart. Do your memories have any knowledge of what this means?"

"Yes, I do know that one. It's the universal salute for a dragon and rider. A gesture of respect and appreciation for their service. Riders also greet each other with that sign."

"People are supposed to salute us? I can see saluting you, but I can't believe I deserved that kind of honor."

"Amáne, you need to understand our station in society as dragon and rider. We have a duty code to serve and protect. Remember, I told you about my royal lineage — unlike other dragons, my line has been sworn to serve the king of the Drekinn dynasty — King Emeric being the last of that line. You and I, as a linked pair, would have answered only to him, which would have put us in the hierarchy of nobles or lords. Now, I'm not sure to whom our duty would be, but as we discussed earlier, we'll find someone of that bloodline. I believe the Healer should be the first we turn to. I sense she'll be able to help us."

"I know, Eshshah. You were right all along. I'm sorry I didn't listen to you before, but then we would never have found this place. So I guess it worked out well for us. We'll leave first thing at day break and seek the Healer's help."

CHAPTER THIRTEEN

The morning broke hot and humid. I resigned myself to the fact we had to leave our magnificent discovery. It was time to confide in the Healer. I went through all of the chambers of our outpost, replacing the dust coverings, and removing the cushions from the entry cavern — preparing the place for our absence. We had no idea when we would be able to return. It was sad to leave after so short a stay, but we planned to come back.

I dressed in the tunic and leggings I'd found in the wardrobe. Rolling up the pant legs, I stuffed them into my boots. There were a few pairs of leather riding boots, but there weren't any that even came close to fitting me. The tunic looked fine once I found a belt that fit perfectly — when wrapped around me twice. I looked in the glass and was actually quite pleased with what I saw. My reflection brought to mind some of the illustrations of the dragon riders I'd seen in the manuscripts. I tried the dragon salute just for my amusement.

The last room we put in order was the library/gallery/ weapons room — my favorite. I would love to have taken one of the books, or several with me, but didn't want to chance destroying them. I did however, succumb to my desire for the beautiful dagger I found on our first day here — the pewter one with the dragon pommel. I slid it into its sheath and attached it at the back of my belt.

The saddle we used the day before felt quite safe. We decided to use the same one for our flight home. I lifted it from its stand and heaved it upon Eshshah. In good spirits and looking forward to our flight, I thanked Eshshah for making me ride yesterday to get over my fear. I was familiar with the phrase 'If you fall off a horse, get back on,' but I never gave it much thought until now. I found it pertains to dragon riding as well.

Finishing our preparations in the entrance cavern, I took a last look, slung my pack on my back and mounted up. After buckling myself in, I gave Eshshah the word. I couldn't avoid a sharp inhale as she plummeted off the ledge of the entry cave. She dropped in a free-fall for several feet before spreading her wings. My reaction was not out of fear, this time, but from pure joy.

Once in the air, Eshshah turned back and hovered close to the cliff. With her nose, she pushed on a rock to the left of the entrance. It tripped a release and allowed the door to slide shut. There was no evidence from the outside our sanctuary even existed on the other side of the stone door. We made a mental picture of exactly where the push-rock was located for when we return.

Our flight back was an enjoyable one. There was not so much as a small gust to interrupt our soaring. We experimented with low flying as well as high flying — now that I had warmer clothing — testing Eshshah's skills as well as our new equipment. At last we had gear worthy of Eshshah.

We landed back on our beach at the cove. Rather than wait for nighttime to fly to my mother's cottage, and then have to wait until the following day to see the Healer, we agreed I should run to her home first thing. Eshshah would wait out the day on the beach and then meet me at the cottage that night.

I took off her saddle and stowed it in a nearby cave. This way she could be comfortable and would be able to go for a swim if she wanted. Giving her a long hug, I kissed her goodbye, and headed off.

It felt good to run. I'd gotten so little exercise since riding Eshshah, I feared I may have been getting lazy. This was what I needed to clear my head. It helped to put my mind on track to try to figure out how I was going to tell the Healer about linking with Eshshah. My fervent hope was that she was not obligated to turn me in if our situation proved to be unlawful.

Free of my cumbersome camping provisions, I traveled much more quickly. Stopping at the cottage first, I went in to check on it, change into a gown and straighten out my unruly hair. I tucked my skirts up and hid my newly-acquired dagger at my waist, then headed for town. I ran on the road outside the walls to the northeast town entrance where the Healer's shop was located. The run was stimulating, but I still couldn't decide how I was going to tell the Healer about Eshshah. My nerves began to get the better of me. Maybe confiding in her now would prove to be the wrong decision.

"Amáne," Eshshah broke into my thoughts, "just go in and tell her everything. I know she'll understand."

I stood outside the apothecary shop and took in a deep breath, then pushed open the door. Her assistant, Gallen, was minding the front counter and he greeted me warmly. Relief reflected in his eyes.

"Hello, Gallen, I've come to speak with the Healer."

"Welcome home, Amáne. I believe she's been expecting you."

"I think she probably has."

I waited only a few moments for her when she came through the door at the back of the room. She exhaled an audible sigh. Relief and anticipation showed in her deep brown eyes.

"Gallen, would you mind watching the shop a bit longer while I take Amáne inside for a while? She looks like she could use some tea."

The Healer's home was behind her shop. I followed her into her kitchen. It was a warm inviting kitchen with delightful aromas. Spices and herbs she used in her concoctions and her cooking drifted harmoniously in the air. The Healer poured us both a cup of tea and sat beside me at her table.

"So, Amáne, tell me what's on your mind." Her eyes searched mine as I tried to gather my thoughts. *Where do I start?*

I turned to face her. "Oh Healer, I'm sorry I didn't come to you sooner — I was afraid to. I didn't know what to do and I didn't know if you would understand. I didn't know if it was legal to have Eshshah as I'm only fifteen and I'm a girl and I would die if she were taken from me, and I'm sure if I died she would die too, and if I told you when you came to my cottage the other day, you wouldn't have let us fly to the island and I have no one to confide in, except of course Eshshah, but she doesn't really know all the laws either and we felt so alone." I couldn't stop my words. A heavy weight had lifted from my chest. I was about to continue with my outpouring when I paused and considered all I had just said.

"Er ... my apologies, I guess I'm not making any sense ... I'm ..." My voice quavered and I broke into tears.

She took me in her arms and let me cry. It was a cleansing for me. I hadn't realized how much pressure I'd put on myself trying to keep this secret from her. Eshshah hummed her calming melody in my head.

"I understood every word you said, Amáne," the Healer said. "You see, in my lifetime I've known many a dragon rider."

I gasped and pulled back to stare at her, not sure if I heard correctly. *How did she recognized I was now a dragon rider?* My eyes opened wide. My jaw dropped.

She smiled and said no more on the subject, but handed me a linen to dry my tears.

The Healer gently asked, "May I see your linking mark — your right shoulder?"

My sleeves were too tight to pull up so I pulled my neckline down at the shoulder and exposed Eshshah's mark — the sign of our linking. The Healer leaned toward me and studied it for a long time. I saw a shadow flit across her eyes, it was gone as quickly as it came. She nodded a couple of times and shook her head once or twice.

Satisfied, she straightened and said, "Congratulations, Amáne, Dragon Rider." To my shock, she finished her sentence with the dragon salute, to which I acknowledged with what I had learned was the traditional response of a nod. Up until that moment, it still felt like a dream. But the reality of my newly-acquired station of dragon rider slowly dawned on me as my shoulders still heaved from my sobs.

"So, your dragon is from the royal dragon line." The Healer looked pleased at that bit of information she'd read in the linking mark. Eshshah — Hmm fire. She has a beautiful name and I'm sure she is as beautiful as her name."

With pride I responded, "She is the most exquisite creature that was ever on this earth. Her scales shimmer red, orange and yellow, and some blue. She has all the colors of a comforting fire — like your hearth. I can't even begin to describe her beauty."

Eshshah uttered her low laugh-like rumble and said, "Thank you, Amáne. Please send my greetings to the Healer. I can't wait until I can meet her in person."

"Sure, Eshshah. Me too. The sooner the better," I said out loud as was my habit.

The Healer politely pretended she didn't hear me talking out loud to my dragon.

"Eshshah sends you her greetings. She can't wait to meet you."

"Thank you, I look forward to meeting her as well. Where is she now and what are your plans of meeting up with her?"

"She's at the cove right now, waiting for dark. We were going to meet at my mother's cottage when she can fly in without being seen."

The Healer was astonished, "She's at the cove? That's at least an hour's ride on horseback from here, if not more, and you can converse with her at that distance?"

"Yes, I hear her like she's in this room. Why? Is that unusual? Eshshah told me dragon and rider communicate by thought transference. Are we doing something wrong?"

"No, nothing's wrong, it's just that the cove is quite a distance away. To my memory, I'm not aware of too many linked pairs who were able to use thought transference at that distance. Interesting. Can you please ask her if she is willing to meet you here instead?"

"She said that would be fine."

"You didn't ask her yet — you spoke to her out loud before, but not this time. She answered as if I had asked her directly. Are you two using open thought transference — she can see and hear me directly through you?" I believe she guessed the answer was yes.

I nodded. "Are we not supposed to do that?"

"Where did you learn open thought transference?" She asked abruptly.

Thinking we were in trouble, I answered. "I read it in one of the books on the island — at the outpost, but we didn't have anyone to practice it with and I wanted to include her in this conversation, so we decided to try it with you ... I'm sorry, Healer, were we supposed to ask your permission first? Are we not supposed to practice it?"

"The island? The outpost?" Her face went ashen.

I started to panic. With every question she asked, my confusion increased. "Eshshah? What did I do?" I asked her out loud.

"Nothing wrong, Amáne. I think the Healer is just having a hard time absorbing your information. I assume she is getting a lot more than she expected from a newly linked pair."

The Healer, still pale, grasped the edge of the table as if she would fall off the bench if she let go. She said slowly, "Please start at the beginning, Amáne. When did you link?"

I proceeded to tell her our whole story. How Eshshah had hatched on my birthday and how badly she felt that she inadvertently injected her entire measure of venom into my veins. When the Healer heard I was unconscious for three days and I had spoken to my mother in the Shadows, she turned a lighter shade of pale — her knuckles went white.

"You saw your mother? What did she say?"

"She said I could choose to stay with her, but that would mean Eshshah would probably perish as well, and that the future of Teravinea would be at stake. What did she mean by that?"

She didn't answer my question. "Please go on with your story."

Despite her growing discomfort, I didn't hold back anything in my narrative. When I got to the part where we were caught in the Valaira and I hung by my wrist, I had to stop and ask, "Healer are you okay? You don't look well."

She picked up the sleeve covering my left wrist and examined the scar that was still raw but healing remarkably. Keeping her voice even with noticeable effort, she said, "I should have seen the signs — I should have been more vigilant.

"At first I thought it was your mother that would be chosen, and I followed her here after she married your father. She trained with me for a time. But then when you were born, we knew you were the One. We were going to tell you when you came of age. I should never have let you go alone on your memorial journey. Amáne, I am so sorry. I feel as if I have failed you. The full measure of venom, a Valaira, seeing your mother?" She groaned. Visibly upset with herself, she looked quite ancient at that moment. I didn't know what to say to comfort her.

She continued, "I've been watching for this since before you were born and I let my guard down. I shouldn't have. A newly-linked pair should never be alone, especially at the hatching. In all of history, I don't recall any pair who linked when they were alone ... and survived." Then recovering slightly, she took a deep breath, "I suspected when I came to visit you the other day and I should have asked you instead of assuming that I was mistaken. I thought

I caught a scent of dragon. I don't know why I didn't trust my instincts. But I didn't think it would be something you would keep from me. I had no idea you would be so foolish as to try a longer flight ... to the outpost ... in a Valaira no less."

I lowered my eyes in shame. She exhaled loudly. "Most linked pairs need at least a week of training and instruction before even trying their first short flight." Then with another deep breath, she said, "I'm all right, please continue."

My story came to the point where we crash-landed at the outpost and I wanted to spare her the anguish of finding out I had visited my mother again in the Shadows. But I couldn't keep it from her, so I disclosed that as well. I kept my gaze on my hands as I continued my narration, afraid to look directly at her.

"What did your mother tell you this time?"

"That, again, it was my decision if I wanted to stay with her, but she thought I should go to my dragon as she was keening for me — I guess my heart had stopped — and Eshshah called me back again from the Shadows." I heard her sharp intake of breath, but I wasn't brave enough to watch her expression as she learned she almost lost us a second time.

I told her about the outpost and how beautiful it was. I was excited at sharing our discovery with her. She listened intently and at last started to relax — her color slowly came back. The Healer was genuinely interested in the outpost. I wondered if she had been there, but she made no mention of ever having seen it.

Our story came to an end and I breathed a sigh of relief as my confessions freed me from the pressure I'd been holding in. It was as if a great weight had been lifted from my chest. I felt badly about burdening the Healer with our secret. But she did say it was the purpose for which she was in Dorsal — that it was her mission. She needed to know.

CHAPTER FOURTEEN

Evening approached and Eshshah's pending arrival created a spirit of excitement between The Healer, Gallen and me. Tonight's meeting was monumental. In my limited understanding of the state of affairs of our kingdom, I began to understand what my mother had said when she implied the fate of Teravinea would rest upon Eshshah and me. We were the only dragon and rider in all of Teravinea.

We moved to the courtyard. For the first time I realized the amount of property the Healer owned. I'd only seen her apothecary shop, via street access, and a limited section of her home. As far back as I could remember, my mother and I would visit and spend the entire time in her kitchen. Other times, while the Healer and my mother talked, I would join Gallen as he worked in the shop. I had never been outside behind her home, except the one time when I rode with her on Thunder. I don't remember much about that occasion. She had a large courtyard and a field that stretched out into the distance. It was bordered on the east by the city walls. Her large home sat on the west most side of her property, built back toward the cliffs that formed the base of the impassable mountains. The mountains continued a distance to the west before the walls of the city picked up again.

The Healer asked me to summon Eshshah from the cove as she, Gallen and I waited in the courtyard for my dragon's arrival. I shook with excitement when I spotted her approach, even while she was still a long way off. Her beauty was shown fresh every time I saw her. Each hour she was more impressive than the last.

She landed gently, the wind from her back-stroke blew our hair and our clothing behind us. I forgot my manners as I ran up to her and threw my arms around her neck when she lowered her head toward my face. I didn't like being absent from her presence for even a short period of time.

I turned to the Healer and Gallen and said, "I would like you to meet Eshshah."

They both stood straight and saluted her. Eshshah responded with a nod. It was hard to read all of the emotion in their faces, but I did see the moisture in the Healer's eyes.

"Healer and Gallen, we apologize we don't know if there's a protocol we should follow for this occasion. We're very informal, please, feel free to approach her."

I could tell straight away Eshshah was attracted to the Healer. She loved her as I did. The Healer was now all I had for family. She wasn't related by blood, but her closeness to my mother made her family enough.

Eshshah made the initial gesture as neither the Healer nor Gallen had moved. Their eyes were riveted on her. She lowered her face to the level of the Healer and nudged her in a friendly show.

In an uncommon expression of emotion, the Healer wrapped her arms around Eshshah's neck and held her. Tears streamed from my eyes as Eshshah hummed her calming tune. It was like a reunion of friends who hadn't seen each other in too long a time.

Then Eshshah turned to Gallen and put her nose on his chest. He reached up and scratched her between her eyes as she hummed her pleasure.

Recovering from her unaccustomed emotional demonstration, the Healer gathered herself and turned to me.

"May I have permission to speak with your dragon?" she asked.

"You don't need to ask for permission, you can speak to her any time you like — Eshshah agrees. She already explained to me the age-old formalities of asking permission from a rider to speak with their dragon. Truthfully, I find it archaic, but you have our permission from now on."

With eyebrows raised in reaction to my dismissive attitude on etiquette, the Healer turned to Eshshah, "Eshshah, your beauty far surpasses Amáne's description. She was correct when she said she couldn't begin to describe you. It is my pleasure to meet you. I've waited for this moment for a long time."

Gallen expressed a similar greeting. Eshshah acknowledged them both with a nod, pleased at their salutations.

She beckoned us to follow her to the back of the long courtyard. This part of her home was built right up to the mountainside — where the building ended, the solid rock of the mountain began. We stopped and the Healer revealed a large dragon-sized door in the wall of her house-proper, before it joined the rock. It was hidden from any that didn't know where to look. She opened it outwards with ease and we found ourselves in a great hallway, the left leading to the Healer's living quarters and the familiar kitchen. The right at first appeared to be a solid wall, but she unlatched another large hidden door that led straight into the mountain. We found ourselves in a sizable cavern that was hewn in a similar way to the outpost, only much less lavish. No intricately-inlaid floor, no tapestries, only clean smooth rock underfoot and on the walls. Various rugs covered the floor. Bright torches on the walls in decorative iron sconces threw their dancing light on our surroundings.

The chamber contained simple, yet beautiful, wood furniture. Chairs, a couch with plush cushions, a table and stools made up the sparse decor. There was a large indentation in the floor in the corner for Eshshah. Next to it, a feather mattress on a carved wooden platform. Above it, heavy cloth draperies hung from a frame that suspended from the ceiling of the cave. A hearth took up the corner of the room.

"I've had this prepared for a very long time, anticipating this moment. I would like to offer this part of my home to you both."

I swallowed, unable to speak. The Healer had prepared a home for dragon and rider, knowing she would see her patience rewarded. I wiped the new tears from my eyes.

Clearing my throat, "We appreciate your hospitality, Healer. Thank you."

"Tomorrow we begin your training, Amáne and Eshshah. I will be your trainer." This took me by surprise, but she disregarded my reaction and continued, "We have lost already more than a week from your linking and I need to make sure you two proceed in the proper direction. I'm sorry, but there will be no more time for leisure. I'll find you a clean night dress and some clothing until you can go back to your cottage and gather more of your things. This is now your home. You can choose to sleep in here, Amáne, or I have a room I can make up for you at the main house if you prefer."

"Thank you, Healer. I'll stay here with Eshshah." Since our linking, I'd never spent a night at any distance from her and had no desire to now.

The Healer nodded her approval as if her question were a test I had passed.

I went to bed that night contemplating the incredible direction in which my life had turned. In no time, my exhaustion overcame me — what a long day this had been. I fell asleep before I could finish reviewing my day.

Chapter Fifteen

The sun had not yet risen when I decided I could no longer lay in bed, feigning sleep. It was the first day of our training. I was tangled in my bed covers from my fitful night, but it was from excitement. My sleep was absent the usual nightmares. I kicked myself free, ready to prepare for my day.

After giving Eshshah a morning hug, I dressed in the tights and tunic the Healer left out for me. They fit me surprisingly well. I attached my new dagger to my belt and headed down the long hall toward the kitchen to find the Healer. She wasn't there. The kitchen was empty but still warm, and the aroma of freshly baked bread filled the room. I helped myself to a piece, along with a mug of tea. As I rushed to eat, Gallen came in and informed me the Healer was waiting for me at the barn.

I crossed the courtyard where Eshshah had landed last night, and made my way across the field. There I found the Healer in the barn inspecting several unsharpened training swords of different sizes and styles. She was dressed in a tunic and tights. This was the first time I had seen her in anything other than her loose gown and surcoat. Her hair hung in a long braid down her back instead of tucked in her usual cap. I had never noticed how striking she was. She must have been a beauty in her younger days.

"Good morning, Amáne. Today starts your training, and let me warn you it will be intense. You've crossed into a new life as dragon rider. There's much for you to learn and little time. You two have been thrown into a conflict you cannot understand yet, but for which you must be prepared. For now you must think of me not as your friend, but as your trainer — it'll make it easier for you." She didn't explain what she meant, but continued to examine the swords and finally chose three and set them aside.

Behind her were suits of armor in various sizes. "You'll need your own armor made for you at a later time, but it's not necessary just yet. This will do for your practice."

She chose a helmet, handed it to me and asked me to try it on. I didn't realize how heavy a helmet actually was. I suppose it would have to be, to withstand the force of someone swinging at you with a deadly weapon. My experience with swordplay was such that I never fully grasped the reality. I grew up sparring with my acquaintance, Kail, because I enjoyed the power, the choreography and the thrill of it. When Kail and I practiced, I didn't process the fact that a sword was, in fact, a deadly weapon. That its use would quite likely result in killing or maiming an opponent was a sudden, harsh realization.

Next, she handed me a quilted tunic for padding under the armor, and then chose a suit of armor that was closest to my size. She named all the parts as she handed them to me and helped me put them on. Greaves, to protect my shins; poleyn for my knees; cuisses for my thighs; a breastplate to protect my torso; the pauldrons for my shoulders; rarebrace for the upper arm; couter for my elbows; the vambrace covered the lower arm; and then gauntlets for my hands. All of this metal felt very restrictive and heavy, not to mention hot as the morning warmed up. Lastly, she handed me a shield. I wasn't accustomed to the extra weight, but she told me it was good to practice in full armor to build my strength.

Eshshah came out to observe and support me. Finding a suitable spot in the sun, she curled up, put her head on her front legs, and followed me with her golden eyes. I looked at her with pride and admiration. The way the sun hit her scales made her look like she was on fire. I had a hard time taking my eyes off of her. She hummed with satisfaction.

With my assistance, the Healer donned her armor, and then, without warning, she picked up one of the training swords, tossed it at me and said, "Let's see what you can do with this."

Instinctively, I reached out and caught it by its hilt. I was pleased the extra weight of the armor only hampered my reactions slightly.

"But, Healer," I protested, "I've never used a metal sword. We only worked with wooden wasters."

She answered my complaint with a lunge, which I managed to parry. Without another word, my training began in earnest. After a series of lunges, which I parried weakly, she swung her sword overhead and threw a wrap shot bringing it around behind me. I read her intention — to work around my back since I had a shield to protect my front. She threw shots to get me to move my shield to defend, which made me work harder than her, conserving her energy and wearing me out. This worked quite nicely — for her.

The noise of our weapons, shields and armor clashing created a din in the series of short bouts in which we engaged — each one lasting no more than a minute. I was no match for the Healer. As she continued her attacks, she shouted at me, "Correct your stance, Amáne! Bend your knees! I thought you used to practice with the grinder's youngest boy. Have you learned nothing?"

I understood she was testing me — pushing me to my limit, which to my shame, was very low.

She feinted an attack to mislead me, and I fell for it. I paid for that mistake with a hit from the flat of her sword. The dust choked me, my legs burned, my arms began to get heavy and didn't respond to what I asked of them. Still she continued. Her age deceived, because she was a formidable sword fighter — she showed no fatigue.

Her lesson increased in intensity. I wasn't prepared for this serious of instruction on my first day. I almost didn't recognize her from the Healer who was my mother's friend. I began to understand her warning, but I was still confused by her severity. *Did I offend her and not realize it?*

"Stop telling me your next move, Amáne."

"I'm not!" I shouted back, my anger starting to build.

"You are. I can tell when you drop that shoulder," she whacked my left shoulder with the flat of her blade, "that you will be moving in this direction. You might as well shout it."

She baited me, throwing the same shot to the same place two or three times and then hit me from another direction as I automatically defended the area she previously tried to hit.

"Your anger is weakening you, Amáne. When you're angry you cannot fight rationally. Control it, or you could make a deadly mistake."

"Eshshah, I need your help," I said out loud.

"No, Eshshah cannot assist you. This needs to be just you. We'll work with her included later, but not now."

"This isn't fair." I complained. "You know I don't have your skills and yet you're not holding back."

"Fighting isn't fair. And I am holding back. Keep your focus."

Try as I might, I couldn't control my anger — I'd held it for as long as I could. Not allowing Eshshah to help made me snap. I lunged in at her, swinging wildly with a high shot to her head. I inadvertently lowered my shield, leaving my torso open. She ducked my swing and went for my undefended side catching me square in the ribs in the one spot where my armor was weak. I crumbled to the dirt clutching my side trying to fill my emptied lungs. When I finally caught my breath, the pain was worse — it felt like she had run me through. I looked at my hand but there was no blood.

"I think you broke my rib," I said between raspy breaths.

"Now Eshshah can aid you. We don't want any broken bones." She didn't even sound sorry. *What did I do wrong since yesterday that she seemed so angry with me?*

Eshshah hurried to my side and put her nose on my ribs. She breathed her warm healing power and relief washed over me. My breath came in more evenly.

"Get up, Amáne. One more bout and then you can go to the kitchen and have your meal. I need to leave on business. Gallen will work with you the second part of the day."

She didn't ease up for the last bout.

When I removed my armor and the quilted jacket, my clothes underneath were dripping with sweat. There was not one dry spot, but I didn't care. I stumbled to the laver outside the kitchen, washed my face and my arms and dunked my head under the cooling water.

Exhausted, I dragged myself to the kitchen. Gallen sat at the table eating quietly. He mumbled an acknowledgement of my presence. I cut a piece of salt pork and some cheese from the wheel, tore off some bread, then took my place across from him. I started eating just as silently. Finally, cooling off both physically and emotionally, I cleared my head enough to review my errors and the new skills I learned that morning. I also tried to determine if there was something I said or did to make the Healer unhappy with me.

The Healer came in before leaving for her obligations and said, "It will be late when I return tonight, but before I leave, Amáne, it's time you knew this truth, since you will be learning dragon skills from him. You have a formidable teacher in Gallen as his true identity is Kaelem, rider of the late Gyan." Then she left the room.

My knife clattered to the floor. I choked on the bite I had just taken as I leapt to my feet. My eyes couldn't get any wider. Coughing and sputtering, I saluted him. He nodded and saluted back, then turned his attention again to his meal. I remained riveted as I tried to catch my breath. I had known Gallen as far back as I could remember. In my childish fantasies I disclosed to my mother I was going to marry him. Then as I grew older, he became my father figure — my substitute for the father I never knew. His kindness meant so much to me. This revelation staggered me.

"I'm the same person you've known all your life." He sounded amused. "Sit down, Amáne. Finish your meal and stop staring at me."

"Oh, sorry, Gallen ... I mean Kaelem."

"Call me Gallen. I'm no longer Kaelem." A dark shadow dulled his blue eyes for a brief moment.

I couldn't respond — my mind reeled. A dragon rider in Dorsal. Right under my nose, and I never suspected, even though he was a personal friend of my mother and myself. *Who would have known?* I called to mind the ballads I had learned but couldn't recall ever learning his story, or how his dragon had passed on. I told myself I would have to do some research. It must have been an unbearable nightmare. One that I never wanted to face. A great sadness began to overwhelm me as I put myself in his place and the thought of ever losing Eshshah.

"Eshshah." I said out loud, just needing to hear her 'voice' inside my head.

Gallen said nothing and politely ignored that I spoke to my dragon out loud.

"I'm here, Amáne. Try to control your emotions. It would not do well to break down here and now in front of Gallen." She hummed her calming sound.

"Thank you, Eshshah." I voiced.

Gallen interrupted, "You'll need to break that habit. It's not wise to always speak to your dragon out loud. When you're alone with her or you need to convey a message from someone to her, then it is acceptable, but at no other time is it necessary. It could result in unpleasant or even dangerous situations for you."

"I'll work on it, Gallen."

We finished eating. He directed me to the courtyard and asked me to have Eshshah meet us there. He was going to work with us as a pair. Still in shock over Gallen being a dragon rider — the first one I had ever met — my eyes were fixed on him as we headed outside.

"Stop staring at me, Amáne."

"Sorry."

CHAPTER SIXTEEN

In the courtyard, Gallen brought out three different types of saddles on saddle stands. He proceeded to explain the differences.

"This first saddle, the smallest of the three, is made to be used in battle. The seat is compact and lightweight. The restraining straps are at the boot pegs. The strap goes over and behind your boot. This gives you full movement during battle. You can stand up completely and twist but still be secure, even in quick maneuvers. The second saddle has a bit larger seat and the restraining straps are at the calf level. It's mostly used for tournament flying and at Faires where you want to execute showy maneuvers — more secure than the fighting saddle, yet it will still allow you to stand up. Lastly, we have this larger saddle."

It was similar to the one we used to fly back from the Dorsal outpost.

Gallen continued, "It's a basic everyday saddle as well as for long distance use. Larger seat and high back for more comfort, more substantial gripping bar in the front, thigh belt for maximum security on longer flights. No fear of losing your seat if you doze off in flight." I wondered how anyone could doze off in flight, but I kept my thoughts to myself ... and Eshshah.

He taught me the proper way to secure each of the three saddles on Eshshah. Then he had me run through drills. I started at one end of the courtyard, grabbed a saddle, ran it to the other end where Eshshah waited, threw it on her and fastened it as fast as I could. The larger one was no problem. We were familiar with that one already, but I had a lot of trouble with the battle one. Its leather ties and straps were thinner and I kept getting tangled in them. He explained that when this one was used, I would need to place Eshshah's chest armor on first and then the fighting saddle. He didn't want to spend much time on this one as he didn't anticipate any battles in the near future.

After the saddle drills, he had me leave the larger one on. We moved next to instruction on different mounting techniques.

"First, show me how you usually mount up."

We showed him how Eshshah bends her foreleg for me to climb up. Holding a ring attached to the side of the saddle, I reached my left foot to the foot peg, and threw my right leg over the back of the seat. The distance I had to extend myself changed often as her size increased daily — although it seemed to be slowing down a bit. Gallen nodded, satisfied with our technique. He went on to explain it was necessary to know many different mounts from different directions. I might find myself in a situation where I was being chased and Eshshah would need to be prepared to spring the second I hit the saddle. It would not be practical for her to have to help me up with her foreleg.

"Let's start with the tail mount. May I?"

"Of course." I granted him permission to speak directly

to Eshshah.

"Thank you. Now, Eshshah, please face the barn and take the preflight position like you're ready to spring, but extend your tail straight back. Amáne, you need to run up her tail, continue on her back and jump into the saddle prepared to take off. Unfortunately, we can't do the full training now in daylight. You can't be spotted flying. But if she were to take off, it would be the second you hit the saddle. You buckle yourself in as she takes her first downstroke. Now, let's try it."

"Wait. You want me to run up her tail? She has ridges all the way up to her back." Her ridges started small above the barb at the end of her tail, increased in size as they reached her haunches, and then decreased to just before her shoulders. At that point her ridges became smooth bumps until higher on her neck, where they grew larger again, then decreased as they reached the top of her head.

"Your feet are small, it should be no problem for you. Step close to the ridges. Plant your feet on either side. You'll be running fast, so you'll probably only take three or four strides before you're on her back."

"You've done this yourself?" I was sorry I was so insensitive to have asked that question, as I saw a shadow of sorrow briefly cross his face.

"Yes, it is a standard mount. Now, go. Imagine you are being chased by a pack of wild dogs, or whatever works for you. Use a mental picture to plan your steps."

I took a deep breath and allowed my natural determination to take over. I wanted to show Gallen I could do this — for him to see I was an able dragon rider. My confidence was up. I was a good runner and had excellent balance. Retreating to the opposite end of the courtyard, I turned and began my run. As I mentally projected my foot placement for my first step, I leapt onto Eshshah's tail. I landed at a good distance and planted my right foot to the right of her ridges. Perfect execution. Spotting my second step, I planted my left foot at what should have been just left of her ridges. But I misjudged. My placement was too much to the left where her tail was more rounded. My foot slipped and I lost my balance. I tried to correct my error and establish traction with my right foot — to push off, jump left and clear her tail. I drove my foot downward, but instead of gaining a foothold, it slipped to the right. I slammed straight down, straddling her tail in a crotch-drop. My breath burst from my lungs. Fortunately, I didn't land directly on one of her ridges, but between two of them. Groaning, I slid off to my left, and landed on my back. I grabbed myself on the way down. My modesty forgotten at that moment.

Eshshah turned her head to where I lay writhing in pain. She mentally cringed and said, "Let me help you, Amáne."

"No... No... I'm good. Thanks." That would have been a little too awkward for me in front of Gallen.

Tears of pain streamed from my eyes. I rolled on my side and tried to even out my breathing. Eshshah was concerned but refrained from helping. Gallen winced and turned away, feigning to find something interesting in his palm. He let me have a couple private minutes to recover, after which he offered me his hand.

"Same thing happened to me when I learned this mount. Get up and try it again. You won't repeat that mistake a second time ... trust me."

He helped me to my feet. Not ready to stand up straight, I bent over with my hands on my knees and took a few more breaths. I paced a bit to shake the pain ... and the thought of having to try it again.

Wiping my eyes with the back of my sleeve, I proceeded to the further side of the courtyard. I closed my eyes, and envisioned my steps. When I had a mental picture of my strides, I opened my eyes and started my run again. I leapt; first step same place as last time; second step, perfect landing. I made a note of where that was. Third stride I planted at the base of her tail. Just as I was ready to exhale in relief of my success, my trailing foot caught on a ridge and I flew forward onto her back, landing with a thud to the right of her ridges, just above her haunches. I slid off behind her right wing, and ended in a heap in the dirt.

Determined, and a bit angry with myself for failing the second time, I ran back to the other side of the courtyard and started my third approach. All else blocked out, I envisioned my three strides and accomplished them perfectly. I ran up her back and, elated at my success, I leaped into the saddle. I had a momentary mental lapse of my first mishap, but upon hitting the saddle, it all came back to me. I clenched my teeth to keep my howl of pain from escaping. "Ow," I groaned to myself.

"Okay, Amáne, I want five more successful tail mounts. Go."

With a few wobbles, I completed my five successful mounts in the next seven tries. Thankfully, I did not repeat the crotch-drop and hoped Gallen was correct when he assured me it would only happen once.

"This next one," Gallen instructed, "is the wing mount. It's another running escape mount. Eshshah if you would, please open your wing for us. See this bony protrusion here?" He indicated a point in the middle of her wing at the joint that bent sharply backwards. In this joint a claw-like *finger* extended from her wing. "This is what you'll be aiming for. The maneuver will involve some synchronization from both of you. The objective is for you to run toward her wing. Eshshah, you will lower it to just within her reach. Then, Amáne, you must jump, grab a hold of her *finger* and Eshshah will raise her wing and propel you as you swing toward the saddle. This will take quite a bit of practice and you need to time your swing while Eshshah needs to time her uplift. Once you've mastered it, you'll be able to launch yourself into the saddle. Eshshah will then be in the correct position to spring into flight. You can start by using two hands, but eventually you will need to learn it with only one hand as it's likely you'll have a weapon in the other.

Okay, that didn't sound so hard. I went through the motions in my mind to get a mental picture of what was necessary for success. Then I retreated to the far end of the courtyard ready to run in on her left side.

"Are you ready, Eshshah?"

"Yes."

Eshshah held her left wing at a height I could easily reach. I started my run, keeping my eye on her wing joint. As I approached, I reached up and grasped it with both hands — she lifted her wing up and in. I swung, propelling myself toward the saddle. The combination of her strength to propel me and too much swing on my part catapulted me several feet over my target and I literally flew over the saddle, landing at a distance on her other side. My feet hit first and I rolled out of the fall without any harm to myself, except my pride — I failed my first try.

"It's okay, Amáne." Eshshah comforted. "You didn't expect to get it on the first try, did you?" She knew I did.

Gallen gave us some pointers. He told us I didn't have to swing so forcefully and Eshshah needed to slow her uplift. Eshshah and I worked on this skill for the rest of the afternoon and into the evening. We tried it from the left side and the right side, with one hand and with two. I don't know how many tries it took us to start getting even close to the saddle. I landed everywhere but where I was supposed to.

He checked in on us every so often and repeated, "It shouldn't take as much effort as you two are exerting."

Finally, success! I grabbed her wing at the right moment and she lifted it at the right speed. I landed squarely in the saddle. I would have celebrated more, but the fresh stab of pain reminded me of my failed first attempt at the tail mount.

The sun had set and we were exhausted. Eshshah decided to wait a little longer for darkness to hunt. I was ready to collapse. I washed off my sweat and dirt, went through the kitchen to grab a small bite, and headed to bed.

CHAPTER SEVENTEEN

The next morning dawned too quickly. Out by the barn again before the sun was up, the Healer had me working with the sword. She started me on my striking techniques using a pell — a man-size wooden post that roughly simulates a human target.

I ran through my cuts and strikes and my footwork. She pressed me to attack the pell with power, emphasizing good technique and accurate range. I practiced combinations as well as single-strike techniques.

"Focus, Amáne! More force. This is your opponent. You're supposed to try to injure him, not tease him."

I put more energy into it, but still she reprimanded me, "Strike with precision! If you don't have control of your strikes then you have less chance to actually hit the target. You must learn to coordinate the movements of your entire body without wasting energy."

We donned our armor and started sparring practice. My body

ached from our previous day's training, but I didn't ask Eshshah to help me out with my pain. I wanted to try to struggle through it myself in hopes it would increase my strength and stamina.

Holding her sword in front of her, point up, the Healer demonstrated, "This is your best defensive position. You can block anything from here." I threw a few strikes and she blocked them with ease. She made it look so simple.

Our morning passed into afternoon. She threw techniques and instructions at me one after the other. The Healer did not lessen her skills, but instead relentlessly challenged me at a higher level. She continued to point out everything I did wrong. Countless times my anger took over and I made costly mistakes. If she had been an enemy, they would have translated into fatal mistakes. That seemed to be when her dissatisfaction in me increased — when I lost my temper. It had always been my worst trait.

Later in the afternoon was spent with Gallen as he worked with Eshshah and me in practicing the mounts we learned the day before. I put saddles on and took them off. I was sorely missing riding Eshshah and asked Gallen if we might have a short flight that night. He said the Healer didn't want me riding for a few more days. My disappointment was not lost on him.

The next day was the same and the next and the next. Day after day, I worked from sun up to long after dark. A couple of times we were even awakened in the middle of the night to practice my mounts so Eshshah could actually take off once I landed in the saddle. Truthfully, I didn't mind that part of our training because it allowed us to fly together. On one occasion we stayed away a little longer than instructed. Both the Healer and Gallen voiced their disapproval. Eshshah and I needed our time alone. I was not sufficiently contrite over my disobedience, and didn't do a very good job hiding my bad attitude. They punished me by not allowing any more night flying practice. I thought it was too severe, but kept my thoughts to myself.

The Healer came up with endless ways to keep me moving. She rarely let me rest, except for meals. I practiced archery, which I was actually pretty good at — it was the only weapon girls were instructed in. She had me run a path around her property for an hour at a time. I mucked Thunder's stall and the donkeys' stalls and moved bales of hay. I worked in her garden. I scrubbed her kitchen.

My frustration at her relentless pressure on me increased daily. Exhaustion claimed my body each night. I hardly had the energy or desire to wash up for bed. Many times I just collapsed with all my clothes on, including my boots. I was even too drained for my reoccurring nightmares. Quite often I cried myself to sleep. Other nights I was too worn out to sleep, which made the following day a disaster.

Try as I might, I felt I could not please the Healer. My only consolation was that Gallen wasn't quite as hard on me as she was.

I cried to Eshshah too often, "What am I doing wrong? I don't understand. I don't know how much more I can take, Eshshah. Is she trying to break my spirit? Is she wishing it was someone else whom you chose?"

"No, Amáne, I don't believe that's the reason at all. I don't know why she's so hard on you. I can feel her heart and it is not vindictive. She must have a very good reason why she is treating you so. Maybe she feels she's helping you learn faster."

"Well, I just wish she would ease up on me before I go mad — I'm that close." I could feel Eshshah's agitation at not being able to ease my pain. This was mental pain, and although she hummed her calming melody for me every night, which did help, she couldn't find a remedy for my anguish. I shouldn't have burdened her so often with my complaints, but I had no one else to confide in.

The next day brought more of the same. The Healer started me on training with a partisan — a spear. This was a weapon I had very seldom worked with. It might have been an enjoyable day for me as I really took a liking to fighting with a spear. However, my concentration was at an all time low and the Healer found it difficult to get me to focus. Adding to that, my lack of sleep made it even harder for me to control my temper. My mood grew dark. Eshshah watched me closely. She suffered with me.

Morning advanced to afternoon, which progressed toward evening.

"Tread back with your hind foot, Amáne!" the Healer admonished yet again.

I'd had all I could take. I closed my eyes and shook with anger as I tried with all my might to compose myself. I didn't want to completely lose control and turn on the Healer. My breathing came in short raspy breaths as I battled in vain for self-restraint.

My fury subsided when I became conscious of Eshshah's heated emotions. I felt her increasing distress. Her tail began to twitch. At first just slightly and then it became more animated. She swung her head back and forth, then rose and began pacing. A low rumble emanated in her throat and then grew louder and stronger. Gallen had come out of the barn to see what was happening. The three of us froze — our attention riveted on Eshshah.

"Amáne, control your dragon." Alarm was in the Healer's voice. "An enraged dragon is not a sight you ever want to witness."

Eshshah was dangerously agitated by now. Her tail quivered. She lost her composure, and raised her head to the sky as she let out a roar. Fire spewed twenty feet into the air.

"She's feeding off your emotions, Amáne, get control of yourself first. Immediately. That's the only way you'll be able to calm her." The Healer and Gallen both backed up to a safe distance, not taking their eyes off Eshshah.

"Eshshah!" I screamed.

Knowing it was her concern for me that had sparked her rage, I assured her, "I'm okay. I'm okay. Please stop."

I ran toward her as the Healer shouted, "No, Amáne! Stand back until she regains her control."

Unaware of the serious danger of my situation, I moved closer to Eshshah. Too ignorant to be frightened, I was only concerned for her safety — I couldn't bear to see her so upset. It was my fault she had gotten to this state. My anger transformed to worry and guilt.

Enraged, Eshshah raised her head again and belched out more flame into the night sky. I was within two arms-lengths of her. I could feel the heat, even though it was directed upward. Had it been toward me, there wouldn't have been even ashes left where I stood.

With my temper under control, I fought to link to her emotions. I'd never seen her like this. My only fear was for her. Without warning, she reared up. Her forelegs beat the air above me. I sprung to the side and rolled as her large mass came down, almost crushing me. Her tail whipped around in my direction. Again, my reflexes saved me. I leapt up barely in time to avoid the sharp barb.

It passed under me with a whoosh of air.

My mind melded with hers as I strained to exude calmness. It brought back memories of us working together to survive the Valaira that seemed like another lifetime ago. I fought for both of us. I had to find a place in her mind to latch on to — to let her know I was there. That we would both be fine. At last, I felt a faint realization in her mind that she caught my presence. I grasped at a thread of her consciousness.

"Eshshah," I said calmly in thought transference. "It's okay. We are okay. Please, you're worrying me. Calm down." Eyes shut tight, I strained with the effort. Beads of sweat formed on my forehead.

Finally, recognition was in her thoughts. It was as if she came out of the darkness and found me. She was confused but I could feel her begin to relax as I hummed my version of the sound she used to calm me.

She lowered her face down to mine, her golden eyes still whirling. I heard a gasp from the Healer. Eshshah became fully aware of me. I put my hand up to her jaws, held on to her fangs that lay outside of her mouth and brought her nose to my forehead. I continued with my silent conversation. "Shh. It's okay. I'm sorry, I shouldn't have lost my temper with the Healer. You were right all along. I'm sure she has our best interests in mind. It was all part of our training. I see it now. It's my fault. I'm so sorry, Eshshah." My eyes blurred with tears.

Slowly, she came back to herself. Still a bit disoriented, she said, "Amáne, please forgive me. I don't know what just happened. I saw you at your breaking point and I couldn't control myself. I couldn't bear to see you suffer, but yet I almost killed you."

"But you didn't, Eshshah. Let's never let anything like this happen to us again. Do you understand me?"

"I'm so ashamed, Amáne. Please offer my apologies to the Healer and Gallen. My behavior is unforgivable."

I turned to the Healer and Gallen who were slowly approaching, one eye on Eshshah, one on me. Both of them visibly shaken. "We offer our apologies Healer and Gallen, we're ashamed of ourselves — both of us. This behavior will not be repeated."

The Healer came up to me, took my face in her hands and looked deeply into my eyes. I don't know what she intended to find, but apparently satisfied, she wrapped her arms around me and Gallen put his hand on my shoulder. Eshshah pressed her nose on my back and the four of us stood like that for a time.

The Healer finally broke the silence, "I don't know ... but that was either the bravest, strongest demonstration of a rider's link with their dragon I have ever witnessed ... or it was the most foolish."

"I'm betting on the former," Gallen said.

"Amáne and Eshshah," the Healer said, "it is I who beg your forgiveness. There's no excuse for the way I've treated you for the last several weeks. But I had to see what you two were made of. You linked and grew together on your own, without any supervision or training. I was worried you'd be difficult to train correctly. I wanted to push you to find your limits. Truthfully, I was amazed at your superior skills for an untrained linked pair. I felt I had to keep testing you. Instead of letting up as I should have, I increased the pressure.

"I'm astonished. I found you're at the level that most dragon riders took at least two years to attain, and some never did achieve. The only explanation I can come up with is the excessive amount of venom you have in your veins. You've withstood more than should have been dealt to you. I'm truly sorry. But you have to understand our very kingdom relies upon both of you."

My anguish subsided. I didn't need to fear any danger with Eshshah. But, I needed to know. "Healer, no disrespect, but I have to tell you that all this time I thought you were angry with us. I thought maybe you were sorry Eshshah chose me and that you were disappointed with me — that maybe I was too young to be a dragon rider, or that I was a girl, or that I wasn't good enough — I didn't know why."

"No, Amáne, that's not true. I wish I could explain it to you right here ... right now. But I can't. It will all eventually become clearer to you. I promise." Her brown eyes reflected her sincerity.

She cleared her throat and looked into my eyes once again, then kissed my forehead. Her expression indicated the conversation was over. "I have business to attend to this evening, so I must go out, but we have a lot to discuss tomorrow. There's porridge in the kitchen. Get some rest tonight."

She turned to walk away, then stopped and faced me. "I am so very proud of you, Amáne. And your mother would have been, too."

CHAPTER EIGHTEEN

The sun shone bright through the skylight when I finally realized I should have been up, prepared to start my day. I jumped out of bed and saw Eshshah was still curled up in her sleeping area seemingly in no hurry to get outside. Finding a note on the floor, I picked it up and read what the Healer had written.

My Dear Amáne,

I had to go out early but I do want to apologize one more time for my mistreatment. I want you to know I never meant it to go as far as it did. Please be assured I was never angry with you, nor was I sorry that Eshshah chose you.

You are free to do what you will this morning. I have heated water and have placed some herbs and aromatics in the tub if you choose to soak in the bathing room. I know it has been a while since you have enjoyed one of your favorite pastimes. Today is also a market day if you want to go into town to see any of your acquaintances. All I ask is that you be back here by the midday meal.

Affectionately,

H

"Eshshah." I exclaimed. "I have a free day. I can do whatever I want."

"Good, Amáne, you've earned it. What are you planning to do?"

"First thing, I'm going for a soak. Eshshah, how long has it been since I've had a chance to do that?" Excited, I grabbed a bath sheet and rushed out of my chambers.

In the bathing room I inhaled with joy. The steam fused with the scent of lavender and herbs the Healer had combined for my benefit. I quickly dropped my clothing on the floor and headed toward the wooden tub that invited me into its fragrant mist.

Passing my reflection in the glass, I came to a standstill. I had always been of slight build and maybe a bit thin as far as body type, but I didn't recognize my own body. My muscles had been toned, cut and chiseled into what reminded me of ancient drawings and sculptures I had seen. I was surprised and fascinated by my transformation. Not like I was anything special, but just that instead of looking plain and shapeless like I always had, I now looked ... well ... athletic. I had no time in the last several weeks to even think of my appearance, let alone ever look at myself in the glass. I lingered in front of my reflection longer than I should have, a little absorbed with myself.

"What are you doing?" Eshshah broke into my vain thoughts. Quite embarrassed, I stuttered some nonsense about getting ready to soak. Sliding quickly into the tub, I vowed to work on my humility.

I soaked until my fingers and toes looked like dried grapes — it was paradise.

After my bath, I told Eshshah I planned to go to the marketplace, just to get out for a while. I hadn't been into town for quite some time.

Wandering the colorful stalls made me feel like an ordinary citizen of Dorsal again. The smells, the people, the buzz. I didn't realize how much had changed in my life — it would never be the same. At least I could enjoy some normalcy for a little while.

I stopped at the fruit stand and bought an apple. I took pleasure in its juicy sweetness while strolling up and down the rows completely enjoying myself. Not paying much attention, I found I had subconsciously wandered into the weapons row — not a big surprise. I came to a halt in front of a booth stocked with blades of excellent craftsmanship and gazed at them with a new appreciation.

"Hi Amáne." It was Kail, the grinder's son, my old sparring partner. "Where have you been? Sorry about your Mother. Were you gone all this time on your memorial journey?"

I greeted Kail, then replied, "I've been back for a while, but I'm staying with the Healer and ... working around her place."

"We should get together to fight sometime. I need someone I can defeat easily," he said with such confidence, yet with a teasing look in his eyes.

"Hey, it wasn't that easy for you. I had the upper hand enough times. You just never admitted it." I shot back. *If he only knew the truth, he wouldn't dare to challenge me now.*

Another of my acquaintances, Fiona, spotted me and came over to where I stood with Kail. She had her twin sisters, Rio and Mila in tow, both of whom ran up to me and gave me hugs.

"Amáne, how are you?" asked Fiona. "I haven't seen you in so long. My condolences to you in the loss of your mother. May she rest with her ancestors."

She turned to Kail with a change of expression and a timid

inflection in her voice, "Hi Kail."

Kail smiled and greeted Fiona a bit shyly, then excused himself, saying he had to help in his father's grinder's shop, sharpening knives, daggers and swords.

I felt the attraction between the two but said nothing. It was actually nice to see Fiona. She had always been kind to me regardless of my quirkiness. And I relished Rio and Mila's affectionate attentions.

"Hmm, of course I would find you at this stall, Amáne." Fiona tilted her head and smiled. "We're on our way to my favorite — the fabrics. Won't you join us?"

She took my arm and Rio and Mila fought for the other. *How could I decline?*

"Where did you go for your memorial journey?" Fiona asked.

As I was dragged to the fabrics and ribbons Fiona always loved, I told her I had gone camping on the cove.

"Oh yes, you and camping. If it were my mother who went to rest with her ancestors, I'd go to the City of Teravinea and wander the market place to see all the noble ladies in their silk gowns. My mother would, of course, approve."

We arrived at the fabrics stall and as she admired the finery, she rambled on, "You're so lucky you are of age, now, Amáne. No more classes and you can concentrate on finding a husband. Who'll make the arrangements for that now, the Healer?"

"Fiona, I'm in no hurry to find a husband. You know that. I have plenty of time in my life before I have to start bothering with that."

"Oh, but then you may not be young and beautiful any longer. You are beautiful, you know, Amáne. You just don't use it to your advantage. Your sapphire blue eyes with your dark hair is rather exotic. Your light olive skin is perfect. You should capitalize on that. Men want beauty in their lives."

"Fiona. Stop."

"Look at that bolt of silk! Can you help me get it down, please?"

I reached for it with my left hand and my sleeve fell back exposing the scar on my wrist. I never had time to work with Eshshah on reducing it, or to ask the Healer for something to lessen the ugly mark.

"Amáne, what happened to you?"

"Er, I just got clumsy, that's all. It's not that bad." I covered it back up as quickly as I could.

"See, that's what I'm talking about. You need to take better care of yourself. A man doesn't want a bride that's all scarred up."

"Fiona, is that all you can think about? Please, we are not having this conversation."

"Well, all right, go ahead and amuse yourself with your swords, and I'll let you know if I need you to fight someone for me. I'll marry my true love and work with my silks, and you can let me know when you're ready to act like a lady — then I'll be there for you."

"Deal."

It was soon time for me to get back home on orders from the Healer, so I took my leave of Fiona and her sisters. I wondered again as I had wondered my whole life how different my existence would be if, like Fiona, I had two parents and siblings. Being an only child was not that great. I looked back wistfully as she was led down the row by a twin on either arm.

It was a pleasure to see Fiona, Mila and Rio. But it was also nice to be on my own again, and away from her preoccupation with marriage. That was a subject in which I wanted no part.

CHAPTER NINETEEN

I leaned against Eshshah and took advantage of her shade as she soaked up the sun in the courtyard. The Healer arrived on Thunder. The blacksmith, Dorjan, rode in on his horse behind her. Gallen joined us just as Dorjan's horse spotted Eshshah and reared up in fright. I was quite impressed with how he remained in the saddle and managed to get the animal under control quickly. He turned his horse toward the barn to get him some distance from my dragon so he could calm him down. Thunder, although not overly fond of Eshshah, was at least used to her. I wondered if they knew what a tasty meal they would make for her. Eshshah let out her laugh-like rumble as we watched them ride to the barn.

Dorjan and the Healer walked back to the courtyard where we waited. The blacksmith's ebony eyes rested on Eshshah. He gazed at her with admiration. Dorjan was a large dark man with a kind face framed in a short dark beard. Walking straight up to us, he saluted both Eshshah and me. We acknowledged the greeting with a nod.

"May I?" He asked permission to speak with Eshshah.

"Of course," I answered.

"Eshshah, red beauty, you've sparked a fire in this man's heart. I am honored to meet you."

Eshshah hummed her pleasure at his compliment.

"She thanks you, Dorjan. She's pleased to meet you as well."

We went inside to the kitchen and served ourselves our midday meal. I was famished, and without any further conversation, I drew my attention to my plate.

At the same instant that I'd gulped a large mouthful of my tea, the Healer spoke, "Amáne, you know Dorjan."

I had known him all my life and we had already greeted each other so I wondered why she thought she needed to introduce us.

"It's time for you to know his true name. He was formerly known as Ruiter, rider of the late Unule."

I think Gallen anticipated my reaction. He ducked just in time to avoid the spray of tea that spewed from my mouth. I jumped up sputtering and coughing, but managed to give Dorjan a decent salute. As soon as he acknowledged it, I ran into the kitchen for a cloth to clean up my embarrassing mess.

Gallen burst out laughing. "Healer, do you think the next time you have alarming news to tell her, you could at least refrain from telling her at meal times?"

We all laughed.

"Thank you, Gallen. I'll try to keep that in mind." The Healer continued, "Amáne, you should be able to handle the rest of what I have to say without losing your food, or your knife, or anything else." She made sure I was using open thought transference so Eshshah would be included in our conversation.

"First, you have to understand you have never known a world with dragons." She looked at me, "The last one died two years before you were born —"

"That was Torin, and his rider was Nara, I know the song. She was my favorite of all the riders." I interrupted.

She paused, nodded and then went on, "But before then, our recorded history always included dragons. Never was there a period of time when dragons and riders weren't seen in the skies. Until this usurper — this Galtero," she spat out the name, "stole the throne by treachery — dragons and riders were a part of who we were."

The Healer revealed what had been her mission for the last twenty or twenty-five years. She had been a member of the court of Teravinea as Healer, close confidant and advisor to King Emeric Drekinn, whose dynasty had ruled Teravinea for the last several hundred years. During times of war and strife more dragons and riders were linked, but in times of peace there were less. While the Drekinns ruled, the kingdom saw relative peace. There were still skirmishes, a few significant battles and border disputes, but generally speaking Teravinea had been in a period of peace for a long time. But even in times of peace, dragons still hatched and chose riders.

"There is a chamber in Castle Teravinea," the Healer explained, "that houses dragon eggs laid by mating pairs duty-bound to the kingdom. A Hatching Gathering is held every year where dragon rider candidates are paraded past the dragon eggs in hopes they would be chosen as a rider. This has been the custom since our history began, so Galtero continues the tradition. But his Hatching Ceremony is a ruse. Since he has taken the throne, there have been no linkings — none. For several years before King Emeric joined his ancestors, less and less eggs hatched, less riders chosen. Many 'accidents' occurred that ended the lives of the kingdom's dragons and more than half of the riders."

The Healer told us about her suspicions that Galtero was to blame for the failure of the dragons to hatch. It was her belief he wanted to guarantee there would be no one strong enough to resist him when he killed King Emeric and took his throne. His sorcerers and wise men surely were behind some dark enchantment of the dragon eggs, prohibiting them from choosing riders and hatching. The Healer shared her fears with King Emeric. Just before they could prove their theory, the royal living apartments of Castle Teravinea were destroyed in an explosion and fire, killing the royal family.

Her life abruptly changed. The Healer dedicated herself to avenging the murder of the Drekinn royal family. Instrumental in her cause, she had to solve the mystery of what evil had been perpetrated upon the dragon eggs. The solution would be necessary to save Teravinea.

Fervently, the Healer spoke of her concerns, "Our kingdom is deteriorating as Galtero sucks the life out of Teravinea. He cares only for power and riches, and does not concern himself with the people who represent the heart of our once-bountiful kingdom. With the dragons and riders we had a cohesiveness throughout the land — we had well-informed citizens. Linked pairs played an important role in communication. They could travel quickly from one end of Teravinea to another, keeping us united. This is what set us apart from other kingdoms. That, and the fact that the dragons and riders were a formidable foe to any who would desire to conquer us. Now we have nothing that would deter invaders, and our kingdom is divided. Galtero would sell us out for a price."

"How can we find out what sorcery is keeping the dragon

eggs from hatching?" I asked.

"The answer to that brings us to the crux of our mission. That is, if you and Eshshah will join us."

"Of course, Healer. Eshshah and I would be honored to be a part of your plan. Whatever it takes to get our kingdom back to its former position — to defeat Galtero and stop his attack on our dragon eggs."

"Thank you Amáne and Eshshah. Our plan is to procure an egg from the hatching chamber and bring it here. It must be an egg from the royal dragon line — Eshshah's line. Only she could determine the lineage. I'll need to discover what trickery is being used and develop an antidote. If I can do that, we hope the following Hatching Ceremony will result in some linkings. This will certainly alert Galtero as to the decline of his power and will assist us in taking our kingdom back. It is the necessary first step."

"I can't think of a greater honor than being a part of taking the throne from Galtero. I'm curious, though, who will rule in his place?" I asked.

"That's something only the future can determine, and we will unfold it to you when we feel it's necessary."

She changed the subject. "In the absence of dragons, Gallen created an ingenious communication device to stay in contact with the other dragon riders throughout the kingdom."

I had no idea there were riders in other parts of Teravinea. Before I could ask, Gallen motioned me to the back corner of the Healer's library. He directed my attention to an apparatus that hung on the wall — a thick glass disc, about two hands-width in diameter mounted on an ornate wooden background. It was framed by two pewter dragons perched on either side of the wood. Behind the glass was an inlay of three dragon scales in a triangular formation.

Below the glass disc was a brass knob. I had seen the same device in the corner of the library chamber at the outpost, but I thought it was a piece of art, and not a functional object.

The Healer indicated, "It is only operable by dragon riders. Gallen would you please instruct Amáne in its use?"

Gallen began, "Due to the decline of dragons and riders, our communication suffered greatly, which, of course, was the intention of Galtero. If we couldn't communicate with other parts of the kingdom, we couldn't gather important information on his doings — nor assemble an army to defeat him. We needed a method where we could still stay in contact with each other, so I designed this communication disc. It allows us to stay abreast of Galtero's dealings. There are twenty-six of us dragon riders left. You make twenty-seven." My eyes went wide with that revelation.

Gallen continued, "We've posted a rider in most of the significant townships, and each has one of these devices. There's also a disc at every outpost. In case you were wondering why Dorjan and I are both here in Dorsal, it's because of a foretelling that an unhatched egg existed here as well as a likely candidate." He looked at me and nodded in my direction.

"We obviously were not as vigilant as we should have been, otherwise, you two would not have been in the dangerous situation of being alone when you linked."

Eshshah and I acknowledged his regret, but assured him that it was meant to be. We held no one to blame.

"This instrument contains the scales of my dragon, Gyan — his name means 'knowledge.'" He took a deep breath. I shuddered at the horror of losing a dragon.

"As you know, Amáne, a dragon's scales exhibit the characteristics of their dragon. Therefore 'knowledge' would be a significant result of communication. These discs have played an important part toward our cause. They've kept us informed of the goings on around the kingdom.

"Here's how it operates. You place your hand on this knob, and say or whisper 'Gyan,' and then the name of the rider who is manning that particular communication device. It must be his true dragon rider name. We will contact Kei, rider of the late Okeanos. Kei is currently known as Farvard. He is in Tramoren, which is in north-central Teravinea. You try it. Farvard is waiting to hear from us."

Things were moving so quickly. I tried to grasp the reality of standing in this room with two dragon riders who included me as their equal. I, Amáne, daughter of Catriona, a fifteen-year-old girl, found myself in a world that had heretofore only been legendary to me. Very nervous, I approached the device. It was hung at a height more suited to these taller men, so Gallen brought me a stool to stand on. I placed my right hand on the brass knob and whispered, "Gyan," and then, "Kei." The disc lit up and shimmered the colors in a prism, which then became muted as a man's image formed in the glass. I startled and immediately withdrew my hand. The image instantly disappeared.

"Keep your hand on the knob, Amáne. Try it again. No need to be frightened."

I repeated my actions and the image transformed again into a visual of Farvard. It was almost like peering into a looking glass, but with someone else's face looking back. He was a handsome man with dark hair and a greying beard.

"Greetings, Amáne, and my salutations to your dragon, Eshshah," Farvard said as he saluted, at which I nodded and then forgetting myself, I saluted back with the hand I had on the brass knob. Farvard's image disappeared once again.

"Sorry," Gallen said. "I should have instructed you to use your left hand on the knob. One more time, Amáne."

I got Farvard back in the disc again and gave him a proper greeting. His eyes twinkled in amusement. "She's younger than you led me to believe, Gallen. And you neglected to mention her beauty. Welcome, Amáne, I hope you will join us."

I blushed, assured him Eshshah and I could be counted on, then listened while they discussed the state of affairs in the kingdom. They shared their opinions of what needed to be done to set in motion a plan for obtaining an egg for the Healer. I had nothing to add, but struggled to follow the conversation, overwhelmed by it all.

The meeting came to an end and I released my hand from the device, after which I fell into the nearest chair before my knees buckled from under me. Farvard was the third dragon rider I'd met in so short a period of time. I was now fully aware of the fact these dedicated men were working with the Healer to save the kingdom — and had been doing so since before I was born, when Galtero first became a threat. They were bound by duty even with the loss of their dragons — making the ultimate sacrifice for their land and what they believed in. I had to take a deep breath as it came to mind that now Eshshah and I were a part of this movement. I could feel their excitement as they realized their vigilance had not been in vain. They now had hope because of our linking. The honor of being their hope pressed upon me.

Dorjan interrupted my thoughts, "I sure wish we could have had some of these communication discs when I worked under King Rikkar. It would have saved us a few trips. He had us jumping all over the kingdom."

"King Rikkar?" I was astonished. "That was King Emeric's

father. It's been more than fifty years since he's rested with his ancestors, and you don't look any older than forty-something. How can that be?"

The Healer, Gallen and Dorjan all laughed at my incredulity.

"You have perhaps forgotten the songs?" Dorjan asked. "Dragon riders do not age at the same rate as normal humans. It'll be interesting to track your lifespan as you're the youngest rider in our history. The reality of a long life is both wonderful and yet can be quite tragic. You have to watch your loved ones age and meet their ancestors while you're left behind — your destiny not yet fulfilled. I still miss my wife of 100 years ago and have finally just remarried."

I reminded myself it was his baby to whom the Healer had me bring the herbs when my mother was ill.

Gallen nodded and added slowly, "That's the most painful part of being a rider. We crave companionship like anyone else — we are human. But knowing that unless we're killed in a battle or a quest, we will be left alone. I've also watched a wife pass to her ancestors."

The elation of being a part of this exclusive band of riders quickly plummeted as the air about me shifted — the sorrow, which was thick in the room, caused my heart to beat in pain.

"Then I shall never fall in love, nor shall I ever marry." I declared to them. This would be my vow.

Gallen responded, "That's not the best solution, Amáne. You may finally succeed in controlling your temper, but trying to control your heart — you would be fighting a losing battle. I would keep an open mind if I were you."

Dorjan added, "Wait a while before you take that vow. You're too young to realize what you're saying."

Neither rider convinced me to retract my statement.

The rest of the afternoon was spent going over everything the Healer could find in her library on Castle Teravinea. Regardless of the plan we would come up with, ultimately, I would be required to know the castle thoroughly. She had some floorplans that I poured over with Dorjan, who knew the castle layout better than most. He had an informant that fed him inside information and kept him current about new construction or any changes. He made the corrections on the large map we had spread out on the table.

The City of Teravinea is located in the central eastern point of our kingdom. Beginning with its vineyards and olive groves that spread through the beautiful lush valley, it then rises to rocky heights. Finally dropping in sheer vertical cliffs to the heavy seas below. It is upon these impenetrable cliffs the castle was built. Surrounded on almost three sides by the sea, it remains a forbidding fortress.

Dorjan pointed out the location of the Castle Outpost. "Its entry is built into the cliffs. The outpost connects to a series of corridors that join it to the castle — if you know the path. It has long-since been abandoned, but it might prove to be useful for our quest."

After a few hours of instruction, Dorjan took his leave. I spent a little more time on my own with the maps. I heard him, Gallen and the Healer speaking quietly downstairs, but even with my improved hearing, I couldn't make out what they were saying. Then I heard horse hooves as Dorjan rode off of the property. Darkness had already fallen.

"Eshshah, are you getting these plans committed to your memory?"

"Yes, but I'm hungry, Amáne. Do you think you'd be

allowed to fly with me tonight when I hunt?"

"Oh, I'd love it. They haven't let us fly together in a long time. Let's see if I have any luck convincing the Healer to let me go with you."

I ran downstairs where the Healer and Gallen were quietly talking at the kitchen table and began my plea. Using my best persuasive tactics, "Healer, may I fly tonight with Eshshah when she hunts? It's been so long. We'll do some practice mounts if you'll let me go. Ten of them — five wing mounts and five tail mounts. Please can I? It's a new moon and it's dark enough that no one will see us." My words spilled out in my excitement as I tried my hand at bribery.

"The darkness of the night doesn't mean it will be any safer for you, Amáne."

"What could possibly happen when I have an almost full-grown dragon to protect me?"

"Have you forgotten all of your bruises, scars and near-ancestor experiences you've suffered since you've been with your dragon?"

"Those were all my ignorance and clumsiness — I know much more now. You've trained us well. We'll be fine. Nothing will happen. I really need to fly with her. Please, Healer?" I tilted my head, my eyes pleaded.

I could tell she was going to give in. I knew she would try to make up for her previous behavior toward me and I took advantage of it. I felt a little guilty, but I didn't let up. She looked at Gallen, who, more often than not, would side with me. I saw him give an almost imperceptible nod. She turned to me and reluctantly, but firmly, said, "Okay, Amáne, but I want you back here in less than two hour's time. That's long enough for Eshshah to hunt. I will expect your timely return."

I threw my arms around her neck, genuinely thankful we had been allowed to fly again. Running out into the courtyard in jubilation, I threw the saddle on Eshshah as quickly as I could. Eshshah, as excited as I was, took position for some wing mounts. We did five successful ones and then worked our way through five tail mounts. I think we had to do six or seven to meet our criteria.

On our last mount, Eshshah pushed off and with a quick powerful downstroke of her wings, we were airborne. I deftly buckled myself in the saddle as she spiraled upwards. There is no feeling like the thrill of her take-offs. It's the most exhilarating feeling to ever experience.

I closed my eyes and breathed in the cool night air. Eshshah's spicy scent mingling with the salty wind rejuvenated me. It was the kind of feeling I wished I could capture in a bottle and pour over myself whenever the need arose.

We flew to our cove and silently enjoyed each other's company. Languishing there for a while, we gazed at the stars in the dark sky and cherished our time alone.

Eshshah originally had thought she wanted to fish, but then changed her mind and had a taste for wild sheep. She had some concerns as to whether she should leave me at the cove or take me closer to where she'd hunt. It had been a while since I'd been to the cove. I preferred to stay on the beach. Reluctantly, she agreed to my request after I promised I would wait for her closer to the cliffs. She felt I would be safer there. If anything, or anyone should approach, I would have the cliffs at my back.

I made light of her concern but conceded to her desire. But I declined her following plea to light a fire for protection. I preferred the darkness so I could enjoy the infinite display of stars, especially since it was a new moon. She gave in.

Marveling at her beauty as she took wing, I sat in bliss and delighted in my solitude — of course, that was solitude with Eshshah in my consciousness. I also shared the pleasure of her hunt, except in her final kill. Per my desire, she blocked me out for that part.

Relaxed for the first time in so long, I started to doze off, but awakened when I heard shuffling and sniffing nearby. My senses sharpened. I slowly and silently withdrew my dagger.

"Amáne, what's happening?" Eshshah's awareness directed toward me.

My sight, even in the dark night, was excellent and I saw the shape of a large dog, probably a wild dog, which were not uncommon around here. They're usually more afraid of people than we need to be of them. Relaxing my concern, I made the mistake of answering Eshshah out loud. "It's just a wild dog sniffing around."

I stiffened as the night's peace was broken by a thunderous growl. The dog turned its large head toward my voice. More than just a common dog growl, it was a ferocious wild snarl from deep in his throat. The vibrating sound continued as the dog approached. I gaped at the biggest dog I had ever seen. He stalked slowly toward me. His eyes glowed in the starlight — red, crazed eyes. His lips curled over large exposed teeth. The animal was not right. Foam collected around his mouth. Saliva dripped from its jaws. This was a rabid dog. I had learned at a young age about the rabies disease when a childhood friend had been bitten. It was a horrible illness and in less than three weeks my friend rested with his ancestors. I held my dagger in front of me and wished I had brought my spear instead. *Why didn't I at least put on my sword before I left the house?* The dagger suddenly seemed so ineffective.

"Eshshah, please." I entreated her to come quickly.

"Amáne, be careful, I'm already on my way."

No sooner had she said this than the dog leaped at me without warning. I ducked to the side and swiped my blade at him, cutting into the beast's shoulder. Its warm blood sprayed my arm. With an unearthly howl of pain, he landed and immediately lunged again. I side-stepped him once more. Just barely avoiding his snapping jaws, I found my mark in another slice, this time to his hind leg.

Instead of slowing him down, it angered him more. With a loud rumble in his chest, he advanced more slowly, calculating. His glowing eyes locked on mine as he came in for the kill.

I stepped back matching his pace. As I retreated closer to the cliff, my boot caught on a rock behind me. I went down hard, but rolled out of the way just in time to miss his spring. In an unexpected move, the mad dog spun around and lashed out as I tumbled. I felt his vise-like jaws close on my calf. Screaming in pain, I called out for Eshshah. A cold rush of panic filled my chest. Realization flooded my mind — I had just been bitten by a rabid dog.

I reached for a branch that lay on the ground beside me. Twisting, I brought it down on the dog's snout. With a yelp, he released me and I rolled to my feet. The branch in one hand, and my dagger in the other, I crouched in a fighting stance to face him. In shifting my weight, a sudden piercing pain shot up my leg. It gave out. Falling backwards I watched helplessly as the dog made his leap to finish me off. His body stretched in its arc of descent toward my throat as I lay on my back, paralyzed in shock and pain.

My life swept before me in slow motion. I regretted my

approaching demise, which would mean the failure of my mission to save Teravinea — even before I had a chance to participate. I grieved that Eshshah would be without a rider. I felt for the people of the kingdom. I felt for the Healer having to prepare another friend to rest with her ancestors.

Wait. What was I thinking? Those were the thoughts of someone who had given up. That was not me.

At that same instant I came to my senses, Eshshah said, "I'm almost there, Amáne, fight!" She melded her mind with mine and gave me the extra strength I needed.

Still on my back, I felt her power flow through my body. Like lightning I slashed with my dagger and severed the mad dog's head halfway off. His blood drenched me as he hovered above in mid-leap. At the precise moment I completed my stroke, Eshshah swooped in and caught the beast as it dropped, saving me from being crushed by his body. She flung it away from me — I heard it splash into the sea.

"Amáne, you're covered in blood. Where are your injuries?"

"It's mostly the dog's blood," I said. "But Eshshah, it was rabid and it bit me." Even though my life didn't end with the dog ripping out my throat, I anticipated it would end in a matter of a few weeks when the symptoms of the disease would begin to show, and the infection became fatal.

"Where, Amáne? Show me quickly."

I unlaced and removed my boot to expose my left calf where the dog's razor-sharp teeth had punctured the leather and sank deep into my flesh. Eshshah immediately placed her nose on the wound and breathed her warm healing breath. I could feel her concentration was more intense than it had been for any of my other injuries. She hummed as well, which also differed from her previous healing practices. The heat from her healing rose in my calf and became almost too hot to bear, but she didn't ease up. My leg no longer hurt from the bite, but the heat became more unbearable. Still she continued her treatment.

After quite a while, and just before I could take no more, she pulled back and breathed a deep sigh, "I think I got it all, Amáne, let's get you back to the Healer. She will never trust me again," Eshshah lamented. "This is all my fault — I talked you into flying with me tonight."

"Eshshah, please don't say that. It was I who talked the Healer into letting us go. And it was I who wouldn't listen to you about leaving me in the cove."

I gathered my boot and hobbled to her side to try to reach the saddle, but had some difficulty getting up to it. She practically had to lay down so I could mount. With shaking hands, I buckled myself in. Eshshah took to the sky and headed back to the Healer's.

I caught sight of the courtyard from a distance. Both the Healer and Gallen appeared agitated as they waited for us outside — we had gone over the two-hour time limit they had given us. Nervous about their reaction to my blood-soaked clothing, I called down to them as Eshshah circled lower and then back-stroked her wings to make a gentle landing.

"Healer, Gallen, I'm okay. Don't worry it's not my blood." Not all of it anyway, but I didn't add that. They both rushed up as we touched the ground, shock on their faces as well as relief.

I slid off, but when I hit the ground my leg buckled under me. I stumbled into the Healer's arms. In a delayed reaction to the terror I had just experienced, both tears and words flooded out of me like a dam that had burst.

"Healer," I cried, "it was awful. Eshshah didn't want to leave me at the cove, but I talked her into it, and she went to hunt, and then there was a rabid dog and I thought I was about to be killed, but Eshshah gave me her strength and then she swooped in before his body could fall on me, after I nearly severed his head, and I don't want to die of rabies, but Eshshah thinks she got it all."

"Slow down, Amáne. You got bitten by a rabid dog?" Her face went pale. "Gallen, please take her in to her chambers. I'll need Eshshah's help. Now, tell us again, what happened, Amáne."

Gallen carried me into my room as I tried again, without much success, to explain the horror we had just been through. As we came into the light I gasped at the blood that drenched my clothing, not knowing which was mine from my cuts and scratches, and which belonged to the dog. I tried one more time to relate my story as the Healer examined my calf.

"Puncture wounds, relatively deep into your muscle, but it doesn't look like major tissue damage. Your boot saved your leg. From the size of the bite marks, it looks like he could have torn your leg off. Eshshah did an exceptional job, but we will need to keep up the treatment until we're sure the virus has been eliminated. Time is the only way to tell."

She rushed off to mix one of her concoctions. When she returned Eshshah put her nose on my calf again as the Healer placed a poultice on the wound. It just added to the burn. I gritted my teeth as the heat rose.

"There has been talk about a wild dog that's been terrorizing and killing the livestock around here." Gallen commented, "They said it was larger than any wild dog anyone has ever seen." He shook his head in disbelief. "You severed his head off with only your dagger, Amáne?"

"Almost," I whispered.

CHAPTER TWENTY

The Healer insisted I take a hot soak. She put a large amount of pungent herbs into the tub — the steam whirled enticingly around the bathing room. I didn't need to be coaxed into one of my favorite pastimes as I sunk down into the comfortable heat. The dried blood and my fears dissolved away.

The treatments continued throughout the night. The next morning found me feeling surprisingly well. My leg was the color of the plums in the fruit market, but I was able to stand on it. And aside from some soreness and a noticeable limp, I could walk fine.

I wanted to start my practice again as it had been a couple days since I'd done any serious sword work. The Healer ordered me to take it easy and kept a sharp eye on me for any symptoms of depression, headache, fever or acute pain — which, thankfully, never came. She did allow me to work a short period of time with a spear on the pell.

I started to think I might prefer the spear as my weapon of choice. Measuring at almost six feet, the longer reach would keep me at a safer distance from danger than a sword. It would take less power to thrust at someone rather than strike with the sword. I had the extra speed as well, which is a great benefit with that style of weapon. It was easy for me to execute a quick backwards retreat, which would give me the distance needed to thrust.

The rest of the afternoon and evening I spent studying the maps and castle floorplans with Eshshah.

The following day, Dorjan rode in to assist in my training. He gave me a strong fatherly hug and then pulled away, looked into my eyes and said, "So you talked the Healer into letting you take flight, and then you convinced Eshshah to let you stay alone in the cove? I believe with your powers of persuasion, you'll make a fine negotiator." He had a deep rumble for a laugh — almost like Eshshah's. "And if your negotiations aren't successful, you can just lop off your opponent's head, like I heard you did with that monster of a dog. Well done, Amáne." His laughter echoed off of the walls. It was contagious. He soon had me laughing with him.

"And it looks like everyone seems to know everything I do around here. Is there no privacy?" I knew the answer to that.

We retreated to the library where we pulled out the castle maps again and began pouring over them. Dorjan placed his finger on a spot just up a mouth of a river from the ocean side of the fortress — again pointing to the location of the Castle Outpost.

"I hear you're familiar with the Dorsal Outpost. Many of our dragon caves and outposts have similar layouts. We never knew where we'd be stationed. To have all the locations similar helped us adapt more readily. Although each had their individual styles, it was easy to settle in, no matter which outpost we were assigned. Some were larger than others, the Castle Outpost being the largest, could house quite a few dragons and their riders."

He went on to explain that outpost was particularly extravagant. "Every rider posted there would buy or create a work of art or some useful object, trying to outdo the rider preceding him ... or her. It was a friendly competition.

"I hope some day you'll have the time to fully appreciate it. Maybe not in this upcoming visit, but sometime in the future."

Afterwards, we put aside the maps and floorplans, then the three of them worked with me in my fighting practice. Dorjan lunged, feinted and parried as he added verbal lessons. "A fighter is always in motion and never at rest. At no time should you remain fixed, Amáne — that's inviting injury. Training is a continual, never-ending process — a path, not a destination."

I absorbed these lessons as well as the physical training they offered. Thus far I had trained only in one-on-one combat. The time had come to start working with multiple opponents. We began with three against one — the one being me. When the three of them rushed me, my goal was to separate them, which allowed me to deal with only one at a time. By stepping to the side, I created a situation where the other two could not get to me without going through the one I had singled out. I could then dispatch the one before I faced the other two. If an opponent got too close, they taught me to use my spear to check him. Or I could step in deep, put the pole behind his leg and use it as a lever to trip him.

"We're only practicing now," the Healer reminded me, "trying to work on your form, techniques and strength, but in a serious fight, there is no fair play, Amáne. Go for the crotch, stab the foot, use the quillon — the hook at the base of the spearhead — if your spear has one, to hook and drag your opponent by the leg, by the neck, whatever it takes."

After the midday meal, Gallen worked with Eshshah and me on our mounts. We practiced our standard foreleg mounts, but with more speed. After dark, Gallen showed us some aerial dismounts. Eshshah hovered several feet above the ground while I lowered myself to her foreleg, and then jumped to the earth, rolling out of the fall and to my feet. Another technique was to secure a rope from the saddle. As Eshshah hovered further off the ground, I descended the rope, and then climbed back up and into the saddle.

By the end of the day Eshshah and I felt pleased with our progress. It made such a difference that there was no longer any misunderstanding between the Healer and me.

Each day was similar, yet different, as new skills were introduced. Excited with every challenge our trainers gave us, we could tell they were pleased with our successes. Not that we mastered everything, but it was obvious we gave our entire selves to our practice.

CHAPTER TWENTY-ONE

As I fell into bed one night, I went over in my head the plan that was beginning to formulate for the procurement of the dragon egg. I was nervous as well as excited that my lifelong dream of a quest would be seeing fruition in just a short time. I smiled to myself when I recalled my childhood aspirations I only shared with my mother. If she could see me now — I mean be here with me — I knew she would be so proud.

With that thought lingering in my head, I faded into sleep. I had a dream I was riding Thunder. I heard the sound of his hooves as they hit the ground. We turned a corner and came upon a group of people who were talking excitedly. I couldn't see their faces, but only heard their voices. Then a woman in the group wailed — it sounded so real.

"Amáne, Amáne! Wake up." It was Eshshah. "Something is wrong."

I bolted upright and heard the Healer from her kitchen. It sounded like she was crying. There were other voices, upset and in an urgent discussion. I could only hear clips of it as I strained to listen.

"We have no choice, Healer, whether she is ready or not, she must attempt it." It was Gallen's voice. "A rider alone could never make it in and out again safely, it would take a linked pair."

In one motion, I threw one of the bed covers over my nightshirt and rushed down the corridor to find out what was wrong. I came into the kitchen to see Dorjan, Gallen and the Healer with stricken looks on their faces. The Healer had tears streaming down her face.

"What's happening?" I ran to the Healer and put my arms around her to try comfort her, she looked so fragile.

Dorjan answered, "The Healer's nephew has been kidnapped and he will be killed within three days time." I didn't know she had a nephew, but this was not the time to ask about him. Dorjan continued, "In the perpetration of the kidnapping, Farvard lost his life." Dorjan took a deep breath. "He now rests with his ancestors." This struck me personally. I had come to know and love Farvard through the communication disc. I groaned, dropped heavily next to the Healer, and heaved a jagged sigh.

Gallen turned to the Healer. "We have no choice," he repeated firmly and with restrained urgency.

She sat up and took a deep breath, then looked into my eyes. "Amáne, this is a long and complicated story and we have no time to go over the details. Just know this, Ansel, my nephew, is currently a lord of a manor in Tramoren, a township northwest of the City of Teravinea — where Farvard was. This is a political kidnapping of a noble, and by our kingdom's code, a kidnapping of this kind should only result in ransom. They have broken the code and raised the stakes — we've been informed he will be executed."

"Who has done this? Can't we just give them what they

want?" I asked.

"They want him dead," she answered.

"Where are they holding him?"

"He's in the dungeons of Castle Teravinea," Dorjan said.

Icy fingers went up my spine as I recalled the stories Dorjan had told me of that dark place.

Like a curtain thrown open to flood a room with the morning light, our destiny was illuminated — I saw what Eshshah and I were meant to do. After a quick mental check with her, I said calmly, "Eshshah and I will go. We've been studying the floorplans for weeks now and with just a little more instruction on that level of the castle," I dared not say dungeon or I might have lost my courage, "we can make our way to his cell. If good fortune is on our side, Eshshah and I can bring him home safely."

I couldn't believe I heard myself say those words. Sounding much more calm and brave than I actually felt, I knew something of immense proportions was behind all this that I couldn't understand. For some reason, the Healer and the two dragon riders weren't ready to reveal it. I realized at that moment all of our training and practice, both mental and physical, was meant for this one quest. Eshshah agreed with me.

The Healer opened her mouth and shook her head as if she planned to decline our offer, but Gallen put his hand on her shoulder. Then he spoke for all of them. "Amáne and Eshshah, you are a true dragon and rider linked pair. At such a young age and after only a limited time of linking, you've grasped your duty with more courage than any newly-linked pair, male or female in our history and I am privileged to know you."

As she struggled to control her tears, the Healer wrapped

her arms around me and held me.

It was Dorjan who spoke next. "We have very little time to prepare. We will do what we can to help you. You must leave at next nightfall. It's too late to leave now. Let's go over the layout of the dungeon and then you need to get some rest."

"Rest? You expect me to sleep?"

"Eshshah will have to help you with that. You have to be alert for this quest. You cannot stay up tonight and expect to be successful tomorrow night, or you'll set yourself up for failure. With the combination of Eshshah's powers and some of the Healer's herbs, you can find sleep. There's not much more you can do tonight, anyway."

So, Dorjan and I retreated to the library and pulled out the plans of the lowest levels of the castle, the place where nightmares were made.

"Dorjan, there are hundreds of cells here. How am I supposed to know where he is?"

Pointing to one section, he said, "I know these are no longer used, so we won't worry about them. This smaller section over here was always reserved for political prisoners. This is where we are certain he is being held. There are only about twenty cells in that corridor."

We went over a couple different approaches and exits so I could have a back-up plan if changes had been made that he wasn't aware of. Dorjan fervently hoped there wouldn't be any surprises — his informant had stayed in contact with him and he felt he was as current as he could be. He instructed me on the best path to reach that part of the dungeon, pointed out where the guard's room was located, and the safest way to get past it to reach the cells.

"I'll leave you now to your rest. I have much to make ready for you. I'll return late morning or early afternoon. Thank you, Amáne and Eshshah. In time you will more fully understand our noble cause."

With that, he left me in the library, had a few quick words for the Healer and Gallen, and rode off. I studied the maps for a while longer and then went downstairs to the kitchen where Gallen and the Healer were quietly making plans. The Healer handed me a cup of earthy-smelling tea and instructed me to take it to my chambers and make sure I drank the entire cup. That, along with Eshshah's humming should put me into a restful sleep. I was doubtful — the butterflies collected in my stomach as I came to the realization of what we were about to do.

CHAPTER TWENTY-TWO

It was mid-morning when I awoke to the sound of horse hooves in the courtyard. Remarkably refreshed, I sat up looking forward to my daily practice. That is until the events of last night came back in a harsh actuality — it was not a dream. The force of reality blasted through my body, first with nausea, then my heart pounded in my ears, followed by a wave of muscle spasms.

Eshshah came immediately to my assistance and hummed her gentle remedy. After a bit, with her help, I regained control. "This won't do. How can I accomplish a near-impossible task if I can't control my nerves? What if I'm unable to even begin my mission?" Doubt threatened to overtake my confidence of last night.

"Amáne, don't think like that." Eshshah admonished. "Your first task is to think positively about your goal. We have no choice but to succeed — so we will."

I dressed and made my way down to the kitchen. Dorjan, Gallen and the Healer were unloading gear and weapons from

Dorjan's cart onto the kitchen table. There were a couple of swords of varying lengths, a shield, and two pole arms — spears — leaning against the wall. I also saw a few items I couldn't identify.

"Good morning, Amáne," Dorjan said in his booming voice, "you look well rested. I've brought you some gifts I've been working on for quite some time. I just finished the last a few hours ago. I may just be known as the blacksmith in Dorsal, but I do know more than just horseshoes, wagon wheels and clipping horses' tails. At one time, my family were cutlers. They made the finest knives, daggers, spears and swords in all of Teravinea. I learned that craft before I became a dragon rider. My skills do not match those of my father, but I haven't forgotten what he taught me so many lifetimes ago."

He reached for the pole arms. "I understand you've taken a liking to wielding a spear, so I've crafted two differing styles. You can choose which feels best to you."

He lifted one that had a blade that widened toward the bottom and had two arms or lugs that curved up from the base of the blade before attaching to the shaft. Handing it to me, he said, "This partisan is a long thrust-and-cut spear. You'll find it a very agile and nimble fighting weapon."

I took it, feeling its weight and its balance. It was light in my hand and had a reach of maybe a little less than six feet.

Gesturing toward the other pole arm, "This one is a glaive. As you can see, it has a longer thinner blade, with a well-defined fore and back edge. It is exceptional for thrusting. And this guard here," he indicated a small cross bar a little below the base of the blade and before the shaft, "will allow you to parry and control your opponent's weapon."

He handed it to me and it felt just as nice, the reach was

maybe a bit longer due to the length of the blade. They were both of beautiful craftsmanship. I raised my eyebrows and looked at Dorjan when I saw Eshshah's scales were inlaid at the base of the blade.

"You've noticed I've made good use of Eshshah's scales, with her permission, of course. You can whisper her name and the scales will ignite for use as a torch. It may come in handy in the dark tunnels under the castle."

The Healer spoke, "You can test them on the pell a little later to see which you prefer. We need to go through the rest of your gear with you first."

There were several swords from which to choose, all well-made and sturdy. I had already made my mind up one of the pole arms would be my weapon of choice. But as a back-up, I chose a beautiful, yet simple sword that suited me.

Next, the Healer handed me some new knee-high boots with buttons up the side. Leather cords laced around the buttons. These were not ordinary leather boots, although their appearance had me think so. They were, in part, a gift from Eshshah, as her scales were used to make them. Between the top leather and the lining were her beautiful fire-like scales. In another era they would not have been hidden, but would have shown in their full beauty. However, in these times we could not chance exposure. Their strength is unmatched and they would protect my lower leg and feet from almost anything.

"These are beautiful. Thank you, Healer and Eshshah."

"There's more from Eshshah and me," said the Healer as she pulled back a cloth that covered something on the table. "I wanted you to see its beauty before we cover it up."

I took in a sharp breath as she held the most beautiful

breastplate I had ever seen. Again, it was constructed with Eshshah's iridescent scales. They were fastened, in an overlaid pattern, to a leather background. It shone brighter than if it were polished metal. I could see why we needed to cover it up as its brilliance would announce my coming from a long distance. It consisted of a front and back piece that attached at the shoulders. Buckles secured the two sections on either side. I found it surprisingly light-weighted. They told me it was nearly indestructible. The pauldrons for my shoulders would be fastened on separately.

To go along with the breastplate were gauntlets, to protect my hands and forearms, again made with Eshshah's contributions. Similar to my boots, a thin layer of soft leather covered her shimmering scales, and made them look like ordinary elbow-length leather gloves. There is no other known substance as strong and lightweight as dragon scales.

Gallen and the Healer put the breastplate over my head for a tentative fitting. They buckled it at the sides, and were please to find it a perfect fit. It was surprisingly supple and didn't hinder my movement at all. This piece of my gear was shaped to make me unidentifiable as female, which didn't prove to be difficult as I was not very well endowed on top anyway — unlike some of my female acquaintances. There was a time or two when that fact was a little embarrassing to me, but now I was thankful for my body style.

Our plan hinged on the fact that I would enter the castle disguised as a male. My hair would be tucked inside my helmet. I learned to move and behave with a masculine bearing. Dorjan and Gallen had taught me to speak with a lower voice so I would sound genuine, like a male my age — not put-on. I'd been working on that part of my training for the last couple of weeks for our original quest. We would proceed with the same plan for the rescue. The

Healer started to explain that in the unlikely event something were to happen and I was captured — if it were revealed I was female ... She shuddered and didn't finish her sentence. I understood what she meant. She insisted I not drop my disguise until I had met up safely with Eshshah. Dorjan and Gallen had both given me last-minute pointers to improve my performance.

To finish off my protective gear, the Healer handed me a riding helmet. Again, Eshshah's scales were between the outer leather and the lining. There was enough room to tuck my long hair inside, without any bulk showing. Gallen showed me a small lever near my temple. When I pushed down on it, a pair of connected dragon scales, treated and polished to be completely transparent, lowered over my eyes. They were of perfect clarity and would shield my eyes from the wind and debris when we flew. Pushing up on the lever hid them from sight.

Then Dorjan selected an object from the table. It was spherical in shape, about the size of a small apple, constructed from the scales of at least three different dragons, judging by the three colors. There was a small brass ring at the top with a leather thong threaded through it.

"This," he said, "is my prize creation. Gallen isn't the only rider to invent something from our dragon's scales to use in our cause." He looked at Gallen in a good-natured taunt. "This is my lightning ball."

These are scales from Torin, Unule — my dragon — and Salama. Thunder, Wind and Lightning. It's a one-time-use-only device and will disintegrate into nothing — no evidence remains after its use. I only had the time to make one, so you must choose the occasion wisely. Ideally, you should take full advantage and wield it to incapacitate a group, possibly guards in the guardroom.

It won't kill them, but they'll wish it did when they wake up hours later. They'll have a headache that will make their worst hangover feel like a soothing massage. You need to remove the brass ring and then say or whisper the three dragons' names as you toss it toward your targets. The noise, the wind and the flash will knock them on their rears — out cold. Remember to put your eye shields down or look away, but the noise and wind will not harm you, only your opponents.

"Wow," was all I could think to say. I was relieved that this device would not kill. My doubt still remained that I could actually take a person's life. I didn't voice these doubts, however, because it contradicted the adamant instruction these three had been instilling. They pressed into me that in any given altercation I may engage in, the result would find someone resting with their ancestors. The preferred outcome — that it would not be me.

"I have a couple more things on my wagon for Eshshah, if you'll join me outside." Dorjan led the way to the courtyard where Eshshah waited.

The items left on his cart were covered in a thick cloth, which he flung back to reveal a double saddle. It was of dark leather with designs similar to the ones on the single seat we used from the Dorsal Outpost — the same style of long distance saddle, only it was for two riders. Two sets of belts, and two sets of boot pegs completed the equipage. The other item was a breastplate for Eshshah. Besides a few of Eshshah's interspersed in the inlay, Dorjan used scales from many different dragons, judging by the multiple colors of nearly indestructible scales. These were attached to a leather lining to protect her most vulnerable part — her heart.

The Healer had loaded a leather satchel with some other necessities. A helmet and some warm clothing for Ansel, some rope, a water skin and some travel cakes with special grains and nourishment for me as well as for Ansel — not knowing if he'd been fed by his captors. She also packed two small vials of a dark liquid in a small pouch to hang on my belt.

"It's important he drinks one of these vials as soon as you find him," she said. "It'll give him the strength he'll need to make it to the other side of the castle where Eshshah will be waiting.

"How do I even know if I've found the right man? What does he look like? How is he expected to trust who I am?" In all of our preparations the last few hours I was surprised these questions had just occurred to me.

Expecting him to be in his thirties, forties, or older, being the Healer's nephew, I was quite surprised when she said he was only seventeen. The Healer gave me a brief description that he was tall, had long dark hair and green eyes. She then took a chain from around her neck that held a man's ring and placed it over my head.

"He knows this ring, give it to him and tell him his aunt has sent him help. Let me just tell you that he can be a bit headstrong, like someone else I know," she raised an eyebrow. "Don't lose this ring, or he may not trust you."

CHAPTER TWENTY-THREE

At the midday meal we went over our plan again. With our permission, the Healer was to ride with Eshshah and me to the Dorsal Outpost where she would wait for our return. It would be daylight when we arrived with her nephew and we wouldn't be able to fly straight into Dorsal. She needed to be at the outpost in case Ansel required medical attention. We were to leave here as soon as it got dark. It should take around three hours to get to Castle Teravinea from the Dorsal Outpost. I had to be in and out of there before daylight, which gave me less than seven hours to find him, convince him I was there to help him, and then navigate the maze of tunnels and passageways to the Castle Outpost, where Eshshah would be.

After we ate, I worked on the pell and decided which pole arm I preferred. I liked the glaive — the one with the cross-guard and the longer blade. I practiced with the Healer, Gallen and Dorjan to get in some final pointers from each of them.

The Healer gave me another cup of her relaxing tea and told me I must get a few more hours sleep. Fatigue would not figure in to my already precarious quest.

A couple hours before dark, the Healer woke me with enough time to eat something and then make my final preparations for our trip. I dressed slowly in dark tights and a dark tunic. Pulling on my new boots, I marveled at their comfort. I twisted my hair and pinned it at the top of my head, then headed to the kitchen.

A large leather satchel leaned against the wall, already packed with the Healer's herbs and concoctions — whatever she felt she would need to treat Ansel, should he need it. There were also provisions in case we stayed at the Dorsal Outpost for longer than expected.

It was quiet at the table. I could hear each of us chewing and swallowing. I'm not sure how I actually got any bites to go down. My mouth was dry and my stomach ready to refuse anything offered. But the Healer stressed again I had to be at my best. For that I needed the nourishment — so I forced myself to eat.

At last it came time to leave. We went out to the courtyard, and while Dorjan put the breastplate and double saddle on Eshshah, Gallen and the Healer helped me with my gear. They eased my breastplate over my head — Eshshah's beautiful scales were now completely hidden. As they buckled it, my teeth began to chatter, although it was a warm night. My muscles twitched and I started in uncontrollable spasms. My stomach went into knots.

Gallen took my face in his hands and looked into my eyes. "Amáne, you are having pre-quest jitters. It's completely normal. I was starting to worry about you not showing any emotion for the last couple of hours."

He placed his hands on the top of my shoulders and exerted downward pressure as he continued to talk. "But, you need to control your nerves. Will yourself to relax. Breathe in, breathe out." He kept the pressure on my shoulders and, truthfully, I could feel the calming effects. I started to pay attention to my breathing. Before I could ask for Eshshah's help, my shaking subsided. Gallen slowly let up his pressure.

Over my breastplate I put another dark tunic that was of a lightweight material but made for warmth on higher flights. I buckled on a thick belt that held both my sword and my dagger in their scabbards. It had several loops in which to attach other objects, such as the lightning ball and the medicine vials for Ansel. I noticed another item hanging from one of the loops on a leather thong. It was a dragon scale, carved into the shape of a key with a flat brass head on the end. Decorated with swirling etchings, the word 'Aperio' was inscribed.

"This key will open any lock that may bar your way. Say the name of the late dragon, Aperio, and it will open for you," explained the Healer.

Lastly, I pulled my helmet over my pinned-up hair and buckled it at my throat. Gallen made sure not a wisp of hair strayed.

"How do I look?"

"Like a very dangerous young man on a serious mission." Gallen tried to make light in this tense moment.

"It's time, Amáne," said the Healer.

With somber faces, Gallen and Dorjan stood straight and gave Eshshah and me a sharp salute. They bestowed their blessings, each giving me a kiss on my forehead.

Adding on a positive note, Gallen said, "We will see you tomorrow night. We expect to hear the details of your successful mission." It did lift my spirits to believe I would be telling my tale to them soon ... I hoped.

Eshshah and I exchanged a silent reaffirmation of mutual

support before I hoisted myself in the front of the saddle. Reaching out my hand, I locked wrists with the Healer. She swung up in the space behind me. We buckled in and I gave Eshshah the word.

With a powerful thrust, my dragon pushed off the ground and effortlessly made her first downstroke. We were airborne — the added weight of the Healer and the extra gear we carried was nothing to her. A slight gasp emanated from the Healer. Gallen and Dorjan's clothing whipped in Eshshah's downdraft as I turned and watched them until they were no longer visible.

Chapter Twenty-four

The night flight was refreshing, and on any other occasion would have been enjoyable. Instead, we rode in complete silence. Just the soft beating of Eshshah's wings as we sailed smoothly through the moonless sky. I concentrated on the plans we'd tried to perfect in such a short time, mentally going over the route I was to take through the bowels of the castle. The names of the dragons to ignite the lightning ball and the one to activate the key were ingrained in my memory. My spear was in its holder to my right. I touched it lightly as I went over some mental strikes and parries. I noted the Healer was also lost in her own thoughts.

In what felt like no time at all, we arrived at the Dorsal Outpost. Eshshah knew exactly where to find the push-rock that opened the outer door. The rock slid open noiselessly and Eshshah flew into the large entry cavern landing perfectly — so unlike the landing we experienced when we first found this place. It seemed like so long ago.

I whispered "Sitara" to turn on the light shields and offered my hand to the Healer as she slid off Eshshah with her satchels over her shoulder. I started to dismount so I could show her around what I considered Eshshah's and my second home, but she stopped me.

"Amáne, there is no time. I can find my way around here. You must leave now. My blessings are upon you. May your ancestors smile upon you and ensure your first quest be a success. You're a noble and brave dragon and rider pair. I thank you. I'll be forever in your debt."

"Thank you, Healer. You'll have no debt in this."

With that, Eshshah turned back toward the entrance and leaped off the ledge. She unfolded her wings after a short free-fall. Our first quest had officially begun.

My mind reeled with the gravity of what we were about to attempt. Quite a contrast from my childhood desires to have a quest, a mission in life — this was not practice with wasters, not sparring with Kail at my cottage, nor was it the training bouts with the Healer, Gallen and Dorjan. We were going forth with real weapons to use on real people, with every likelihood that any given confrontation may end in death — even that of my own. I began to see our success was of more consequence than I had ever thought.

We turned toward the north and flew almost parallel with the eastern coastline, heading for the point that juts out at the center of our kingdom — the City of Teravinea. We flew high but not at the height where the cold was unbearable. Eventually, we would swing wide around the point and come at the castle from the sea. We hoped Dorjan was correct in his assumption that the battlements on that side would no longer be guarded. There, we would find the Castle Outpost. Under Dorjan's instruction, Eshshah knew how to find the push-rock to open the stone door.

Earlier that day Eshshah and I had forced ourselves to discuss my possible demise. I fervently begged her to not take her own life, but to choose another rider for the good of Teravinea. My death would not be in vain. It was a short conversation neither of us wanted to bring up again.

We had a three-hour flight. I knew I would do better than to worry and agonize over all of the ramifications should we fail. I pushed out of my consciousness any thoughts of what my death would mean to Eshshah. Nothing negative was allowed in my head or my heart. I avoided any unfavorable influence that would affect the success of our mission.

I closed my eyes and began even breaths before panic could rise in my chest. Once I started the actual search for Ansel, it should go easier for me. Adrenaline would kick in and my mind would be occupied instead of imagining unpleasant scenarios.

"Amáne, I see the castle," Eshshah said at last. Her eyesight was far superior to mine, even with my added abilities. A few minutes later I saw the fortress majestically rising from the towering cliffs — the water churned white foam at their base far below.

Eshshah slowed her pace to study the castle from this angle as it appeared to grow before us. I had never seen nor imagined such a massive structure. Suppressing my awe and small twinges of fear, I clicked into fight mode. Training my eye on the battlements, I searched for any sign of a guard. Thankfully, as Dorjan had predicted, this side was not patrolled. They had no need to keep watch, as any ship would have been sighted from another part of the fortress. This area was only accessible by dragon, and everyone assumed there were none left to worry about.

We came to the corner of the cliffs that towered above a rocky beach at the mouth of a river. This was the landmark

Eshshah was looking for. She turned in. We flew only a short distance. At about the same height as our Dorsal Outpost, she spotted the push-rock.

The stone door slid open silently and we landed in a large entry cavern. It was a similar layout to our Dorsal Outpost, hewn into the cliff. But unlike Dorsal, the wall to our right had a door that connected to a passageway leading into the corridors of the castle. It was through this door I would return with Ansel.

As we surveyed our surroundings, our hearts sank. We could see there was truth in what Dorjan had said when he marveled at its extravagance. There was certainly evidence that at one time it must have been lavish. As we took it all in, it was obvious not much remained of its former beauty. The hooks were still on the walls where tapestries had hung, and there were areas where it looked like paintings had been removed. Anything of value was no longer at the Castle Outpost. Broken pottery lay in shards at our feet. Dorjan would be sorely disappointed.

My anger was immediately directed at Galtero, who, I was sure had played a large part in the looting of this outpost. I had a good idea that whatever he didn't want from here, he gifted to foreign kings to impress them. Maybe one day I could help bring the Castle Outpost back to its grandeur.

Pushing my disappointment aside, I slid from Eshshah's shoulders with my spear and my pack, landing silently. Both of us sniffed the air to make sure the outpost was not occupied. Like the Dorsal Outpost, a faint dragon scent was present. Eshshah detected a trace of human presence, but she assured me there had been no one in this place for a long time.

Our first task was to create a ruse. We needed to make it

appear we had escaped with the castle's prisoner by a rope down to the beach and made our getaway in a small boat. There had to be no hint a dragon was involved.

I retrieved a small grappling hook from my pack with a long rope attached. Searching for a suitable spot near the entrance, I wedged the hook to make it look like it had been cast up from the ground below. I threw the other end of the rope over the edge. It was just long enough to be believable that someone could both enter and escape the cave using this method.

Leaving my pack in the entryway, I leaped back onto Eshshah and tied another rope to an anchor on the saddle as she dove out of the cave. She hovered while I climbed down and dropped to the beach at the mouth of the river. Eshshah stayed airborne and circled low — we couldn't leave dragon prints. This part of our plan required that I run back and forth between the beach and the rope dangling from the cave entrance. It would appear that rescuers had come in from a boat, taken Ansel and escaped the same way. The only bad part of this plan was that my feet are small. If anyone actually thought about the prints or were skilled in reading them, it might not be wholly believable. But what would their other conjectures be? I was sure a dragon would not figure into their theories. Lastly, I dug a trench at the waterline where a small boat would appear to have landed and been dragged up onto the beach.

Satisfied I'd set the scene as well as I could, I caught a hold of the rope hanging from Eshshah, climbed up to the saddle, and we flew back to the cavern.

I dismounted and retrieved my pack. Removing the lightning ball, I secured it to my belt along with the pouch that held the two small medicine vials. I hoped I would not find him in poor condition. If I did, I trusted the contents of the vials would be enough to aid in Ansel's escape. I doubted I would have the strength to carry a man all the way out. The last loop held a small skin of water.

I closed my eyes and took long slow breaths until I could unclench my hands and still my shaking body. Taking hold of my glaive I turned to my dragon as she softly hummed to me. "Okay, Eshshah, this is it. Are you ready? Will I even be able to do this?"

"Yes, Amáne. You can. You must. I will be with you in open thought transference. You're not alone. Remember that. Please be careful."

She put her face down to me and grabbing her fangs I pressed a kiss on her nose, then leaned my forehead against her for one last comforting breath.

Astride Eshshah once more, I gave her the word and she dove off the ledge.

CHAPTER TWENTY-FIVE

We flew along the battlement wall following the river, watching for any sign of guards in the towers. We saw no one. I made a mental note of the distance I would have to travel to get back to the outpost where Eshshah would wait for us. I fought my discouragement as I saw it was much greater than I had hoped.

At last we came to the tower that rose above the dungeons far below. I gave Eshshah's neck a long hug and another kiss. Grabbing my spear, I quickly slid off the saddle and made my way down the rope, silently landing on the battlements. Swallowing my fear, I watched her fly off. Time pressed on — I had to be in and out before daylight and already the ruse we set up at the river mouth had taken up more than we had counted on.

Getting my bearings, I checked my surroundings before sprinting from the shadows where I'd landed. I headed toward a tower door where the stairs would take me down into the recesses of the castle.

Dorjan explained that these stairs, and in fact all of the steps in the towers and outer walls, were built unevenly. This was to trip up enemies who hadn't learned this particular castle's stair pattern. He taught me the pattern, but even still I had to catch myself a few times as I miscounted. I decided I should slow down a bit. It would be a disaster if I were to clatter down to the bottom should I lose my count.

Descending the tower's spiraling stairs, I checked the arrowslits in the wall to see where I was in relation to the ground level. My one consolation was that since the Castle Outpost was much lower than the battlements, where I started my run, we would not have as many levels to climb back up to the entry cavern. In fact, once I got to the dungeon level, we would only have to go up three levels to get to the Castle Outpost height.

The drop in temperature told me I had reached the underground level, but I continued to descend. The air became more dank. The stairs grew slick with moss the further down I went. My progress slowed. At each level a doorway opened up into a corridor. I carefully peered out the door to check for guards. To my surprise the corridors were always empty. Was Galtero that egotistical to think no one would dare oppose him; or that ignorant not to guard his fortress better? I was, however, very thankful. Either way, it was to my advantage.

Four levels underground, I finally reached the level of the dungeon. The stench was nearly unbearable. Death, vomit, stale ale, urine and other unidentifiable odors wafted toward my sensitive nose. I had to sip some of my water and swallow hard more than once to keep from retching. *How could the guards even stand to work in such conditions?* I couldn't imagine ever getting used to these vile odors.

The stairs ended at a long corridor which led me to another

passageway that ran perpendicular to the one in which I stood. I checked both ways. The passage was clear. I entered and turned right — my senses sharpened to any sound or movement. A short distance up the corridor I saw light casting out from a doorway, and heard voices. I had reached the guardroom. Sweat flowed in rivulets down my body. I needed to stop for a second and take some breaths. I felt Eshshah's gentle encouragement as she stayed with me in open thought transference.

Noiselessly, I made my way to the doorway. The gruff voices of the guards grated on my ears. They were engaged in dicing, a favored gambling pastime. Boisterous outbursts and foul language assaulted me. I smelled a strong odor of ale.

"I'll roll ya for the boots off of that cursed rich one we're ordered not to touch," said one voice. "The second we know someone is comin' to take him to the executioner, we'll take 'em. He's not gonna be needin' 'em anyway, with no head on his shoulders."

"What're they waitin' for?" asked a second voice.

"King Galtero to get back. He wants to watch the execution himself — make sure he's good 'n dead," a third voice answered.

Repulsive laughter echoed from the room. The first voice added, "I don't want 'em after they're filled with his blood. I'll roll first." They laughed even harder. I had the urge to turn and run. My guess was they were talking about the Healer's nephew.

I craned my neck around the doorway to establish their number and positions. Thankful for my good fortune, I noted there were only three of them. They stood close to each other with their backs toward me, near the far wall. I unhooked the lightning ball from my belt, hoping all of the guards were present, and that they'd stay interested in their game.

Taking a deep breath, I steadied myself for my first

encounter. I leaned my glaive against the wall, and wrapped my fingers around the lightning ball. I pulled the brass ring out and prepared to toss the device. Exhaling slowly and evenly, I brought my arm back and whispered Torin, Unule, Salama, then lobbed the ball against the wall just as one guard threw the dice. Immediately, I ducked back into the passageway. The explosion, wind and flash took them quickly. I'm sure they never knew what hit them. When I looked again, they lay crumpled in a heap on the ground.

With a sudden sense of smug accomplishment I grabbed my glaive and carelessly rushed into the guard room to make the door on the far side.

This was a serious error on my part.

As I bolted for the door, I nearly collided with a large guard — his blade drawn. A brief sense of relief passed through me seeing he was only armed with his sword, not his halberd. Even better, he didn't have his shield.

I didn't miss the change in his expression from alarm to that of amusement as he looked me up and down. He relaxed his defenses when he saw the size of his adversary.

This was a serious error on his part.

Without hesitation he lunged at me. I stepped to the side and used the shaft of my spear to trip him up. He thudded heavily to the ground. I should have followed through instantly and stuck him with my blade as he fell. The voices of Gallen, Dorjan and the Healer echoed in my mind. "If you are confronted, be prepared to kill. Do not hesitate, or it could mean your life. It will not be practice, Amáne, you may not get a second chance."

Instead, I froze. I couldn't finish him. He rolled over and noted my indecision. A self-satisfied sneer curled his lip as he leaped to his feet, and swung his blade at my head. I moved fast, ducked his swing and ran backwards to open up the distance between us —

I needed the gap to make full use of my spear. He raised his sword for his next strike. I faced an unexpected opportunity — a second chance. I thrust my blade into his armpit that was left unprotected. Warm blood spattered my way as his eyes opened wide with the realization he would be meeting his ancestors.

I yanked out my glaive and stood motionless as he toppled to the dirt floor. A loud huff of air released from his lungs. Shock coursed through my body. My chest heaved as I tried to catch my breath. Comprehension washed over me — I had just taken my first human life.

"May you join your ancestors in peace." I whispered as a wave of nausea overtook me. Leaning on the wall, I emptied the contents of my stomach onto the floor. I wiped my mouth and the tears from my eyes with the back of my glove.

I pulled myself together, grabbed the guard's sword from his limp hand and ran cautiously to the passageway that contained the cells. I needed to keep moving. I summoned all my willpower and with Eshshah's presence, managed to move forward. Our duty was to bring the Healer's nephew home. I was determined we would succeed.

A long row of cell doors filled the corridor both to my left and to my right. Dorjan said Ansel would more than likely be in the cells to the right. I fervently wished he was correct. There were about twenty cells to check in that direction alone.

The small observation windows in the cell doors were almost too high for me. But if I stood up on my toes and used my spear for balance, I could just reach to open them and see who was inside. The first cell held what looked like an old woman in chains on the far wall. Moving to the next cell, I found a man who had already joined his ancestors — mouth gaping, eyes staring. I checked cell after cell as I hurried down the corridor, but found no prisoner that fit Ansel's description.

Two more cells left. I raised myself to the window one more time to peer inside. Suddenly a twisted face popped up at me from the other side like a hideous toy jack-in-the-box. The prisoner let out an insane shriek. I stifled a scream and fell backwards. My spear clattered to the floor, as the mad man inside laughed hysterically. I was ashamed and angry at myself for my reaction. Picking myself up, I fought the urge to cover my ears from the continued ranting of the demented man.

Finally, I reached the last cell and opened the observation window. This time I listened before I looked inside. Toward the far wall was a figure in chains, slumped over. His head rested on crossed arms positioned on top of his bent knees. His long dark hair fell over his arms. From the looks of his fine clothing, though filthy and disheveled, and the description the Healer had given me about his long hair, I was sure it was Ansel. I breathed a sigh of relief as I pulled Aperio's key from my belt.

Silently whispering, "Aperio," I unlocked the cell door and crept inside. I closed the door behind me, and softly called Ansel's name. There was no response. He remained in the same position. I moved closer and whispered his name again. My heart sank — *was I too late?* He may already be close to his ancestors. I laid my spear and the guard's sword down and moved closer to where he sat. Fearful of the worst, I put my hand out to try to rouse him.

I was not prepared for what happened next. With lightning speed he leaped behind me. He raised his hands above my head and brought them down in an attempt to choke me with the chains that bound him.

My reaction was instantaneous as I dropped into a crouch and ducked my head. I leaped out of his reach, then wheeled around to face him. We both stood frozen in our fighting stances — our eyes locked.

I held his green eyes, where a mixture of emotions played. First a hint of alarm — I don't think he expected me to move that quickly. Then instantly, they flashed with disappointment — he had missed his chance to kill me. And finally they were filled with hatred and anger as he glared at me.

There was something familiar about him, a kind of connection I made, although I was certain I had never met him.

My train of thought was broken as a string of curse words flew from his mouth and then he almost growled, "If these chains hadn't stopped me, boy, I would have killed you. Unchain me and fight fairly."

I knew otherwise, but said instead, "I have no doubt you'd like to kill me. I don't want to fight you, but was sent to release you."

"Release me? To the executioner?"

"No, Ansel. Your aunt, the Healer, sent me. I've come to take you home."

"My aunt sent a boy to rescue me? Were there no men available in all of Teravinea that she had to send a boy? That doesn't sound like her." His eyes narrowed, and with poison in his voice, "Tell me who you are, swine herder."

"She told me to give you this ring." I slipped the chain from around my neck and held it out. "She said you would recognize it and that I was to tell you that your father would want you to have it, as the time will be nearing for you." I couldn't make sense of the message, but delivered it word for word.

His eyes told me he understood what I'd said, but he remained wary. "Are you going to hand it to me, or just stand there gawking like a fool?"

I gave him the message and it's obvious he knows what I meant. So why does he have to be so rude?

He was an admirable foe — and quite full of himself. However, I was glad he was on my side, even though he didn't realize it at the moment. I reminded myself he was probably in shock from the trauma of Farvard's death, then his abduction and ending up here in chains.

But, my stubbornness got the better of me — *two can play this game.* "Well, if you would use your brain, and stop playing the fool yourself, you'd see I'm telling you the truth. Hold your urge to kill me — maybe then I can hand it to you."

The look on his face told me he wasn't accustomed to being spoken to with such disrespect, especially by someone of a lower class. But he slowly relaxed his stance and held his hand out for the ring. I came closer cautiously and put it in his hand, then quickly stepped back.

"So, you believe me now? If I unlock your chains, you won't attack me? We need to get out of here before daybreak."

He held out his hands for me to unlock the chains, his eyes still fixed in a glare. His attitude was starting to annoy me.

I pulled the key from my belt and whispered "Aperio," unlocking the bands that held him. The shackles opened and dropped to the ground. Ansel rubbed the raw skin on his wrists. For a moment he looked so vulnerable and weak, I almost pitied him. Even still, his arrogance irritated me. I wasn't so sure if we were to have met under other circumstances, we would have gotten off to a better start. I doubted it.

I handed him the water skin. He looked suspiciously at it, then at me. Snatching it from his hands, I took a swig to prove it was safe. I shoved it back at him, and didn't hide my angry stare.

He nearly drained the entire skin.

"Here, now drink this. The Healer sent it to give you some strength." I held out the vial of the dark liquid.

Ansel hesitated and shot me the same suspicious look.

"Go ahead, take it, it's not poison. You'd be wise to start trusting me if we're going to get out of here alive." I couldn't keep the urgency from my voice.

He grabbed it from my hand and tossed back its contents. His face scrunched and he nearly choked. I didn't bother to hide my amusement. I was not ashamed of my bad attitude toward this young arrogant lord.

Ansel's condition improved noticeably after he finished the Healer's concoction. I picked up my spear and the sword from the dead guard. Still piqued at him, I thrust the hilt toward him and said, "Here, take this. I hope you know how to handle a sword."

"Probably better than you can handle that spear." He shot back.

Fighting a sarcastic response, I pressed my lips together, turned and inched the cell door open. Peeking around the corner, I made sure no other guards had shown up, then motioned it was clear. I had found him alive, and now I had to get him back to the Castle Outpost and meet up with Eshshah. I was thankful for the adrenaline that had kicked in — and for Eshshah's venom that ran in my veins.

CHAPTER TWENTY-SIX

"We're on our way, Eshshah, stay with us," I said ... out loud.

"What?" Ansel asked, looking to see if I had an accomplice.

"Nothing."

We had to go back through the guardroom to get to the corridor that would take us to the outpost. Ansel eyed the three guards in a heap by the wall as we stepped around the one lying in a pool of blood. He turned to me with eyebrows raised. Ashamed of what I had done, I shrugged, but kept moving.

Ansel and I stayed on the same level as the dungeons and found the passageway that led back toward Eshshah. I mentally went over the path we needed to take. My confidence started to build. The hard part was over and now it was just a matter of navigating the maze of corridors and tunnels back to safety.

We were in a passageway with no exits when I heard voices around the next corner. I put my hand on Ansel's arm and stopped him.

"There are men coming and there's no place to hide. We

have to fight."

"I can't hear anything."

"Why can't you just listen to me and trust that your aunt sent the right person? I can hear them coming. It sounds like four different voices. Get ready."

After a scowl in my direction, he reluctantly followed my lead. We flattened our backs to the wall at the corner where they would make their turn. Just before they were upon us, we jumped into the corridor and lunged at them. Surprise was our ally as we each dispatched a guard, dropping them at once to the floor.

"May you rest with your ancestors," I whispered, suppressing a wave of nausea.

The two left standing had the extra seconds to react. Recovering their wits, they faced us with their halberds. I would have preferred, of course, that they only had swords, especially for Ansel, as a pole axe versus a sword was not an even match.

Sizing up the large man in front of me I took in his slovenly appearance, uncharacteristic of a trained soldier. I could only hope he was as sloppy with his skills. I ducked as he swung at my head, then sidestepped to get behind him and trip him. He stumbled, but didn't go down as I had expected. I noted a flash of rage in his eyes as he spun around on me and swung again. This could work for me.

"Is that all you have?" I taunted as I ducked his second stroke. "You swing like a girl." I sneered.

His face reddened, his eyes blazed. He charged at me and threw a shot. I parried his careless blow and jumped back. The man's anger interfered with his decisions, just as I had hoped.

I heard a clatter to my right and realized Ansel's opponent had managed to knock away his sword. He lunged toward Ansel for the killing stroke. Ansel dove and rolled out of reach, barely evading the blade. In the split second I had before my guard closed the gap, I drew my spare sword.

"Ansel!" I shouted as I tossed it to him. He sprang to his feet. To my relief, he caught it just in time to fend off the next strike aimed at him. I turned my attention back to my fight.

Backing up to get my distance so I could thrust my glaive, I slipped on a dead guard's blood and went down hard, landing on my back. A rush of air forced out of me. I struggled to refill my emptied lungs. My eyes opened in time to see the man with his weapon poised directly above my head — a glare of death in his piercing dark eyes. He brought his pole-axe down on me just as I succeeded in finding my breath. I instantly rolled to one side, but the edge of his blade caught me on my unprotected upper arm. I yelped in pain but managed to leap to my feet. Spinning to face him, I allowed a slight smile as I caught him wrestling to release his blade from the grip of the dirt floor. It was the opportune moment that I needed — the advantage turned my way. Again, a second chance. I thrust my blade into his ribs between the buckles of his sloppily fastened breastplate. He fell with a thud as I relinquished him to his ancestors.

My attention turned to Ansel. He was tiring, but still holding his own. With my success he found a sudden burst of energy, and got the upper hand. I rushed to his aid. At the same moment I thrust my blade into the back of our opponent's knee, Ansel swiped at his neck. The guard dropped where he stood. One more time, I wished a man to rest in peace.

We looked at each other wide-eyed. Our chests heaved as we fought for air. We were pleased with ourselves that we took them, two against four. I remained mindful of the fact I had taken human lives yet again.

Pushing that thought to the back of my mind, I grudgingly complimented him, "Not bad with a sword, I guess."

"Looks like you can handle that spear after all," he returned. "Thanks for the sword. But you were taking your chances taunting him like that, weren't you?"

I shrugged. "I know all about anger and the mistakes it causes." He gave me a puzzled look. I let him try to figure it out for himself.

"We're fine and on our way," I told Eshshah. I could feel her anxiety.

"Yes, I know." Ansel responded. "I'm standing here with you. I can see we're fine."

"I'm not talking to you."

As we took another moment to catch our breath, I realized my arm was bleeding more than I had thought. Using my dagger to cut off some of my tunic I handed the cloth to Ansel who quickly wrapped my wound. I couldn't help but notice his skill and speed.

We continued running in the direction of the outpost. Advancing through all the turns I'd memorized, I started to feel relief that we were closer to our destination. But it was short-lived — we found ourselves at a dead end.

"Oh no, did I make a wrong turn? Which way do we go, now?" I asked Eshshah out loud ... again.

"How should I know? You're the one rescuing me, remember?" Ansel answered.

"I'm not talking to you!"

"Oh, great, you ask yourself questions. Do you hear voices, too?"

Eshshah answered me. "You didn't make any wrong turns,

Amáne, but that way must have been recently blocked in. There's another passageway that runs parallel to the one you're in. If you can go back and find an entry to it, then you can go around the blocked wall and return back to the correct corridor. Do you remember seeing it on the map?"

"Yes, I do," I answered Eshshah. But it seemed Ansel took it as the reply to his question on whether I hear voices.

He cursed and threw me a bewildered look as he shook his head. "I probably would have had better odds if I'd stayed in my cell instead of running in this sewer with a half-mad boy."

That was it. I had all I could take from him — the Healer's nephew or not. His aristocracy meant nothing to me at that moment, though it should have. I was not about to overlook this self-centered man's last statement. Turning on him, I unleashed my temper.

"Who do you think you are? You act like you're someone special. Well, you're not. You're just some stupid rich lord who got himself kidnapped. And a friend of mine died trying to protect you. Now, if you don't mind, I'm trying to get us out of here alive."

I regretted what I said about Farvard dying while trying to protect him. Ansel's shoulders slumped, like the air had been sucked out of him. It was pitiful and I almost apologized, but I was too stubborn — and angry.

Without another word, he followed me back up the corridor until we found a door. I listened to see if I could hear anything on the other side. It was relatively silent.

I made the decision. "Okay, let's try this way." I said. "Yes, I'm talking to you this time."

I turned to look at him and noted his face had gone pale. Pulling the last of the Healer's vials from my belt, I uncorked it and handed it to him. A little gentler this time, I said, "Here, you look like you could use this. We're not there yet so you'll need the boost. Stay with me. We'll be out of here soon." I sounded a little more confident than I actually felt.

He took it and drank half, then handed it back to me. "You could probably use some, too. Finish it."

His action surprised me and I locked eyes with him. I took the vial from his hand and drained the last half. The elixir was harsh and burned going down, but I managed not to choke. I felt revitalized almost immediately.

Hmm, I thought, *he could actually be kind when he wanted to*, which improved my impression of him a bit. I would have to make a real effort to stop talking out loud to Eshshah. I couldn't really blame Ansel for being confused, but he did irritate me ... he also fascinated me.

CHAPTER TWENTY-SEVEN

We stood outside the door and I hesitated for a moment to reassure myself that it was, in fact, the way I should choose. I nodded, then leaned into it. We found ourselves in another corridor, but much larger than the one we had come from. A low hiss echoed off the walls. I figured it was the steam from the workings in the bowels of the castle, or maybe the lit torches sputtering on the walls.

The odors from the dungeon we had just escaped were seemingly mild compared to this passageway — there was an abnormal stench I couldn't identify. A putrid smell, like rotting flesh. It was nauseating but we had to enter and see if it would lead to our way out. It might be the only way around to connect with the corridor that would take us to Eshshah.

We had not gone a great distance when my stomach tightened — a rock wall stood before us, blocking our path. It was not built to the ceiling, but was maybe eight feet tall. If we had to, I thought we could get a running start and scale it to the other side. At least I knew I could, and was hoping my pampered companion would be able to as well. I wondered if maybe we should retrace our steps to see if there was another door further down the corridor.

"Great, another dead end. We're getting nowhere fast," Ansel grumbled half to himself.

I jerked my head at him, and gave him a black look. Fighting the urge to strangle him, I said, "If we have to, would you be able to scale it with a running start? Or would that be too difficult for you?" I couldn't hide my irritation. I had no apologies for my rudeness. He was rude first and I had reached the end of my patience. *Don't cross me*, I thought to myself. Besides, I was starting to fear that maybe I wouldn't be able to get him out of here alive after all — which added to my dark mood.

"I'll have no trouble with that wall. I can get over it. The question is, can you?" He said, taking note of my height and turning my sarcastic remark back around to me. He was good — I had met my match.

I bit my tongue, and with some effort managed to ignore his retort.

"First, let's just go back to the passageway to make sure there's not another way around," I said.

The low hiss echoed again. As we turned to go back the way we came, my blood ran cold. Blocking our way was a hideous misshapen reptile-like creature — as black as a nightmare. Choking back a scream, I stood frozen as it crept slowly forward into the torch light, its claws scraping on the ground. I had never seen anything like this monster. It was as if someone's demented experiment of breeding a dragon had failed. Such a noble being as a dragon could never be bred by humans.

The creature had underdeveloped wings, no longer than my arms — much too small to get his hulk of a body airborne. His distended belly dragged on the ground supported by his short stubby legs. Bulbous eyes, a long snout with sharp teeth, and huge fangs dripping with venom. At first impression, I thought he was dense, and sluggish. I actually had pity for him, for just a split second. It was evident he was mistreated. An iron collar cut into his neck, obviously used to chain him. But at the moment, there were no chains. He was free and heading straight at us — and he looked hungry.

"Eshshah what is this thing and what do I do?"

I heard Ansel take a breath like he was going to answer my question or point out that I was talking to myself again, but he remained silent.

Good, I thought, *he's finally learning to bite his tongue.*

"I know of no name for that creature," answered Eshshah. I could feel her anxiety. "I believe you're correct, it must be Galtero's cruel attempt at breeding a dragon. You can have pity, but do not underestimate his strength, his speed, or his deadliness. Amáne, please be careful. Go very slowly. No sudden movements. Don't try to fight it, you cannot win. The only chance you have is to outsmart it and buy yourself some time to run to the wall. Ignite my scales that Dorjan inlaid in your spear. The flame will help keep him at bay. Tell Ansel he must not look into the creature's eyes."

I warned Ansel, "Move slowly when I do and don't look into his eyes." I could sense he was ready to ask why, but again he remained silent. Slowly, I extended my spear and whispered "Eshshah." The scales ignited. This startled the monster. It stepped back with a snarl.

"Now," Eshshah instructed, "walk backward slowly and I want you to look into its eyes. You're linked to me and its gaze will not affect you. You can hold its eyes, which will keep Ansel from being drawn to him. Use your gaze and your torch to distract it enough for Ansel to start his run for the wall. The timing on this is of the utmost importance. You have to get close enough to the wall to make your break, yet far enough to get a running start to scale it. I have no doubt as to your capability, but I don't know about Ansel's."

She continued, "Instruct Ansel to wait for your word to run. He must start at the precise moment you say, and you need to stay locked on the creatures eyes. Do not break your gaze. Then when you hear him reach the wall, you break and run. Ansel should have scaled to the top and you can spring up after him. It must be timed right."

I whispered these instructions to Ansel, and stressed to him the importance of the timing.

As we inched backward, I held the brute's eyes in mine and could feel the strength in his stare. A normal human would have been drawn in and made easy prey. Thanks to Eshshah's venom running in my veins, it didn't affect me. I kept my spear-torch extended in front. The flame held him from charging while I waited for the moment for us to make our escape.

When we were the right distance from the wall, and I felt the creature was distracted enough as he focused on my eyes, I said steadily to Ansel, "Okay, now, run."

For some reason he hesitated. He didn't run when I gave the word. *What's wrong with this stubborn man?*

"Run, I said!" Trying to hold the terror from my voice.

Finally, he broke and ran for the wall. I could hear him behind me and was thankful that at least he was faster and more agile than I thought he would be. He reached the wall and scaled it without a problem.

The problem, however, was now mine. The creature's gaze was broken. I had lost my concentration in telling Ansel a second time to run. It shook its head to get back into the present before the remainder of his meal could escape.

That was my cue. I thrust my torch in his face, which bought me a split second. Wheeling around, I literally ran for my life. Ansel's hesitation had broken the timing, and the creature was much faster than I anticipated. I tossed my spear over the wall — the black lizard hot on my heels. The stench of its putrid breath burned my nostrils. I leaped on the wall and scaled toward the top. Ansel had his hand ready to grab mine and pull me to safety. Just in time. I made it. I grabbed his wrist as he locked his hand around mine.

Instantaneously, my right foot burst into searing pain. The beast's powerful jaws clamped down on my foot. I screamed in excruciating agony, but kept my wits about me enough to shove my left foot down on his snout with all the strength I had left. He let out an enraged snarl and released me. Ansel yanked me over the top. We slid and tumbled in a heap on the other side. The black creature gnashed his teeth and clawed furiously on his side of the wall.

The feeling was familiar — it was a venomous bite. I strained to keep my mind in focus as Ansel and I gathered ourselves. The shock in his face, I'm sure reflected mine. My pain bordered on unbearable. Eshshah called my name, urging me to keep going. Her call and concern gave me the encouragement I needed. I switched into survival mode.

"Hurry, this way!" I said.

"Are you okay?" Ansel asked with terror in his voice.

He looked at me in disbelief as I moved down the corridor, using my spear as a walking stick. I had been through similar agony. Only with Eshshah's urgent plea as she melded with me and poured her strength into me, was I able to keep my sanity and my will to go on. I convinced myself my injury was not that bad.

"Keep moving," I said through clenched teeth, partly from anger, partly from pain. I could feel the venom as it spread upwards, but knew it wouldn't overcome me just yet. I was sure bones were crushed, but I was not about to look.

My spear helped take some of the pressure off of my foot, but with each step a new stab of lightning shot up my leg. I looked back at the way we had come and my heart skipped.

"I'm leaving an obvious trail."

Ansel turned, saw my bloody tracks and made a quick decision.

"Sit here," he said as he took my arm and helped lower me to the floor — my back against the wall.

It didn't appear that anyone was following us yet. I could still hear the creature howling in the distance.

"Hand me your dagger." He cut strips off his tunic then knelt in front of me. A curse escaped from his lips when he caught sight of the damage.

"I'm not going to look," I told him. I didn't want to lose consciousness ... or anything that might be left in my stomach.

"No. No need, you'll be fine. It's not that bad."

He didn't make a very good liar.

"You think it'll leave a scar?" I tried to joke.

After another bewildered glance in my direction, he wrapped my foot and halfway up my leg with a speed and expertise that surprised me. I didn't look until he finished.

"Where did you learn that?"

"I may be a stupid rich lord, but I am related to the Healer, you know. I've learned a few things from her."

My face got warm but I still refused to apologize for what I'd said to him.

Ansel helped me to my feet, positioned himself at my right side, and wrapped his left arm around me bringing it under my arm. Modesty had no room at that moment and situation. But I was thankful I had my breastplate on or my impersonation of a boy would have been discovered. I needed to keep up my male charade until we got to Eshshah in case he decided to try anything chivalrous — if he even had that in him.

With my spear in my left hand and his support on my right, we were able to move more quickly down the corridor. We had to find the door that would connect us to the passage from which we had detoured.

I started to think better of him after his attention to my injury, yet I debated whether I would ever forgive him for his hesitation. It was his fault I was bitten.

We found the door that led back to the original passageway. It took every ounce of my willpower joined to Eshshah's strength to successfully make the last two turns down the long corridors.

With my dragon's assistance, we managed to reach the stairs that led to the outpost and safety. The creature's burning venom threatened to overcome me by that time. Ansel half carried me up the first set. When we got to the landing, I had to stop to catch my breath and try to deal with the pain that rose up my body. I bent over holding on to my knees as the fire reached my thigh. I needed to get to Eshshah quickly before it ascended to my chest. It would be too difficult for me to breathe, and I would surely pass out.

"I am so sorry. It was my fault that creature bit you. It should have been me." Ansel said.

"Then you would be dead," my voice flat and harsh. "We're almost there. Let's go." I threw aside all pretense of politeness as my pain dictated my mood.

Two more flights of stairs and we came to a gate that I unlocked with Aperio's key, then closed and locked it behind us.

We turned the final corner and at last had reached the door into the safety of the Castle Outpost. Unlocking it, we entered the cavern. My lungs nearly burst from the effort to get here and from the venom rising. We took a moment to lean on the wall as we both gulped for air.

Ansel let out a curse as he realized we were in a cave high up in a cliff. He could see out the entry that it was a long drop to the ground below.

"What now, do we grow wings and fly out of here?"

I rolled my eyes and clenched my fist, barely managing to hold my punch.

"You're not far from the truth. Eshshah, come around slowly, please."

We had decided we didn't want to scare Ansel any more than necessary, although, seriously, I would have loved to scare him senseless. Maybe show him some manners. But, I probably would have regretted it later. Besides, I was not in the right frame of mind to enjoy it. My body was on fire.

Eshshah set foot in the entry cavern. As was natural upon a surprise meeting with an almost full-sized dragon, Ansel jumped back and cursed. Then realizing Eshshah was a true dragon, he did something that I didn't expect. He greeted her with a salute. I was shocked, yet pleased he actually knew the proper way to show respect to my dragon.

"This is Eshshah."

"Greetings, Eshshah. I stand in awe of your beauty."

Eshshah nodded to him, pleased with his compliment. Without delay, she moved to me, concerned only for her rider. Putting her nose to my foot, she exhaled her healing breath to stave off the venom and ease some of my pain. Ansel turned to look at me with wonder, mixed with confusion in his widened green eyes.

"You're a dragon rider," he stated, and saluted me.

With Eshshah's healing attention, my pain became bearable. My pride got the better of me. I stood up as straight as I could with my spear for support, nodded and pulled off my helmet. My long hair cascaded over my shoulders in a tangled mass.

I should have been a little more ashamed of the pleasure I took upon noting the shock on Ansel's face.

"And you're a girl!"

Once more, I nodded. Switching to my normal voice, "My name is Amáne." I hoped my smug look wasn't too obvious.

"You're Amáne?" He asked in astonishment. I could see his mind starting to put it all together, now. "My aunt has been telling me about you. Please accept my apologies, Amáne, for my disrespect."

I saw the blood rise in his face behind his tan skin as he said, "I owe you a double apology for my foul language. I don't make it a habit of speaking like that in front of a lady. I'm so sorry."

"Well, if I'm going to go about impersonating a male, I should probably try to get used to it."

"I had no idea who was sent to rescue me," he said almost to himself. His eyes were riveted on me. "... a Chosen One ... a dragon rider. And a beautiful one at that. My aunt neglected to share that detail, otherwise, I would have begged her to meet you weeks ago."

I rolled my eyes but couldn't stop the heat as the blood rose in my face. Before I could think of a response, Eshshah surprised me with her behavior. She lowered her head and put her nose on the ground in front of Ansel.

"Eshshah, what are you doing?" I asked.

"Amáne," she said, "meet the true heir to the throne of Teravinea. This one you call Ansel, is a Drekinn, son of the late King Emeric Drekinn of the royal line of the Dragon Kings of Teravinea. I felt the bond between my line and his and knew who stood before us."

It was my turn for incredulity and I think my eyes got as wide as his did.

"You are a Drekinn? King Emeric's son? The songs say you died in the explosions at the castle. Now it's my turn to offer an apology for my disrespect. I had no idea who I was sent to rescue — the heir to the throne, the crown prince." I didn't add any compliments as he had. I was not completely over being angry with him. But, I curtsied as well as I could with my injuries.

"No, don't curtsy to me." He put his hand out and said, "I guess we're even now. Truce?"

"Truce." I answered as I took his hand.

Emotions, exhaustion and pain all conspired to overwhelm me, as my head started to spin. I leaned back against the wall and slid down, as I reached for Eshshah. Ansel's hand was still in mine from our handshake. He helped lower me gently to the floor.

"Amáne," Eshshah said, "please ask Lord Ansel to remove the bandages." 'Lord Ansel' sounded strange to my ears as I was still in disbelief about his true identity.

He did so, and against my better judgement, I looked at the damage to my foot. The blood drained from my face as I saw the mangled flesh and bone barely held together by my boot. I gagged, but sheer willpower kept me from actually throwing up. I was convinced had it not been for my dragon-scale boot, the creature would be digesting my foot, and I would be looking at a stump.

Eshshah placed her warm healing nose on the devastation and hummed her tune. The heat of her healing overcame the burning pain of the venom. I clenched my teeth and closed my eyes as her heat became much more intense, even than when she healed me from the rabid dog bite.

"It'll need to be wrapped again, if Lord Ansel wouldn't mind. Keep the boot on. I have no time for a proper healing, but this will have to do for a while. It's almost daybreak — we have to leave."

Handing him my dagger, I gave Ansel Eshshah's instructions as I removed my outer tunic for him to use. I hoped I could find a tunic left in one of the sleeping chambers. After expertly wrapping my foot again, he helped me to my feet.

"We need to tell Gallen we're heading home. The communication disc should be in the library, this way." I said.

Using my spear on one side and Ansel supporting my other, we made our way down the long hallway to the library, which was in the same general location as the library at the Dorsal Outpost, except there were many more bed chambers to pass before reaching it. Moving to the disc, I placed my hand on the brass knob and said, "Gyan," and then, "Kaelem."

The disc shimmered and then muted into an image. Gallen appeared in the glass.

"Amáne, thankfully you're safe." Relieved to see my face — as relieved as I was to see his. I tried to hide my pain, but he knew me too well.

"You're not okay." His face paled. "What happened? Is Lord Ansel with you?"

"Yes, he's here. We're fine. We're heading home."

Then Ansel stepped up and saluted. He knew Gallen had been a dragon rider. "Greetings, Gallen. Since it appears Amáne is not going to tell you, I will. She's been seriously injured saving my life. She was bitten by a venomous creature — some kind of relation to a dragon. It'll take all of the Healer's skills to save her foot. Bones are broken. There's a lot of damage. I wanted to prepare my aunt so she'll have everything she needs to attend to her."

"I'll tell her. Thank you, Your Grace. Amáne, please get home safely." This news upset him. I was furious with Ansel for causing Gallen to worry. I glared at him through my pain.

We said farewell, and I removed my hand from the knob. Ansel helped me find a warm tunic in one of the sleeping chambers, and we hurried back to the entry cavern.

"Ansel, or Your Grace, or whatever you want to be called, there's a gear pack in the corner over there. Get out your helmet and put on the outer tunic. Prepare to fly." My pain should not have been an excuse for my lack of respect. Diplomacy was not high on my list at that moment as my self control waned.

"Please, just call me Ansel."

He donned his gear as Eshshah treated me once more. Attaching the pack to the saddle, Ansel put my spear in its holder. He helped me up to Eshshah's leg so I could climb into the saddle, but I didn't have the strength to pull myself the rest of the way up. Under any other circumstance, I would have been mortified, but one more time, modesty was set aside. Ansel looked embarrassed as he tried to decide where best to place his hands, but I didn't care just then.

I glared at him, "Just get it over with!"

He quickly pushed me up from behind, then took his place in the rear saddle. He helped me buckle in and get my helmet on.

I gave Eshshah the okay to take off. She proceeded to the entrance and leapt off the ledge. I could hear Ansel gasp behind me as we did a free fall for several feet before she spread her wings and took flight. Shamefully, I took some gratification in his reaction to her dive.

CHAPTER TWENTY-EIGHT

We flew east over the sea until we were sure we would not be spotted from the castle. Daylight was just breaking, although the sun had not yet risen over the horizon. We left none too soon. Turning south, we headed toward the Dorsal Outpost.

The fresh sea air in my face, after the fetid odors of the tunnels, did a lot to lift my spirits. I contemplated with satisfaction that Eshshah and I had completed our first quest successfully. I turned to Ansel and saw that he began to relax as well. He thanked Eshshah and me countless times, repeating he couldn't believe he was actually riding a dragon. I caught the joy on his boyish face. His smile was unforgettable. I was almost able to overlook the fact that I had been so angry with him. *Maybe I could try to forget our ill-fated meeting and start fresh ... maybe.*

My enjoyment was short-lived — the burn of the venom increased in my veins. Eshshah's healing skills held my pain in check temporarily. Frightened that she and the Healer would not be able to save my foot, I voiced my concern out loud to Eshshah. Of course it drew a response from Ansel. This time it didn't annoy me so much.

"Amáne," Ansel said over the rush of wind, "I know my aunt's healing skills, and I have no doubts as to the fantastic skills of your dragon. I'll bet my right hand you'll be dancing with me on my eighteenth birthday in a couple of months. Deal?"

"You're willing to wager your hand? Quite confident aren't you? I hope for both of our sakes you're right. Deal." I made an effort to smile at his encouragement.

The pain escalated as time passed, but I managed to keep it to myself. Eshshah, of course, knew, and helped as best she could. I was glad Ansel couldn't see my facial contortions — each minute the fire intensified. Soon, not just my face reacted to the stabs of agony, but my body stiffened as the heat of the venom increased.

"Amáne? — Are you all right?" Ansel asked.

I couldn't open my mouth to respond for fear a scream would be my reply. I nodded, but I didn't think he believed me. Eventually, my groans could no longer be contained as I fought to keep from crying out. The sound carried back to him.

He leaned over to me and turned my shoulders gently. I didn't have the strength to resist. He winced, seeing the pain on my face and the beads of sweat from my fever, even in the wind from our flight.

"Permission requested, Amáne." He knew dragon protocol, but was too distressed to wait for my response allowing him to speak directly to Eshshah.

"Eshshah," he pleaded. "Can you not help her? She's burning with fever. She's suffering."

Eshshah answered him directly, "Yes, I know, Lord Ansel. I'm with her mentally to help control her pain, although it's only partial in effectiveness. It would be much worse if we didn't have that link. But in flight I'm not able to do any more for her. Our best option is to get her back to the Healer as quickly as we can. Amáne understands that. She will live, do not torment yourself."

My dragon put on a brave front for Ansel, but her concern for me echoed in her thoughts. She knew my injuries and my fever were not life-threatening — but my pain still affected her.

A spasm blasted through my body. My back arched with agony and I could not suppress the shriek that forced itself from my lips. Ansel wrapped his arms around me and pulled me back to him. I could feel his strong arms as he tried to restrain me from thrashing. One final burst, like lightning, shot from my leg up through my head. The last I remembered was falling back into his chest as all went black.

CHAPTER TWENTY-NINE

I found myself in a strange radiant place with marble floors and a bright blue sky for a ceiling. Joyful — just what I would imagine it would be like if I were truly with my ancestors. But it was only a dream. I knew because it differed from the shadows I'd visited twice before. And, unlike my usual dreams, this was not a nightmare. No beasts, no lizards, no horrifying visions that had me running for my life.

My mother stood across the way. She looked lovely and I waved at her, but I had no desire to join her. Instead, I watched as dragons circled overhead. All were the same light color but one. The one was an emerald green. He spiraled down toward me and landed. Then, it was no longer a dragon but a young man. He looked familiar as he gazed at me with his cool green eyes — the same color as the dragon that had hovered above me. I recognized him from a dark and terrifying dream — a nightmare of death and of monsters that played in the back of my mind. He smiled as he strode toward me. Our eyes met and I smiled back, then he bent over and kissed my forehead. Warmth spread through my body. Then the dream began to fade. I fought to keep it from ending but it slipped away. I could see the light from behind my eyelids. Upon opening them, a pair of green eyes stared back at me. I jolted and caught my breath. My reaction in turn startled Ansel, who sat on the edge of my bed.

Confusion encircled me. I wondered what he was doing there. But as I took in the familiar surroundings of my chamber in the Dorsal Outpost, it all came back to me. Ansel's rescue; the unnamed creature; the venomous bite; the flight from the Castle Outpost. After that, I had no knowledge of the rest of the story. I realized it had not been a terrifying dream, but stark reality.

"What are you doing?" I asked, my voice raspy.

"I'm watching you sleep." As if it were a common pastime for him.

"I would think you have better things to do than watch me sleep."

"No, not at all. What were you smiling about?" He managed to keep the amusement out of his voice, but it showed in his eyes.

"What do you mean?" My eyes narrowed.

"You smile in your sleep ... and you talk, too. I don't think you were talking to Eshshah this time."

At that he couldn't keep a straight face. If it wasn't such an attractive one, I might have swiped his smile right off. I tightened my jaw and fought the urge.

"What was I saying?" I asked, wary of his response. I was rather embarrassed but wanted to know if I needed to be more so.

"Well, I did hear my name mentioned," he said, obviously pleased.

"That's not true." The blood rose in my face. I hoped it wasn't true. *Why is he trying to antagonize me?*

He relented from his taunting, "I'm sorry, Amáne. I

shouldn't be annoying you. How do you feel?" His eyes gave away his genuine concern. "You were quite ill. We were all worried about you. It took all of the Healer's and Eshshah's powers to save your foot. They worked on you for a long time."

"They saved my foot," I said slowly as I heaved a sigh.

"Yes," he said, seeing my relief, "I told you that you would be dancing with me for my birthday."

"Dance? My foot hurts just thinking about dancing." I shuddered at the thought. "How long was I out?"

"We arrived early yesterday morning and it's the middle of the afternoon, now. The Healer is taking a rest and Eshshah is out hunting."

"Yes, I know where Eshshah is," I said, a little too harsh. He didn't have to tell a rider what her dragon was doing. He certainly had a knack for irritating me. I think he enjoyed it.

"If you'll excuse me," I said. "I need to get out of this bed."

"I have orders not to leave your side. You can't get up without my help."

"I don't know if I'm presentable. I'm not getting up with you still in here." My irritation fought for dominance over my discomfort of his presence in my chambers.

"The Healer made sure you were dressed properly. I won't let you hurt yourself on my watch. I'm not leaving."

With an exasperated huff I lifted the bedding to peek, and sure enough, I was dressed in a tunic and tights — not my night clothes as I thought. Throwing back the covers I sat up a little faster than I should have. All the blood drained from my face and my head spun. I fell back onto the bed.

"Ouch," he grimaced. "Easy, Amáne. Maybe you should

take it a little slower." Ansel took my arms and gently helped me sit up. Butterflies danced in my stomach — I found myself uncomfortable with his attentions. As soon as he helped me up, I removed his hands from my arms.

I stayed in this sitting position for a few minutes before he stood up to help me ease my legs over the side of the bed. I gasped as the blood rushed into my injured foot. Gritting my teeth, I breathed through the pain. I tried to hide it, not wanting any excuse for him to prohibit me from leaving my chambers.

"Slowly, Amáne," he repeated. "There's no rush. Just hold there for a bit so your body can get accustomed to sitting up. Wait right there, I have something for you."

Ansel ran to the corner of my chamber and grabbed a staff that leaned against the wall. He handed it to me as a child would hand his latest creation to his mother. His eyes were bright as he sat beside me on the bed to watch my reaction.

"I made it for you. I didn't have the time to finish it, but I promise I will."

It was a walking stick cut from a beautiful piece of wood at just the right height for me. But what caught my attention was the carving of a dragon at the top of the staff. Not just a dragon. It was carved in the likeness of Eshshah. Her tail curled down in a spiral around the wood. She was stained a beautiful deep red.

"You made this for me?" *Why would he spend his time making something for me?* "It's beyond words — it's ... beautiful." Again that boyish face as he drank in my genuine appreciation. "Where did you get the red stain for Eshshah? It's the perfect color."

"Eshshah showed me a tree on this island, and listen to this, it's called a Dragon's Blood Tree. The sap is red and it makes a very fine stain."

A tear fell from my eye as I threw my arms around his neck in a spontaneous reaction. "Thank you. I love it." And then instantly realizing my boldness, I pulled away. "Er ... I'm so sorry. I ... I was just excited. I didn't mean to throw myself at you. I tend to overreact sometimes."

"Any time you want to fling your arms around me, Amáne, is just fine with me."

I blushed but laughed with him, "Well, let's see if this art piece is as functional as it is beautiful."

The throbbing subsided enough for me to try to stand up. I put my new walking stick in front of me. Ansel was poised to help me should I need it. I was pleased he'd recognized my stubbornness and let me try to stand on my own. Taking a deep breath, I released it as I rose and made it to my feet without his assistance. I did, however, accept his arm when I started taking steps.

We slowly moved down the hallway to the entry cavern. It was such a relief to be back at our outpost. The entry flooded with the afternoon sun and I breathed in the fresh sea air. The ocean view from this room was unmatched.

I eased myself slowly onto one of the couches and was thankful for so much at that moment — my life; Eshshah; the Healer; the success of our quest; and even for Ansel — his presence, proof of our triumph.

He seated himself rather close to me on my right — even though there was plenty of room on the couch. His eyes met mine. "Amáne, I never really thanked you and Eshshah properly for saving my life. I'm forever indebted to you two. I also want to apologize once again for my rudeness to you."

I smiled, "You're welcome. You've already thanked us — countless times. You owe us nothing. It was our duty. As for your rudeness, yes, you were quite angry to find that your aunt had sent a boy to rescue you."

"I'm so sorry."

"No need to be sorry. You were probably angrier when you found she actually sent a girl."

"Truthfully, no. That didn't really bother me as much."

"Even a girl who could wield a blade better than you?" I teased.

"Wait a minute, I'm not so sure about that. Should I take that as a challenge?"

"It's your pride, not mine. Once I'm healed, and we get the opportunity, I'll be happy to take you on. Deal?"

"Deal." We shook hands.

Ansel sat back. I felt his stare. After a minute of uncomfortable silence, he leaned over, took a handful of my hair and brought it to his face. He inhaled slowly as if he were savoring the aroma of a fine meal only the privileged could know.

"What are you doing?" I moved to my left, pulling my hair away from him.

"I love the smell of your hair. It smells like your dragon."

I would have to agree with him on the fascinating scent of Eshshah, but I didn't realize I smelled like her. Nevertheless it was inappropriate for him to be so familiar with me. I hardly knew him.

"I'd appreciate it if you wouldn't do that again."

"My apologies, once more. That was rude of me. It just feels like we've known each other for longer than we actually have.

Forgive me." He sounded contrite, but his eyes were smiling.

A bit confused, I nodded and smiled.

"Will you tell me the story of your linking with Eshshah?" he said with true interest.

Thrown off by his request, I asked, "You want to hear how Eshshah and I linked?"

"Yes, I study dragon lore and I love to hear the stories of linkings. I made poor Gallen tell me his so many times when I was a young boy. I see now how hard it must have been for him. But he always obliged whenever I asked."

"Of course he would, you're heir to the throne! It's his duty to serve you, no matter what you ask of him." He took my admonishment well.

At that moment I understood what he meant when he said it seemed like we had known each other for longer than we had. I found I also felt a kind of bond with him, but we were still practically strangers. He was royalty, yet I was still comfortable to be myself around him. Truthfully, I should be practicing the same respect as Gallen, but conforming to formalities was something I didn't do well.

I did, however, oblige him and told him of my memorial journey for my mother; the building of my fire ring at the cove with Eshshah's egg; her hatching; and what I remembered of my dragon fever. It was easy to talk to him. I even told him of our first flight and how I cracked my nose.

He leaned in closer and scrutinized my face. I pulled back — my eyebrows knit in confusion. "You'd never know it," he observed. "Your nose looks perfect to me."

My mouth twisted up on one side, and my eyes went wide.

He ignored my reaction and continued. "You probably

already know this, but you're only one of three female riders, and by far, the youngest — male or female — to link."

"Yes, I'm familiar with the ballads."

"Can I be so bold as to ask to see your linking mark?" he asked.

I wasn't used to this kind of attention, especially from a male — and it was a bold request. I felt the red rise in my face. But like most people, I enjoyed talking about the things I love — and Eshshah was the love of my life. I hesitated, then decided it wouldn't be too immodest to bare my arm for him. I had loose sleeves on my tunic so I hiked the right one up to expose my tattoo-like linking mark.

He examined it closely and while lightly tracing parts of it, he explained how it tells a story. "This part here tells your dragon's name and her properties — this means fire. And right here," he traced another section, sending chills through me, "is the meaning of your name — water." He nodded in thought, "Nice combination, fire and water. There's much more to read, but I'm not really fluent in deciphering all of the information. My aunt is very good at it."

"Oh. I wondered about that. She studied it for a long time when I finally confided in her."

As we spoke, I'd elevated my injured foot on the table in front of me and absently poked at the wrappings.

"This thing is really starting to itch."

"That's a good sign," Ansel said. "It means it's healing."

"It's driving me mad. I'm going to unwrap it. I want to see how it looks."

"That's not a good idea, Amáne. You should wait for Eshshah to get back, and the Healer to be in here, too."

"Why? I just want to see what it looks like, and I can't scratch it through the wrappings." I searched for the end of the cloths to start unwinding them.

Ansel sat up straight. "Amáne, I'm serious. Please. Wait for the Healer. She wants to be present when you unwrap your foot."

An odd suspicion engulfed me, as a sharp twinge of panic rose in my chest. *Maybe they couldn't save my foot. The extra dressings are to hide that fact — and I really only have part of it left!*

My eyes narrowed as I glared at him. "What's wrong with my foot? Why are you trying to keep me from unwrapping it?" My voice rose. I frantically pulled at the cloths.

"Amáne!" Eshshah called from her hunting. "I'm on my way, please wait for me."

"Why, Eshshah?" I shouted in full panic.

Ansel called out for his aunt as he took a hold of my hands to keep me from unveiling my injury. He didn't know my strength. In my hysteria to block his efforts, my elbow struck him in the nose. I heard a crack and his blood flowed freely. His hands shot to his face, giving me leave to finish throwing off the wrappings — shamefully ignoring what I had done to him. The cloths fell to the floor. My heart felt like a fist had squeezed it to the bursting point. I went numb as I stared at what had been hidden from me.

A blood-curdling shriek burst from my mouth. "Eshshah! No! What does this mean?"

I desperately scratched at my leg, drawing blood, thinking my nails were enough to remove the linking mark — the perfect image of the black creature from the bowels of the castle — staring at me from my ankle.

CHAPTER THIRTY

My sobs came in great gulps as the Healer rushed into the room and pulled me close. That same moment Eshshah swooshed in.

"What does this mean?" I shouted again, as I pushed away from the Healer. "Am I linked to that creature? I would rather have lost my foot! Eshshah, why didn't you heal it? Why didn't you make this hideous mark go away?"

"I'm sorry, Amáne. I couldn't. We don't really know what it means. He was a poor attempt to create a dragon. It seems that some of the same properties were probably bred into him." I felt her disappointment, as if she took it as her failure.

Instantly ashamed of my behavior and remorseful for how I'd made her feel, I fought to gain control of my hysteria. She put her head down to my face and breathed her aromatic soothing scent on me as my sobs began to subside.

"Eshshah, I'm the one who should be soothing you for my heartlessness. I'm sorry." I looked at the Healer and Ansel and asked for their forgiveness, as I wiped the tears from my face.

My eyes rested on Ansel. I gasped as I noted his swollen face and the blood that still flowed from his nose. Mortified at what I had done to him, "Eshshah, can you please help him?" I said out loud.

"No — thank you — I'm okay. Really." He said and pulled back as Eshshah's large head lowered down to his face.

"It's all right, Ansel. She'll make you feel better. Please, Eshshah, go ahead." I put my hand on his chest to hold him still as Eshshah put her nose down and breathed her healing warmth on his fracture.

He literally melted back into the couch. The swelling and bruising all but disappeared. Letting out a huge sigh of relief, he placed his hand over mine that rested on his chest. His touch surprised me. I withdrew my hand and looked away to hide my blush.

The Healer had gone for a wet cloth for Ansel. When she handed it to him, the shawl she had thrown in haste around her shoulders slid down her arm. My eyes widened at what I saw on her right shoulder. I made an effort to say something, but nothing would come out of my mouth. She caught my stare and realized her linking mark had been revealed.

I jumped to my good foot and saluted her — still no words would come.

She saluted back. "Thank you, Amáne. Yes ... well ... it was time you knew. Please sit down before you damage anything else. Close your mouth and stop staring. At least this time you're not eating or drinking anything."

Ansel looked puzzled. I was embarrassed. She sat heavily beside me, suddenly appearing ancient and tired. Her eyes gazed somewhere far away and long ago. They looked so sad.

The realization hit me like a Valaira. "You were Nara. Rider of the late Torin," I stated in reverence. The Healer was the greatest dragon rider that ever lived. My mother's friend all my life and I never knew. I took her hand in mine and held it tightly — my inadequate attempt to comfort her.

"The songs say you died with ..." I couldn't finish my sentence.

"That was what we needed people to believe. Galtero had to think he'd won. But we were so close to revealing his plot."

The Healer sighed, "As I said before, we sensed Galtero was responsible for the failure of the dragon eggs to hatch. I think he may have recognized our suspicions. One afternoon King Emeric came to me and urgently pressed me to take my sister's great-granddaughter, Queen Fiala, and the prince, who was just three days old, to safety." Her eyes rested on Ansel before she continued. "There was treachery under foot, and the king had a premonition that something terrible was about to happen. Fiala, barely well enough to flee, having just given birth, was to be ready to leave after dark.

"That evening, I was in the Royal family's apartments on my way to Fiala's chambers when the first blast went off. It was King Emeric's quarters. I ran to the nursery and grabbed the baby from his nursemaid as the second blast went off. It was Fiala's chambers. It was too late for my relative and her husband. My only choice was to save the prince. I was barely clear of the apartments when the third blast went off. It was the nursery. That same instant Torin flew in between the blast and myself. He caught the full force in his chest and the baby and I were thrown several yards.

"I rushed back to Torin, but there was no hope for him." She swallowed hard, her eyes glazed in the memory of that fateful night. "In his death throes he prophesied there would be an egg that would hatch to a female rider in Dorsal before twenty years were completed, and I needed to go there and keep watch — only after that linking would Prince Ansel gain his throne. Torin sealed my fate that I must accept my duty to save Teravinea." Her voice lowered to a whisper.

The Healer looked at me with such sorrow in her eyes. My tears matched hers.

She took a deep breath, composed herself and continued, "We went into hiding for about two years. I couldn't even let the riders know we were alive. Not because I didn't trust them, but if they were captured and tortured, I couldn't have Galtero know that the heir lived. I found a wet nurse for the baby and raised him as my own. If it were not for this boy, my nephew, I would surely have gone mad. He reinforced Torin's plea for me to hold on to the thin thread of my sanity. He gave me hope." She looked lovingly at Ansel.

"I made the difficult decision to relinquish my care of him to a cousin of mine and her husband who became his foster parents — they had no children of their own. I had work to do for our cause, and Ansel needed a stable home. I came out of hiding and worked to organize the riders that still lived. We vowed to avenge King Emeric's death and get his son, the true heir, on the throne."

She closed her eyes, and shook her head slowly, "And now, seventeen years later, when I thought we would soon see the first part of our plan come to fruition, we have lost ground. Galtero is now assured of the fact that Ansel is alive, and he missed his chance to eliminate him. There is no doubt he'll put higher security on the castle because of what you and Eshshah just accomplished." Her eyes rested on me. "This will make it more dangerous for you to procure a dragon egg. It means we have to reformulate our plans to get you back inside the castle."

I felt Ansel tense up beside me. I glanced over at him and

his eyes, already full of remorse, were now lit with alarm.

"Wait. You're saying Amáne has to go back into the castle?"

"Yes, Ansel, we will stay with our original strategy, as we've already discussed, which was to send the linked pair to obtain a dragon egg. It is imperative we solve this mystery before we can advance our plans to get you on the throne." The Healer's patience had been stretched like a bow string.

"It's too dangerous to send her back in. Why not send Braonán, or Calder, or Bern?"

I shot an angry glare at him. There was enough tension in the air already, so I held my temper, but not my tongue, "Ansel, this is Eshshah's and my quest. We are the only linked pair. This is what we have been training for. We're ready. Don't forget, we already got in and out of the castle once." He flinched — *I shouldn't have said that.* "We can do it again, I have no doubts."

Why should it matter to him that Eshshah and I had to go back to the castle to complete our original quest? I was, in truth, a Chosen One — a rider, with a commitment to the Royal line of Drekinn. And Eshshah was of the Royal Line of Dragons, bonded with the Drekinn line. It was our duty to do whatever it took to get Ansel on the throne. I hoped he was not going to be a problem in the carrying out of our mission.

The Healer didn't address his concern. Looking like she had the weight of Teravinea on her shoulders, she rose slowly from the couch. With a sigh that came from deep within, she said, "I'm tired. I'll be in the library. I need to speak with Gallen."

A blanket of depression floated down on Ansel and me as she left the room. We sat in silence for a while. When I finally stole a glance at him, he looked devastated. Without a word, he leaped off the couch, picked up a cup from the table in front of us and hurled it out of the cavern. I heard it shatter on the rocks below. He stormed out and retreated to his chamber. If these doors didn't glide silently, I'm sure he would have slammed them all the way to his room.

I grabbed the bandages and rewrapped my ankle so I wouldn't have to be reminded of the mark from the hideous black lizard. Limping over to where Eshshah lay taking in the afternoon rays of the sun, I slumped down in the crook of her neck. My need to be close to her was strong. I fell into a restless sleep, dreaming of fires, explosions and dying dragons.

Chapter Thirty-One

When I awoke, darkness had fallen. I had missed the sunset. There was no sign of the Healer or Ansel. I whispered "Sitara" to light the shields.

"Do you feel like fishing for me, Eshshah? I should fix something for them to eat."

Eshshah brought back a large fish, for which I sang a song of thanks for its life. I prepared the fish and some potatoes in the local Dorsal fashion and served up two plates. I hobbled with them down the corridor, balancing them in one hand while I used my walking stick with the other. Entering the library, I found the Healer asleep, slumped across her books and maps that were spread on the table. I didn't disturb her, but left her plate with her.

Limping my way to Ansel's chamber, I softly called to him before I pushed the door open. I found him sprawled across his bed, but I knew he wasn't sleeping.

"Ansel, I brought you something to eat."

"I'm not hungry."

"But you have to eat something. It'll make you feel better."

"I said I'm not hungry," he snapped.

"Fine. Then, just starve and wallow in your self pity." I barked back as I slammed his plate on the small corner table — bits of potato escaped.

He sprung up to a sitting position and in barely restrained fury said, "Is that what you think I'm doing, Amáne? Feeling sorry for myself?"

"Well what do you call it?"

"You don't get it. This is all my fault."

"You had nothing to do with your parents joining their ancestors."

He ignored my statement.

"You had it right when you said I was a stupid rich lord who got himself kidnapped."

Now I definitely regretted making that statement. I opened my mouth to finally apologize for my careless words when he cut me off.

"Farvard's death ... your injuries," he waved his hand at my ankle, "... the ruin of all the riders' strategies and planning, including you having to go back into the castle — which I am telling you now I will overrule — are all because of my selfish stupidity."

Shocked at his statement of overruling our quest, I nonetheless decided not to address it at the moment. He was under enough pressure already, but this was one issue where he wasn't going to get his way — I would fight it later, not now.

Instead, I agreed with him. "I guess I don't get it. Why is all of this your fault? It wasn't your choice to be abducted." He heaved a heavy sigh. I could see he needed to share his story, so I lowered myself slowly into one of the chairs at the table. With genuine concern, I coaxed, "Why don't you come sit over here and eat? Then you can tell me how it happened and why you think it's your fault."

He trudged to the chair opposite me and slumped into it. I pushed the plate toward him and he drew his knife to eat. Instead of spearing pieces to put in his mouth, he stabbed at the fish and potatoes, scattering them around on the plate. I leaned back in my seat with my arms crossed, trying to be patient while he poked and mutilated his meal. Finally, I was done watching. I yanked the plate away from him.

"Are you going to talk to me or just sit there with a scowl on your face while you play with your food?"

I barely finished my sentence when he raised his knife and brought it down in fury, burying the point deep in the table. I didn't feel threatened, but I startled, then cringed at the abuse to the beautiful wood table.

We both watched as the knife quivered back and forth in smaller and smaller arcs until it was still. I looked up and met his eyes. I could see regret for his behavior, and behind that, pain. He pressed his lips together and said nothing.

I stayed silent and waited while he struggled for the right words. Ansel began his story. "My foster parents were good to me. How do you raise a prince that you have to hide from the world? To make sure he is brought up to understand his future role — should he ever get that opportunity — yet at the same time try to protect his identity? They took an impossible task and did the best they could.

"My foster father met his ancestors when I was eleven. If it weren't for the dragon riders assigned to me, I think we would be in a worse position than we are now. They had to work hard to keep me in line ... to teach me some discipline. I'm thankful my foster mother joined her husband last year so she wouldn't have to suffer on my account any longer. I'm sure I played a role in both of them passing too soon.

"I didn't go to classes to learn math, archery, our ballads or our history songs. My education progressed under private tutors. Malory came highly recommended, even though he was only three years older than I. His services were enlisted for me shortly before my foster mother went to rest. Unknown to her, he was a bad influence. I take full responsibility for my indiscretions," he said fervently. "But that said, he convinced me quite often to sneak out with him to visit pubs and other unsavory places. Truthfully, it didn't take much to persuade me. He merely pointed out what had been my mantra for a long time — that I was overly protected all of the time and not allowed to have any fun. I didn't see a problem with his point of view, so I went along with his plans whenever he decided we should enjoy a night out.

"We were quite lucky never to have been caught, he was very clever. Looking back, I see now he was diabolical. He must have drugged the household on the nights we went out. We were never caught. I had dragon riders guarding me — and they don't normally miss much. I, on the other hand, was too blind to see what he had been doing.

"Three nights ago Farvard heard of our plans for a night in the village. He forbade me to go, but I was used to getting my way. He finally relented, on the condition that he would go with us. Malory said we were going to meet up with some friends of his.

"We started the evening at a pub we were familiar with. After a couple of ales I noticed Farvard suddenly looked ill. Malory's friends assured me he just needed some fresh air. Two of them supported him on either side and we all left the pub. Instead of going out the front way, we went out the back into an alley."

Ansel stopped, took in a deep uneven breath and squeezed his eyes shut. He swallowed hard and made an effort to gain control.

I wanted to let him know he didn't have to finish, but I felt he needed to relate his story. I looked away and gave him some time to gather himself.

"When we got to a dark corner of the alley," he pressed on, "the man on Farvard's right drew his dagger. Before I knew what was happening, he slit Farvard's throat and let his body fall, like a sack of manure." The agony in Ansel's face broke my heart. His green eyes locked on mine. "Farvard was my friend, Amáne. He did not deserve to die like that. He passed to his ancestors because of me — because of me!" He repeated. "Do you understand? I might as well have been the one wielding that blade." His volume increased with each sentence.

After a pause, his voice thick with pain, "And then they tied me up and took me to Castle Teravinea — I didn't even put up a fight. I couldn't believe Farvard was gone."

He pounded his fist on the table and then let his head fall forward on his arm. If it had been me in his position, I would be heaving with sobs. I guess that's not a manly thing to do, so he just lay there breathing heavily. It was heart-wrenching to watch.

I was never very good at comforting, but I couldn't just walk out and leave him there alone in his depression. Rising from my seat, I shuffled closer to him. I rested one hand on his shoulder and ran my fingers through his hair with my other hand. I remembered when I was little, my mother used to stroke my hair to soothe me. It was the only thing I could think to do. I had no words that would relieve his anguish. I also hummed Eshshah's calming tune.

My foot throbbed, but I didn't want to stop until I was sure he had calmed down. Finally, his breathing evened out and it sounded like he fell asleep. Careful to not make any noise, I grabbed my walking stick and silently slipped out of his chamber.

I heard Ansel whisper, "Thank you, Amáne," as the door slid shut.

CHAPTER THIRTY-TWO

The next morning I was awakened before dawn by a scream — it was mine. Another of my nightmares had robbed me of my sleep. My heart raced as I bolted upright. All the heartache and unhappiness from the day before enclosed me in its gloom — I needed to get away. It felt like I had a weight on my chest and I couldn't breathe.

"Eshshah, let's go for a ride. I'm sure the Healer and Ansel are still sleeping. We can just go for a short flight."

"Amáne, what about your foot? Do you think this is a wise decision? The Healer may not appreciate us sneaking out."

"We won't be sneaking. If she were awake, I would ask her, but I'm sure she's not." That sounded quite rational to me. I convinced Eshshah, and we silently made our way to the library to get the saddle. I chose the tournament saddle because the straps secured a rider at the calves. This made sense as it would not interfere with my damaged foot, yet would give it support.

I had a bit of difficulty in saddling her, but I finally tightened the last strap. On our way to the entry, I stopped at my chambers where I found a large riding boot in the wardrobe that would fit over my bandages. I laced the boot and felt it braced my ankle sufficiently, after which we headed to the entrance cavern. I climbed up on Eshshah's foreleg and managed to place my walking stick in the spear holder.

Trying to figure out how to hoist myself up into the saddle without putting weight on my injured ankle, I heard what sounded like a snicker behind me.

"Do you need me to push you up there again?"

I jerked my head around and found Ansel standing with crossed arms, leaning against the wall. He didn't even bother to hide his amusement. I'd been so distracted that I didn't hear him enter. Scowling at him, I tried to keep the red from rising in my face. I remembered how he had to push me into the saddle when we left the Castle Outpost.

"No thanks. I've got it." This gave me the motivation I needed, and I pulled myself up. A slight stab of pain shot through my ankle, but luckily, my back was toward him and he didn't see my grimace. "I didn't think you were awake," I said, buckling myself in.

"A girl screaming in terror is usually enough to wake me."

"Oh. I'm sorry. I, er..."

"I would have come in to check on you, but I knew Eshshah was with you. She, I'm sure, was all you needed."

He had a way of saying things to which I didn't know how to respond, so all that came out of my mouth was, "Thank you anyway."

"I'm surprised my aunt gave you permission to go on a flight."

"Well ... she didn't exactly. She's sleeping."

"You're going to sneak out without telling her?"

"I'm not sneaking! I'll explain it to her when I get back. My acquaintance, Kail, always says it is easier to ask for forgiveness after you do what you like, than it is to ask for permission beforehand."

"Sneaky friend."

"It's not sneaky! Are you going to go tell your aunt now, to keep me from going?"

"My lips are sealed. Just be careful, Amáne. Take it slowly."

"No, Ansel, we're going to fly fast and take chances." When I saw the alarm in his face, I added, "I'm teasing you. We'll be careful. See you soon. Let's go, Eshshah."

She dove off the ledge and did a free fall until we neared the rocks below. At the last second she spread her wings and headed toward the water. My heart was in my throat, but I swallowed the whoop of joy that I would have let out. *I wonder what Ansel thought of that take off.*

There were no words to describe my feelings and closeness to Eshshah when we flew. It was pure joy — complete freedom. I took in the fresh ocean air as we skimmed the glassy sea. Her wing tips splashed the briny spray into my face. This was exactly what I needed. I hadn't realized the pressure I'd been holding in until this glorious moment of complete euphoria.

Sailing smoothly through the air, we explored some of the surrounding islands. We weren't going to chance a landing as I had no intention of getting down from the saddle. It would be too painful to have to get back up. Eshshah and I were perfectly content to just soar. Life didn't get any better and for this moment I was thankful.

I'd intended it to be a short flight, but when I looked at the angle of the rising sun, to my dismay, it was apparent we were gone for more than an hour. We didn't dare stay out any longer.

"Hurry, Eshshah, we need to get back."

As we approached the outpost I could see from a distance

that someone was waiting for us in the entry. I hoped it was Ansel. As we neared the cavern my stomach twisted — it was the Healer. She stood with her arms crossed. Her body language told me she was not pleased.

She retreated to the side as we glided in and landed. I gulped as I noted her angry countenance and realized I would have to face her wrath. Ansel sat sunken in on one of the couches looking like a child who had been scolded. A wave of regret went through me as I realized I had gotten him in trouble as well.

"What do you think you're doing, Amáne?" The Healer shot me a menacing look.

"I'm sorry, Healer. I needed a break and you were sleeping. I thought we would go on a short flight so I could clear my head. I had no intentions of staying out this long."

"Dismount this instant." She was livid.

"Yes, Healer."

I unfastened the buckles on my right side first and swung my hurt foot around in front of me. Usually, I dismount swinging that leg over the back of the saddle. I thought bringing it over the front would be less painful. It proved not the best solution as my entire leg throbbed with agonizing pressure. I took a sharp inhale as I tried to breathe into the pain. Luckily, Ansel read my face and jumped up to my assistance. Before he could take one step, the Healer put her hand up to stop him. He lowered himself back into the cushions.

"Dismount, Amáne." She repeated.

Knowing I was on my own, I put on a determined face. I unbuckled my left calf straps, grabbed my walking stick and lowered myself down to Eshshah's foreleg. I didn't understand why the pain was so severe. I could put no weight on my foot. Unlacing the large boot, I let it drop. I cringed as more pressure rushed into my injury.

Turning my thoughts to Eshshah, I made a silent plea for her help. As if the Healer could read my mind, she said, "Eshshah, leave her be."

I fought my temper enough to suppress it, but my stubbornness kicked in. Setting my jaw, I made an effort to hide my pain. I slid off of Eshshah's foreleg to the floor and hobbled to the couch near Ansel. Easing myself down, I exhaled slowly and raised my eyes to face the Healer.

"It appears to me you have a problem with authority, Amáne. That's a poor trait in a dragon rider." I winced. There was nothing more devastating she could have said to me. I had no reply.

"Do you need to be reminded that you are indeed a dragon rider now and that you are part of a bigger picture?" I shook my head in answer, even though it was more of a rhetorical question. She went on, "You were on your own for too long at the start, but it is not just about you anymore. You have an obligation to the other riders, to Ansel and to all of Teravinea. You are now our hope — everything you do affects us all. This joy ride, when you don't even know the status of your injury, could have had disastrous results. Like it or not, the survival of the kingdom hinges upon your health. Do not play so lightly with it."

Turning to my dragon, she said, "Eshshah, you know about duty more than any other creature in this room. You also know the power of persuasion this girl has on all of us. You must not let her talk you into this kind of foolishness when you know better."

My remorse knew no bounds — I had brought Eshshah down with me. Ashamed, I silently asked for her forgiveness, which of course she granted.

The Healer turned her wrath back to me, and continued,

"You will not jeopardize everything we have worked for — more so than it already has been." She shot an angry glare at Ansel, then back at me. "Did you not pay attention to Ansel's story and how a desire for self-satisfying pleasure ended in disaster?"

I sunk even lower at that cut. Chancing a glance at Ansel, he looked like he had been punched in the stomach — a wave of darkness crossed his face.

Finally, the Healer appeared to be calming down, if only slightly. "Maybe one day you will lead, Amáne, but until that time, you will answer to me. Is that understood?"

"Yes, Healer."

With that, she stormed out of the chamber.

I stared at the floor, fighting the tears and wished this was another of my nightmares that I could wake up from.

Ansel turned to me. In an angry whisper, he said, "Maybe your sneaky acquaintance doesn't know the Healer very well." Then he rose from the couch and headed out of the room.

Closing my eyes, I released the breath I'd been holding. I picked up the bowl on the table in front of me. It took all of my self control to resist launching it at his head. Instead, I hurled it out the entry — like he had done the day before with the cup.

CHAPTER THIRTY-THREE

I awoke a couple of hours later, still on the couch where I had cried myself to sleep. My recent shame washed over me making me want to close my eyes again to try to forget. Ansel sat at the ledge working on my walking stick. He followed through on his promise to finish it, although I thought it was perfect already. Evidently, he wasn't angry with me anymore. Absorbed in his project, I watched as he buffed the carved dragon at the top of the staff. I didn't want to disturb him, so I lay still and followed his hands with my eyes.

He must have felt my stare. Before long he turned around and caught me watching. Ansel met my eyes and shot me an easy smile. It seemed to light up the entry even more. After a final swipe with his polishing cloth, he jumped up and brought me my staff, taking a seat beside me to observe my reaction.

I examined his new addition, small gold stones for Eshshah's eyes were inlaid into the wood. He had found the perfect color.

"I love it. Thank you. It's beautiful."

He paused in anticipation, "I believe this is the part where you throw your arms around my neck."

I rolled my eyes.

Then changing his tone, "Amáne, first of all I'm sorry it

took me so long to say this to you, but I haven't offered you yet my condolences for your loss. My aunt told me you were very close to your mother, and I'm sorry she was taken from you. Secondly, I want to thank you for being there for me last night, and I apologize for my childish behavior."

I didn't know if by 'childish behavior' he meant his show of emotion because of Farvard's death — which was not childish at all in my opinion; or the stunt he pulled when he jammed his knife into the table. I refrained from asking and simply nodded in acceptance of his apology.

"Ansel, now it's my turn to apologize for getting you involved in my bad behavior this morning."

He replied, "It was my fault. I should have stopped you. You know the Healer is right — the three of us are bound by duty, through no choice of our own. You as dragon rider; Eshshah, born of the Royal Dragon line; and myself as heir to the throne. In addition to duty, Eshshah's line has an ancestral bond to the Royal House of Drekinn, which in turn binds you ... to me." He smiled, shrugged and added, "In truth, I'm not opposed to that bond."

I ignored his comment but needed to address something that troubled me, "Yes, you're right. We are bound by our obligations. That's why you can't oppose us going back to the castle for a dragon egg. The Healer says we need an egg ... so —"

"Can we not discuss that now?" He entreated.

I would have preferred to get it out of the way — to make him understand that Eshshah and I have been training for this mission and that he must not deny our quest. I reminded myself of the trauma he had undergone through his capture. I wasn't up for a fight, so I let it go with a shrug of assent — for now.

Pleased that he had gotten his way, he completely changed the subject. "Tell me about your life in Dorsal ... your friends ... the suitors who seek your affections. Your poor mother probably had plenty of eligible men knocking at your door to negotiate for your hand."

I laughed. "Absolutely not! Thankfully, no one is interested in me. If any had been foolish enough to ask my mother, then she would have put them to right. I have no inclination for anyone to have my hand, or my heart for that matter. My mother would not have participated in any such negotiations, anyway."

It could have been my imagination, but I thought I caught a hint of relief or satisfaction, along with slight disappointment cross his face — just briefly. Why, I couldn't guess. But he continued his interest in my life. Being the topic of this conversation made me a bit uncomfortable. But strangely, it didn't really matter — I actually enjoyed his company at that moment.

"What about your sneaky friend, Kyle ... or Kole ... or ..."

"Kail. No. He only has eyes for Fiona, for which I'm glad. I think most of the time he forgets I'm a girl, anyway."

His eyebrows raised in surprise. "What? I'm liking him less and less."

"Oh, that's never bothered me. If you haven't already noticed, my femininity is not one of my finer attributes." I waved my hand over my tunic and tights as an example.

"I have noticed ... and I disagree." I met his eyes to see if he was teasing me, but they showed his sincerity. A nervous twinge rippled through me. He continued. "May I tell you what I think is your finest attribute? Besides your beauty, of course."

I blushed. This was the second time he had referred to me as beautiful. No one except for my mother, and Fiona, had ever said anything about my being beautiful. My mother didn't count and Fiona, I thought, was just being kind. I found compliments were not pleasant for me, but I tried to hide it. Still, as awkward as I felt, I was also curious as to what he might reveal.

"Sure, I guess."

"I think it's the fire in you — your spirit — your courage. Your mother named you well. Amáne, Water, it quenches the raging fire — it gives you your balance. Then you link to a beautiful dragon named Fire. It all fits."

Eshshah hummed in approval.

I sat there dumbfounded. Finally my profound response was, "Oh."

This was all too embarrassing for me. I couldn't continue any more discussion that involved me as the subject matter. Before it led to my irritation, I recovered my senses, cleared my throat and turned the conversation.

"So what's life like being a prince hiding behind the title of lord of a manor? It must be magnificent to be surrounded by lavish things — elegantly beautiful ladies vying for your affections."

Disappointment crossed his face as he realized the conversation was now directed back at him. He could only return the courtesy and answer my question as I had answered his.

"It has its advantages. The ladies are elegant, yes, some are beautiful, but mostly they bore me. Weak, oblivious to anything outside their small circle of concerns. 'Who is hosting the next ball?' 'When will the latest fashions arrive?' 'What new expensive silks has the mercer imported?'"

He turned to me and sighed. "In truth, Amáne, it's all rather frustrating. A long time ago I used to know who I was. It pained me to see the destruction of all that my father had worked for, yet I was not able to do anything about it. My people suffered under Galtero's rule and I couldn't help them. It was killing me, so I guess I just gave up — my gaining the throne became an illusive dream."

It was as if a dark cloud obscured the sunlight that had been in the room. Instead of giving in to the vortex that threatened to take us down, I fought it. I sat upright, leaned in to him and rested my hand on his arm. "You can never give up hope." I said fervently. "You must have faith in the future. Remember what the Healer said about Torin's prophecy — the first part has already come to pass.

"Look at me." I brought my face closer to his and drew his eyes toward mine. "It will be through Eshshah and me that you will see victory. Hope, Ansel — hope does not disappoint — you must believe that to be so.

"You said I had fire in me ... well, then let me share my fire with you. I'm sure there was a time you fought for what was right for the kingdom. You must take up your fight again. I won't let you give up. Not when it's so close ... not when Eshshah and I are fighting alongside of you."

I could see a spark light his eyes — a small flame ignited. The dark cloud passed, and he allowed a slight smile to change his countenance. That smile alone was like sunshine. We held each other's eyes for a few heartbeats — until my heart pounded in my ears. The sound frightened me. I became aware of how close we were. I felt the heat from his body. Confused, I removed my hand from his arm, turned my face away and stood up with the help of my walking stick.

"Come on, let's go find the Healer," I said, hoping he had not heard my heart beating so loudly, "If I'm lucky, she's not angry with me anymore, and we can see if she wants Eshshah to catch us a big fish. I can teach you how to prepare it, Dorsal style. Maybe this time you'll at least try to eat it instead of mangling it." I shot him a sidelong look and then went in search of the Healer. Ansel followed.

That afternoon found the three of us in the kitchen working together on our midday meal. Well, the Healer and I were working and Ansel just got in the way. Every time I turned around I practically ran into him.

Finally, before I got too annoyed with him, I gathered the last of the potatoes from the bin and deposited them on a table. "Here, I have a job for you." I handed him a knife. "You can chop these potatoes. Please cut them small."

The Healer gave me such a look of disapproval, I stopped short. Then she looked at Ansel, who was already happily employing the use of his blade. Pursing her lips, she shook her head, and then turned back to her task without saying a word.

It dawned on me I had just ordered the Prince of Teravinea to perform the menial labor of a scullery maid. At first I was ashamed at giving him such an assignment, but when I glanced over at him I noted he was completely engrossed in his chore. I had to turn my face and hide the smile that came to my lips. Only with concentrated effort did I manage to stifle my snicker.

Seriously, I thought to myself, *I need to start thinking of him as who he really is, and start giving him the respect due him.* He was King Emeric's son, and someone so above my station. The fact that I'd treated him as my equal shamed me — *how dare I be so insolent.*

Truth was, he had a way about him that allowed me to be comfortable in his presence — as long as he kept his distance ...

and didn't look at me too intensely ... or try to inhale the scent of my hair. I, however, needed to reflect upon my place as dragon rider in regards to my future king.

These thoughts ran through my mind while I prepared my pan with oil, garlic, dried red chili peppers and spices. That task completed, I went to retrieve the cut potatoes. Expecting he would have diced them into cubes, I wasn't prepared for their appearance. He'd cut them into the thinnest slivers. They lay on the board like a stack of hay. I inadvertently raised my eyebrows at their presentation.

"Did I cut them wrong? You said make them small."

"These are great. Thank you." I hoped he didn't catch my hesitation.

They ended up being the favorite of the meal. He had created a new twist on Dorsal's specialty of chili pepper potatoes.

After our meal, the Healer excused herself to the library. I cleared the table and straightened out the kitchen. Ansel joined me. I declined his help, but he stayed and kept me company. I fought the urge to give him a task so he would stay out of my way, but reminded myself of my place. By the time I finished, I was more than ready to get off of my aching foot.

My mind reeled as I thought about how, in just the short time I'd known Ansel, I had allowed myself to think of him as a friend. Friend — I liked the sound of that. I've had plenty of acquaintances, but never permitted anyone close enough to call a friend — girl or boy — I had always been a loner. Yes, he annoyed me plenty of times as I'm sure I annoyed him, but I dismissed that easily.

In the same instant I considered him my friend, I also conceded that I had allowed myself to step over the boundaries of duty and respect. The line was not clear to me and I didn't know how this friendship would affect our working relationship. I knew that soon we would have to return to our respective responsibilities — he to his obligations as prince to save his kingdom, and I to assist in those plans.

We retreated to the entry cavern. I postponed my need to rest my foot as I limped to the ledge to take in the scene before me — the blue ocean against the cloudless sky. Ansel followed closely. The heat of the day relaxed into an enjoyable temperature.

Looking out onto the calm sea, I breathed in deeply. "I just love this view."

"So do I," Ansel responded.

Something in the way he said it made me turn toward him. He was not looking at the ocean view as I was — he was looking at me.

I fought the panic rising in my chest, but before the situation continued in a direction I didn't want it to go, I nonchalantly put a bit of distance between us and then went back to the topic that had bothered me for long enough.

"Could you really overrule the Healer's plans and oppose sending Eshshah and me for a dragon egg?"

"Amáne, I really don't —"

"No, Ansel, I need to know. We have to talk about this."

He exhaled deeply and under protest, he answered, "Yes, I could. And I will if I deem it necessary."

"You would send Calder, or Braonán or one of the other riders. Why not me?"

"They have more experience than you. They're not..." he hesitated, trying to carefully formulate his words.

"What? They're not a fifteen-year-old girl?" I advanced on him and pounded my walking stick on the stone floor. It echoed through the entry cavern. "That's not fair to think that way! They don't have Eshshah — their dragons no longer live." I choked at the thought. "Do you realize when we were running around in those tunnels that it was only because of my dragon that we got out alive?" He winced. "You didn't see or hear her, but it was due to her strength alone we were saved. She gave me what I needed to fight for my life after that creature bit me. And she brought us out of that nightmare. Calder, Braonán, anyone else would have died down there, and you along with them." I realized I was talking through my clenched teeth.

I lowered my eyes and my voice. "I'm sorry, I don't mean to be disrespectful, but I can't keep my mouth shut and have you just decide you don't want us to fulfill our obligation. I don't understand why you would do that. We will swear our fealty to you, yet you threaten us with your right to deny our quest."

He responded firmly and evenly, "Don't forget, you aren't officially sworn in. That needs to be done at Council in the presence of the other dragon riders — and I also have final say on that matter."

My head snapped up and flames must have shot from my eyes at that moment. He held up his hands, palms out in surrender.

"Amáne, I would be a fool to decline yours and Eshshah's services. You will be sworn in at Council. I'm just saying all those decisions are ultimately my responsibility. I need to be convinced that your quest will have a strong chance of success before I can bear to see you subjected to that kind of danger again."

I feared there was more to his statement than just our allegiance to him. He was making it more personal and I couldn't let him go in that direction. How could I make him see that he cannot make it personal and I cannot elevate our relationship to anything higher than friendship. I didn't want it to be anything more. I was prepared to forfeit even our friendship, if it interfered with our mission.

"Ansel, Eshshah and I offer you our lives as is our duty. We were chosen for this obligation, it is our destiny. I cannot offer you anything beyond."

I hoped he understood what I had tried to tell him. I couldn't meet his eyes, but kept my gaze somewhere around his chest. I saw his shoulders drop almost imperceptibly.

"So, it's just duty and your allegiance that you offer?"

Still refusing to look up, I could only force a nod. "... and friendship." I added in a small voice. It was the only answer I could give him — I was fairly sure I understood his question.

"Amáne. Look at me."

When I resisted, he put his finger under my chin and gently lifted my face, giving me no option but to look at him. I was held there by his green eyes, unable to look away. Something inside of me was reluctant to admit that I didn't want to look away, but only to remain lost in his gaze. *What is happening to me?*

His eyes bore into mine — searching. He found what he was looking for and a slight smile turned the corners of his lips.

"That's not true — there's more," he said. "You're not listening to your heart, Amáne. Your future is tied to mine ... and not just by duty."

He drew his face close to mine. I stood frozen, expectant, silently protesting ... yet also hoping. But mostly, angry with myself that I was so weak. I made no effort to resist. All these emotions and more churned in my chest, along with a thousand butterflies in my stomach. I closed my eyes and felt his breath on my face.

At that moment, the Healer walked into the room with a roll of maps under her arm.

Startled, I spun around and lost hold of my walking stick. It echoed as it clattered to the ground. Accidentally putting weight on my bad foot, I lost my balance and surely would have ended in a heap on the hard stone floor if Ansel hadn't caught me. He helped me regain my balance and retrieved my staff. I composed myself and stepped away from him as I tried to bring my breathing back to normal.

"Oh good, the three of you are here," the Healer said, then stopped short, as she took in the scene before her. She tilted her head and raised her eyebrows. I steadied myself for another dose of her wrath, but she said nothing. She showed no sign of whether she was aware of what almost happened between Ansel and me.

I, however, was quite aware of what she interrupted, and I was shaken — my body still trembled. With some effort, I stilled my heart and convinced myself that I was relieved she came in when she did. Something had occurred that left me confused. I knew I had to work on staying strong if the situation repeated itself. I could not encourage Ansel's infatuation with me.

"I've been studying these maps, conferring with Gallen and the others," the Healer began, her eyes on Ansel, "and we've decided where you'll be residing." She spread the maps on one of the tables and then explained.

"Ansel, you know you are no longer safe in Teravinea. We have been in negotiations with King Tynan of the Kingdom of Serislan, just north of us. Of course, he doesn't know your true identity, but he believes you are a noble of some stature. He was told that Galtero has confiscated your lands and that you have escaped and ask for sanctuary from him, which is mostly the truth. He has agreed to allow you Trivingar Manor, on his southwest coast." She pointed to a location on the map.

She added, "He was a great ally of your father and has no love whatsoever for Galtero. There is trouble brewing — he's informed us Galtero has plans that do not forbode well for Teravinea. You must leave tomorrow night —"

"Tomorrow night?!" Ansel and I said in unison.

It was too soon to accept that our time here was up. This place seemed to do that to me. I would stay here forever and gladly if it were my destiny, but I knew that was only my wishful thinking.

"You will leave tomorrow." She repeated. "Eshshah and Amáne, I would appreciate your assistance in transporting Ansel to Trivingar."

"Of course, Healer," Eshshah and I both answered.

"It's about a four hour flight to the Arevale Outpost," the Healer continued, "which is just this side of the border from Trivingar. Braonán will meet you with a horse. From there you will ride to your new residence. I've heard Trivingar Manor is quite beautiful."

She looked at Ansel. "I am so sorry your life has been one of hiding and running, but I assure you we are getting closer to our goal. The Royal House of Drekinn shall rule again. Nothing worth achieving is done without cost."

Chapter Thirty-Four

Just before sunset found me again at the ledge looking out over the shimmering sea. As the sun descended in the sky, the air stirred slightly, whispering in my ear. Eshshah lay curled up behind me.

Growing up in a coastal town had taught me love for the sun and the sea. Watching the sunset had become a ritual every evening. My mother and I used to stand at our doorway and watch the great ball of fire quench itself as it sunk slowly into the horizon. I looked forward to it here at the outpost as well — it was my favorite time of day. I was loath to miss the ritual. Watching it reminded me again how much I missed my mother. *Why was she taken from me at such a time in my life?* In my confusion I needed her even more now. I remembered her words, "You will need to use your intuition and your intelligence in deciding which paths you choose — remember to follow your heart." Did she have any idea what paths I was going to be facing? How could I follow my heart and choose the correct path for Teravinea? I could not see that they went any way but two different directions. I had no other option — I couldn't let Ansel get any closer to me if it meant jeopardizing our quest.

As the sun lowered, the wind started to find its voice. Whitecaps formed on the waves, and I knew we were in store for a Valaira. My hair and my tunic rippled gently as the hot wind began to build. I shuddered as I remembered the last Valaira when Eshshah and I had fought for our lives, and this outpost had saved us. Memories of our ordeal, mixed with a need for my mother, caused a tear to escape. How my life had changed since she gave me her blessing.

I heard the door behind me glide open and footsteps approach — it was Ansel. I swiped the tear from my face and blinked several times in hopes the arid wind would dry the moisture that had built in my eyes.

He came up beside me and put his arm around my shoulder ... which I gently removed.

"Amáne," Ansel said.

"— Ansel," I said simultaneously.

"Go ahead." Again simultaneously.

"You go," Ansel said first.

I sighed and gazed out over the churning sea. "Tomorrow we'll be preparing to leave. I was just thinking how quickly time goes by, but I guess all things must come to an end. We've been through a lot in just a short period of time and now we've arrived at the point where we need to move on — and we don't know where that will lead, do we?" I turned toward him. "Ansel, I'm thankful I was able to meet you and I hope you will let me consider you as my friend." I wanted so desperately to keep him as a friend. I wasn't ready to give up on that yet, and was going to try to make it work — before I had to sacrifice that as well, for Teravinea.

"Hmm. Friend." He said.

"Well, older brother, if you prefer?"

242

"No. Friend is fine," he said quickly, and then under his breath, not realizing how good my hearing was, "... for now."

I ignored the last part and continued. "I've never been very good at making friends. I've always been kind of a loner, but I see it's rather nice to have one, and I just wanted to let you know." I really had so much more to tell him but I had to keep it simple. I couldn't give him hope of anything more.

He smiled and nodded.

"What were you going to say?" I asked.

"Pretty much the same thing, I guess."

I breathed a sigh of relief — a little surprised this proved easier than I thought it was going to be.

After a pause, he exhaled, studied my face and said, "No, that's not true. What I want to tell you is that besides the fact I am indebted to you for my life, I want you to know these last few days have been the best days I've ever known. I've grown very fond of you. Truth is, I care for you, Amáne." He bit his lower lip. "I never really cared for anyone before, other than myself. I've had a hard time trying to make you see that. For some reason, you're closing your eyes to what's right in front of your face."

I groaned inwardly. *Of course he wasn't going to make this easy. What was I thinking?* I reminded myself of my vow in front of Dorjan and Gallen that I would never fall in love. However, I didn't think I needed to worry much about the vow. It should be easy to remain on a level of friendship and nothing more — for my quest as well as my vow. Love was just not in my destiny. I would not allow it to happen. I could not.

"Why do you have to complicate things, Ansel? Can't we just leave it as it is?"

"'As it is' is not the same for me as for you. Can you just give me a reason why you're closing your eyes to the obvious — and fighting me on this?"

"Ansel, first of all, there is nothing obvious. And secondly, I'm a dragon rider!"

"Yes, I know. I had to step around your dragon just now. She's hard to miss."

"Ugh! Now who is the one closing their eyes to what's obvious, Ansel-the-Dragon-Lore-Lover? You of all people know we don't age the same as normal humans. I will not watch you grow old and meet your ancestors and leave me still looking hardly any older than I am now. I can't do it. I won't." It was a weak excuse, but it was all I could offer.

As my frustration increased the Valaira intensified. A powerful blast of wind rushed in, nearly knocking me off of my good foot. I reached for Ansel's arm for balance as he steadied me by my waist.

"So, Amáne, tell me," he smiled, "do you think you won't be watching me grow old and pass on if we just remain friends?"

I took a deep breath, and let it out slowly. "Why do you have to be so annoying?" I was getting nowhere — he was as stubborn as I.

"At least I'm being honest with myself as well as with you," he returned. "You, on the other hand, are twisting the truth of your heart to some personal version of reality."

"I don't understand what you mean," I said, trying to make myself heard over the howls of the Valaira as her fury increased.

He took my face in both of his hands and kissed my forehead. I closed my eyes. I didn't want to look at him. His eyes were too much for me to resist. Before I realized what was happening, he tilted my head back and pressed his warm lips gently against mine. A wave of heat rose through my body — the wind intensified, whipping in circles around us as our long hair intertwined.

"That's what I mean," he breathed.

I willed my racing heart to be still and worked to slow my breathing. *How could I have let this happen?* I had slipped. I was weak. Closing my eyes, I set my jaw and reluctantly but gently pushed him from me. I looked up at him — my eyes pleaded.

"Ansel, please."

With a triumphant gleam in his eye, yet unable to hide his frustration, he conceded, "Okay, Amáne. You win round one. Just friends." And he stuck out his hand.

I took it firmly in mine and said, "Deal. Just friends. Thank you, Ansel." Although, I think we both knew I didn't really win that round, but we left it alone.

The Valaira blew in full force thrashing wildly around us as she drowned out any chance of further discussion. I whispered "Sitara" to light the shields, then closed the front entry, shutting out the tempestuous noise. I excused myself, and retreated to my chambers, still shaking.

Chapter Thirty-Five

The next morning the air was still. The three of us sat in the dining chamber silently eating our morning meal. Depression dimmed the room like a fog — each of us brooding on our own versions of our upcoming departure.

Most of the day I put myself to the task of preparing the outpost for our absence. I cleaned, put items in storage and covered the furnishings. The remainder I spent moping around. I halfheartedly packed my satchel for the journey. The Healer allowed Eshshah and me to take a short flight together. She sensed I needed to be alone with Eshshah.

The flight to the Arevale Outpost would be around four hours. Braonán would meet us at the field near the outpost, and from there he and Ansel would ride less than half an hour to his new home. Eshshah and I would fly back to Dorsal.

Ansel and I more or less avoided each other throughout the day. I was afraid I would have another weak moment — I couldn't begin to guess Ansel's excuse.

That evening I stood at the ledge and watched alone as the sun set. We were supposed to be resting, but I couldn't sleep. My tears flowed freely.

All too soon, it was dark and time to leave. I put on my helmet, without pinning up my hair, letting it fall loose. I mounted and waited in the saddle as the Healer gathered her belongings and said her farewells to Ansel. My throat tightened watching the two of them. He would wait here while Eshshah and I flew the Healer back to Dorsal, then we would return for him.

As we spiraled into the Healer's courtyard, Gallen came out to watch our approach. Eshshah landed lightly and I helped the Healer dismount before grabbing my walking stick. I swung my leg over the back of the saddle and lowered myself to the ground.

Limping, I rushed to Gallen, who welcomed me with his arms opened wide. He wrapped them around me and swung me in a circle, locking me in his fatherly embrace. I didn't realize I'd missed him so much. It had only been a few days since I departed, but it felt like a lifetime — almost like I was a different person now.

"Amáne, welcome back. I'm so proud of you." His eyes settled on my staff, "Is that your new weapon of choice?"

"I guess if I needed to, I could knock someone senseless with it." I laughed. "Ansel — I mean Lord Ansel — made it for me."

He walked up to Eshshah who lowered her head for him to scratch between her eyes. She hummed in pleasure as he greeted her. "Thank you Eshshah for bringing Amáne and Lord Ansel back safely. Congratulations on the success of your first quest."

She nodded.

Gallen took the Healer's satchel and gave her a warm embrace, then with his arms around both of us, he led us inside. It was so nice to be back here again with Gallen, even if only briefly. The Healer looked relieved to be home, too.

He put some cheese and bread on the table. As we ate, he asked endless questions about my quest. He wanted to know about the creature from the tunnels, and to examine my new hideous linking mark. I was sorry I had such a limited amount of time before I had to leave.

The Healer got up and asked me to follow her into her library. Directing me to a couch, she sat close beside me and took my hand in hers.

"Amáne, I know I am hard on you at times. I feel it's necessary — you are so often too headstrong, which has its moments of necessity, but at times hampers your progress." She sighed. "I see myself in you so often. I know I'm no replacement for your mother, but I do love you. I can see how you miss her, but if you need to confide in me, please be assured I'm here for you. Don't forget that."

Then, more softly she said, "Your most difficult task will be learning the delicate symmetry between your happiness and your duty. There is a fine line between the two and you must learn to balance them. I don't want to see you make the same mistake I made." Before I could ask her what she meant, Gallen came in and pronounced it was time I should leave.

I gave the Healer and Gallen long hugs and limped toward where Eshshah waited in the courtyard. Gallen gave me a leg up. I stowed my walking stick and buckled in, saluted the two and gave Eshshah the word. She leaped up into the night sky. I watched as the Healer and Gallen became small specks in the courtyard.

Back at the outpost, Ansel had a satchel packed with some things he wanted to take from there. He had dressed in a floor-length cloak, black with purple trim. His long hair tied tightly in a queue at the nape of his neck with several ties evenly spaced down the length. For the first time since I had known him he actually looked like royalty. I was taken aback at his striking presence.

My eyes remained fixed on him as I dismounted. "Wow, Ansel. If I didn't know better, I would say you look like a prince or something." I teased. "Where did you find that?"

"It was in one of the wardrobes. You think I can pull off the prince thing?" He smiled.

"Most definitely!" But I really wasn't teasing this time — he took my breath away.

I kept my distance from him for fear I would lose round two should it come to that. I grabbed my small pack and mounted back up. It was getting easier with my foot as it was healing nicely, thanks to the Healer and Eshshah's efforts several times a day.

Ansel pulled on his helmet and tossed me his satchel. I secured it on the saddle, then reached down to lock wrists with him as he swung up. It was customary, when using the double saddle, for the rider to be first up and last off. Ansel knew that his position on Eshshah was always behind me, regardless of who he was.

I took one last look at our Dorsal Outpost and whispered "Sitara" to turn off the light shields as I flipped down my eye protectors. I gave Eshshah the word and she leaped out of the entry. For Ansel's sake she spread her wings quickly to start her glide, rather than execute her free fall that I loved. She pushed the rock to close the stone door and we were on our way.

Eshshah's powerful wings pumped with ease, as we climbed until the air was thin and the cold penetrated my bones. Although the extra weight of Ansel was really not a hardship for her, the distance made a difference with two riding. She was still a very young dragon. Flying higher created less stress for her. I had on my riding tunic, which was meant to keep a rider warm.

For most people it would probably have been fine, but living my whole life in the warmth of Dorsal left me with a low tolerance for the frigid air.

After the initial thrill of taking off, I settled down and we flew without conversation for quite a while in the darkness.

"Amáne, you're cold," Eshshah said. "Do you want me to fly lower?"

"No, thank you Eshshah. I know it's easier on you at this height. I'll be fine," I answered in thought transference. I was getting better at it and especially up here, it would be too hard to converse out loud anyway.

"You could always ask Lord Ansel to keep you warm," she said with her laugh-like rumble.

"Not funny, Eshshah."

"But seriously, Amáne, why are you so determined to push him away? I can sense the attraction you each have for the other, but you fight it and bury it deep inside you. You have an opportunity for a relationship and a possible future mate. Isn't that what humans look for?"

"Whoa, Eshshah! I am not looking for a future mate. I believe other female humans my age are, but I'm not. I vowed I will not fall in love, and I definitely cannot think of Ansel as anything remotely close to a mate."

"Do you have a justification for your vow?"

"Yes, Dorjan and Gallen lament the loss of their wives having watched them grow old and pass on to their ancestors, while they hardly aged. I don't want to put myself through that tragedy.

"But that's only my selfish reason." I admitted, "I have a more pressing argument for my decision to keep any attraction to

Ansel in check. Eshshah, you and I have a duty with our lives to protect him. Do you think for one moment that if I accepted his attentions, he would send me on dangerous quests?

"I think back to the tunnels in the castle and that horrible creature. The reason I got bitten is because he hesitated. I understand now why he did that. It was because he didn't want to be the one to run and have me fight for him — he's no coward. That was before he even knew me — and that was when he thought I was a boy. And now, if I were to accept his overtures he would never want to send us into danger. That decision could cost him his throne. I must stay my distance."

I went on with my thoughts. "Eshshah, I think this exile will be advantageous. He can put his mind to setting up his manor and taking care of whatever it is lords are concerned with. And, he can occupy himself with the riders and their plans to defeat Galtero. Besides, he'll be so far away, we probably won't even see each other for quite a while. Then maybe he'll forget his feelings for me, or find someone else." I choked at the thought of him with someone else. "Eshshah, I just have to live with the fact that my duty comes before my happiness."

"I heard the Healer tell you that there is a balance."

I had no response — we flew on in silence.

My head began to hurt from the thin air, and my heart hurt from the fear of Ansel forgetting about me. The cold pierced my skin. I shivered and my teeth chattered. I was miserable.

Ansel put his hand on my shoulder and leaned into my ear so I could hear him over the rush of wind, "Amáne, you're freezing. Can I help you stay warm?"

"No, thank you, Ansel. I'll be fine." But my words came out stuttering, I could hardly control my muscles as they worked unsuccessfully to build heat in my body.

"Please, Amáne. I promise, it will be only as a friend. I can't stand to see you uncomfortable when I'm so warm in this cloak."

"Only as a friend? You promise?" I stammered. Numb to my bones, if I didn't do something about it, Eshshah would have to fly lower — I didn't want to make her do that.

"Yes, I promise."

Without waiting for me to reply, he unhooked his cloak and pulled me back, clasping it in front of me. Then he wrapped his arms around me and drew me closer. I don't know how I could have discerned the difference between his arms around me as a friend or as something more, but at that moment, it didn't matter. The heat of his body coursed through mine and relaxed me like a hearth fire on a cold night. Before I knew it, his warmth eased my tremors and I fell asleep in his arms.

CHAPTER THIRTY-SIX

"Amáne, we're almost there." Eshshah broke into my dreams.

"Eshshah, I'm sorry, I abandoned you and made you fly alone."

"You were with me the whole time."

"Ansel, wake up." He had slumped forward over my shoulder.

"No, I don't want to," he mumbled, half asleep. "I'm having a beautiful dream. You're in it. And your hair smells so good." He tightened his arms around me.

"Ansel, stop!" I elbowed him in the ribs a little harder than I needed to.

"Ow! What was that for?" Completely awake, now. "I think you broke a rib."

I knew he was teasing, but it would have served him right if I did. I was embarrassed as I guessed his dream was about more than just being friends.

Up ahead I spotted the fire that Braonán had lit for warmth and protection. As we approached I could see him jump up to tend to the horses. They were spooked at the sight and smell of Eshshah.

We landed lightly in a clearing and Braonán ran up to meet us, stopping with a hearty salute. I saluted back and watched his face as he looked admiringly at Eshshah — as only a rider could. I felt pity for his loss.

Ansel tossed Braonán his satchel and then dismounted. I grabbed my walking stick and followed him down.

"Braonán, this is Amáne, rider of Eshshah. Amáne and Eshshah, this is Braonán, formerly Yaron, rider of the late Volkan." He formally introduced us. We saluted each other again, both going through the usual greetings of 'Pleased to meet you.'

He faced my dragon, "Eshshah, your power and beauty show bright in your golden eyes."

Eshshah nodded, pleased at his compliment.

He looked at me and then at Ansel, and laughed gruffly, "Tiny little thing, isn't she?"

I rolled my eyes.

The rider was a huge man, good looking in a rough way. In obvious pleasure at seeing Ansel, he locked hands with him. They both embraced and pounded each other on the back.

"So good to see you're safe, Your Grace!" He boomed.

'Your Grace.' *I'm not sure I could get used to addressing him that way.* I'd better start, as the respect was rightfully his — he was a prince, the true heir to the throne of Teravinea. I had to keep reminding myself of my position in regards to his.

Braonán continued in a loud voice, "Lord Ansel, Trivingar Manor is awaiting your arrival. I trust you'll find it to your satisfaction. Besides some of your old staff, the new help has been well chosen — the grounds are spectacular. And wait 'til you see all the fine wenches they have in the township of Trivingar."

Ansel cleared his throat so loud I thought he was going to choke.

"Braonán!" He said, not too kindly. "We have a lady present."

My heart constricted. I removed my helmet and shook my

hair out just to emphasize I was the lady present. I really couldn't blame Braonán for overlooking it — I was, as usual, dressed like a boy, and the helmet didn't help much.

He was truly repentant for uttering such an ill-mannered statement in front of me, "My apologies, Amáne, I meant no disrespect."

"Apology accepted," I said rather monotone.

Isn't this exactly what I had spoken to Eshshah about? That I wished there were distractions here for Ansel so he would get over his infatuation with me? I should be happy. This is what I hoped for. So, then why did I feel like a dagger had just been thrust into my heart? I nearly doubled over with physical pain.

Breathe in, breathe out. I thought to myself *You cannot have it both ways.* I struggled to control my emotions, blinking back the threat of tears.

Ansel could see my pain and quickly tried to alleviate the damage.

"Braonán, please take my bag and prepare to leave. I'm going to ride up to the outpost with Amáne to help her re-saddle Eshshah and let the Healer know we've arrived safely." Braonán looked relieved at an excuse to leave my presence.

In a daze, I let Ansel lead me by my elbow back to Eshshah. I mounted at nearly the same time as he did. Eshshah leaped into the air without my word. She followed Ansel's lead to help me cope with my reaction to Braonán's statement.

We flew to the edge of the field which dropped off sharply to the beach below. Eshshah then banked right for the entry to the Arevale Outpost hidden in the cliffs above the rocky shore. She located the push-rock and opened the entry cavern. We landed, and I slid out of the saddle as I whispered "Sitara" to light the shields. The three of us walked down the corridor to the library in silence. I still struggled to breathe — angry with the turmoil of emotions churning inside of me. Reaching the communication disc, I put my hand on the knob and whispered "Gyan," and then "Nara." After a moment, the disc shimmered as the Healer and Gallen came into view.

"Good, you've arrived safely. Eshshah made that distance in record time. I didn't expect you to arrive for another half hour or more." Gallen said.

Any praise for my dragon was welcomed by me. It lifted my spirits somewhat. However, my countenance did not improve enough for the Healer not to notice. Alarmed, she asked, "Amáne, are you ill?"

"No, I'm not ill, Healer." I changed the subject. "We will be leaving here soon."

Ansel greeted them and said he would contact them once he settled in. Braonán had set up a communication disc at the manor.

We signed off and I released my hand from the disc, then headed toward the back of the library to choose a single saddle for the ride home. Ansel helped me secure it on Eshshah — we worked in silence. I wished he would quit staring at me. For once he seemed at a loss for words.

When we made our way back to the entry cavern, he put his hand on my shoulder and gently turned me to face him.

"Amáne, Braonán is a rough character. Don't let what he said upset you. It was just one of the pointless things that men say. It didn't mean anything to me."

"Well, it should!" I snapped. "You would do well to be interested in the beautiful women in Trivingar. You deserve a fine lady on your arm. One of your station, who will be beneficial to your throne, and who will return your affection." The dagger in my heart twisted. My torment increased.

Hurt showed in his eyes, which magnified my pain. "I know you don't really mean what you're saying, and I know you have feelings for me, Amáne. It's written all over your face. I just can't figure out why you're working so hard to deny it."

"Of course I ...er, care for you, Ansel — as a friend ..."

How could I make him understand? It was for his own safety. My obligation to his throne came first — it was too dangerous for him to be emotionally involved with someone whose destiny it was to protect him. Why couldn't he just relax his attentions?

He held his eyes on me, waiting for an explanation.

My shoulders dropped. "Anything other than friendship just will not work, Ansel." I said, "We're from two different worlds."

"Opposites attract."

"You're destined to be the King of Teravinea — I was born a nobody ... a commoner from a tiny corner of the kingdom."

"I'm currently without a throne — still basically a nobody myself."

Frustration building, I tried again. "You have a lavish lifestyle accustomed to beautiful rich women dressed in silk and lace — I'm a plain girl who wears boys' clothes half the time."

"And your beauty far surpasses those women in silk and lace."

Blood rushed to my cheeks — a combination of anger and self consciousness. I uttered an exasperated sigh, and said, "You're not going to give up, are you?"

He shook his head. "I know what I want." He said pointedly. "Look, Amáne, I understand you're not ready to commit yourself to anyone, yet. I have time. I want you to know I won't give up on you — I'll wait for you. I promise." He emphasized the word 'promise.' "I want you to be sure ... to follow your heart. I have a good idea where it will lead you, but you need to figure that out for yourself."

I couldn't tell him that I can't follow my heart. I had already figured that out. Maybe after my quest for the dragon egg I could rethink my position — if an option still remained. But until then, I had to fight my heart. I had to build a wall around it that he could not enter.

Ansel drew closer and gently pushed my hair back from my face, first one side, then the other. He tenderly brushed the tear that had escaped the corner of my eye. Bending toward me, he kissed my forehead first and then moved to my lips.

The part of me that wanted him to forget me lost ground to the part of me that wanted to offer him something to remember. This was to be the last time I would allow him to kiss me, so I might as well make it memorable ... for both of us. After tonight, we will go our separate ways and maybe the next time we see each other, he'll have moved on.

There was a desperation in my actions as I wrapped my arms around him and pulled myself closer. I kissed him back — lingering longer than I should have.

If time could have stopped right then, I would have been where I wanted to stay for all eternity. But that could not be. Too soon I pulled back and put my fingers on his lips to hold him from another kiss. I put my hands on his chest and slowly pushed him away — both of us frustrated.

Still trying to catch my breath, I felt ashamed of myself for my boldness — and for giving him false hope. I whispered, "I can't, Ansel. We have to leave it as friends ... or nothing. Maybe some day I can explain."

The pain in his eyes added to the agony of my heart. I

turned, stepped up onto Eshshah's forearm and pulled myself into the saddle, then reached down to lock wrists with him. He mounted up without my help, settled behind me and held on to the saddle as Eshshah moved to the ledge.

We flew back down to the clearing where Braonán was putting out the fire and preparing to depart. Ansel slid off. I had planned on leaving right then, but Braonán said he had a parcel he wanted me to take to the Healer. Dismounting, I followed him to the horses. He pulled a package out of his saddle bag and handed it to me.

As I turned to leave, Ansel said my name softly.

I looked back at him and pleaded in a whisper, "Please don't."

He bit back what he was about to say. Instead, he unfastened his cloak, swung it over my shoulders and clasped it at my chin.

"You'll want this for your ride home."

I lowered my eyes, tears already flowing, and executed a low curtsy, "Thank you, Your Grace."

Without thinking, I glanced up at him. I saw the flash of absolute disapproval in his eyes.

This is how it has to be, I thought. I turned and walked slowly to where Eshshah waited — I could feel Ansel's eyes boring into me.

But, I didn't turn around. I couldn't ...

Acknowledgments

I found the daunting project of writing my novel called for a sense of reclusiveness — an existence in my own little world with only my characters for companionship. This was not a problem for me. I love my characters and have no regrets spending so much time with them. But even so, it is a solitary undertaking. Luckily, I'm a loner. That said, I could not have managed a project like this unaided. If I didn't have the support of my family, I probably wouldn't have arrived at this particular moment.

My husband, Lloyd, my biggest fan — You proudly told everyone you knew about my project ... even before I wanted anyone to know. I had to remind you for two years that I was not an author, yet, but a writer, never having been published. I no longer need to go against your claim. My daughters, April and Alanna — Your editing skills exponentially improved my work. Their daughters, Rio and Mila (sound familiar?) — You were inspirations. My sons-in-law, supportive. Jason, I salute you. — Your enthusiasm is like a Valaira. You'll make a fine rider. My brother, Dan — I valued your suggestions. My sister, Doreen — Your eagerness for more kept me going. Thanks for double-checking my facts. Nolan, your support was priceless. Scott Saunders, my expert in combat and weapons — Without your recommendation, Amáne would only be wielding a sword. It was because of you she took a liking to the glaive. Scott's friends, Julie and Gerry Adams, who also belong to The Society for Creative Anachronism, Inc. (SCA), local kingdom of Caid - You welcomed me to your home where my attention was riveted by your sword and spear practice with Scott. Ouch. The SCA (www.sca.org), is the place to turn for all things Medieval. Eric Magruder — Despite my early rough draft, you gave me hope. My favorite line was when you said, "... the only thing I'd change is the name of the writer — I'd put my name on it and submit it." Linda Armstrong and Armstrong School of Highland Dance, including mother/daughter Pamela and Alison Ashworth, Kaylee Finnigan, Erin MacNeil, Katherine Arthur and Clementyne Vega — You were my first young-adult readers. Your fire and spirit for my project boosted my desire to see it to fruition.

Jessica Hamabe — I laughed at your comments in the margins. You may recognize a few of your suggestions. Mia Stefanko — Your editing skills and time you took out of your busy schedule went over the top. Forrest Vess, my ear, who had to listen to me rambling on and on about dragons and tattoos and query letters — Your artistic opinion and suggestions for the cover art were what I needed for those who judge a book by its cover. Pete Walker, your linking mark/tattoo art is a hit. My Tuesday night writing meet-up group, including, but not limited to Al, Candace, Craig, Devon, Donna, George, Pam — Thanks for your attention to detail. Your input was indispensable. All my friends and acquaintances who read and enjoyed my story, you know who you are, thank you, thank you, all. If I have left anyone out, my sincere apologies. This has certainly been an exciting ride, exceeded only by a flight on the back of a dragon.

    ... now on to book number two ...

*Page 18 - "Be sincere of heart. Accept whatever befalls you, in great misfortune be patient; for in fire gold is refined." Book of Sirach 2:4-5

*Page 233 - "Hope, and hope does not disappoint." Romans 5:5

Character Names and Their Meanings

Some of these names I've taken liberties with their spellings and full meanings. But most are not far from the original.

Amáne - Water - derived from Native American

Ansel Drekinn - Protector - German; Drekinn - Dragon - Icelandic

Bern - Brave and gallant - German. Formerly known as Koen (Brave - French) - Rider of the late Heulwen

Braonán - Sorrow/tear drop - Irish/Gaelic. Formerly known as Yaron (to sing or shout - Hebrew) - Rider of the late Volkan

Calder - Violent Stream - Welsh. Formerly known as Vahe (strong - Armenian) - Rider of the late Bade

Catriona - Pure - Old Greek

Dorjan - Dark man - Hungarian. Formerly known as Ruiter (rider - Afrikaan) - Rider of the late Unule

Duer - Heroic - Scottish

Eshshah - (Pronounced ESHAW) Fire - Hebrew

King Emeric Drekinn - Leader - German. Ansel's father.

Farvard - Guardian. Formerly known as Kei (sand - African) - Rider of the late Okeanos

Queen Fiala Drekinn - Violet - Czechoslovakian

Fiona - White/Fair - Gaelic

Gallen - derived from Galen - Healer/Calm - Greek. Formerly known as Kaelem (honest) - Rider of the late Gyan

Galtero - Ruler of the Army - German

The Healer - Formerly known as Nara - Happy - Greek. Rider of the late Torin

Kail - Mighty One - Celtic/Gaelic

Malory - Bad Luck - French

Mila - Favor, Glory - Slavic

King Rikkar Drekinn - Strong Ruler - Nordic form of Richard. Ansel's Grandfather

Rio - River - Spanish

King Tynan - Dark - Gaelic

D. María Trimble lives in Carlsbad, California with her husband. Her days are spent as a graphic artist at a local company. She has been a student of dragonology from a very young age.

www.ingramcontent.com/pod-product-compliance
Lightning Source LLC
Chambersburg PA
CBHW051421170626
46809CB00006B/2256